"Every once in awhile, you start reading a book and you start to smile. The images on the page begin to unfold, and you realize that this writer has, in some unaccountable and miraculous way, lived in your skin. Reading Brad Whittington's prose was like that for me. By the time I'd finished the first couple of paragraphs, it was as if I'd found an old friend I never knew I had. Do yourself a favor: read *Welcome to Fred*."

— THOM LEMMONS —
author of *Jabez: A Novel* and the *Daughters of Faith* Series

"I know a good, insightful coming-of-age story when I read one. *Welcome to Fred* is a joy. There are lessons to be learned here, but they're all couched in Brad's winsome prose so they don't hurt. I commend this to you. This is good stuff. And I'm not just saying that because he's from Fred.

"Brad Whittington is a funny guy. And I know from funny. Everything he writes about Fred, Texas, is true. And I know from Fred because I once lived in Woodville, only twenty miles away as the crow flies through the Big Thicket of East Texas. According to some people, not far enough away from Fred."

— ROBERT DARDEN —
Assistant Professor of English, Baylor University;
Senior Editor, *The Door* Magazine; Author of *Corporate Giants: Personal Stories of Faith and Finance* and more than twenty-five other books

"What do you get when you cross Dave Barry and Garrison Keillor? Two very irritated men. Besides that, you also get a great talent like Brad Whittington. Brad can take the awkward moments of growing up and turn them into something really ridiculous. But don't take my word for it—visit Fred yourself."

— ROBIN HARDY —
author of the *Strieker Saga,* the *Sammy* Series, and the *Annals of Lystra*

"It is always a joy to find a new writer that knows what he is doing. *Welcome to Fred* presents us with just such an author. Written with gravity and levity, this coming of age novel is a delight to read. As a young city boy is transported to very rural Texas, he must discover who he is. The process is both thoughtful and hilarious. I look for more good things from this author."

"Whittington is a welcome new voice in the world of fiction and faith. His fresh story of a young pastor's son's coming of age, filled with nostalgia and interesting characters, will make you smile."

WELCOME
TO FRED

{A NOVEL}

BRAD WHITTINGTON

B&H
BROADMAN
& HOLMAN
PUBLISHERS

NASHVILLE, TENNESSEE

Published by Broadman & Holman Publishers,
Nashville, Tennessee

Dewey Decimal Classification: F
Subject Heading: SELF-ACCEPTANCE–FICTION\MOVING–
FICTION\CONVERSION–FICTION

Page viii, partial lyrics of "Child of the Wind," written by Bruce
Cockburn, © 1991 Golden Mountain Music Corp., used by permission.

Unless otherwise stated all Scripture citation is from the RSV, Revised
Standard Version of the Bible, copyrighted 1946, 1952, © 1971, 1973.

1 2 3 4 5 6 7 8 9 10 07 06 05 04 03

For Robin Hardy,
who deserves most of the blame for the
fact you are holding this book in your hand right now.

Little round planet
In a big universe
Sometimes it looks blessed
Sometimes it looks cursed
Depends on what you look at obviously
But even more it depends on the way that you see

— Bruce Cockburn, "Child of the Wind"

ACKNOWLEDGMENTS

I sat down and wrote this book, but that seems minor in comparison to all that others did to make this thing a reality. First there's Dad, who kept saying for years, "You need to write this stuff down," and Mom, who said, "*Apogee?* Are you trying to help sell dictionaries on the side?" Then there's Sueann, who endured all the early incarnations of this work, and Jeannette, who not only did that, but also committed the serendipitous act of foisting it on a friend by the name of Robin Hardy. And Daniel and Sarah, who insisted I tell these stories over and over. And of course Milly, The Woman and the last word on what will work and what must go.

Thanks to Jodi Wheatley for suffering through many hours and regrettable manuscripts in the dark ages to convince me to quit writing junk, Lanny and Eric Hall for being an early fan base, and Don Woodliff for many years of support and inspiring the creation of Jolene over egg drop soup and kung pao chicken in 1989.

More thanks than I can possibly document goes to Robin Hardy, who single-handedly promoted this manuscript over more than a decade until somebody finally relented, an act that never fails to inspire and awe me anytime I think about it. (Go out and buy all her books, right now! Yes, I'm talking to you.) A very large amount of credit goes to Milly and especially Sam Lott, the Texas Outlaw, for pointing out when I'm being lazy and not giving the big scenes the effort they require. Without them, this book would not be half as good as it is today.

Thanks to my editor, Gary Terashita, who gave me an education on what it takes to get a book in the store, and what it takes to get it out of the store, and who tells me what he thinks is the truth even at the risk of inflating my ego. And to Lisa Parnell for a gimlet eye and a light touch.

It only seems fitting to acknowledge my primary sources of information for corroborating details in the past year: biblegateway.com, dictionary.com, cdnow.com, amazon.com, about.com, and yahoo.com, through which I found the more obscure sites. And thanks to everyone out there named Arthur.

Finally, thanks to God, who shows up with the baseball bat when I need it and showed up with the cross when everybody needed it.

— BRAD WHITTINGTON —
www.fredtexas.com

CHAPTER ONE I found it in the back of a drawer in his roll-top desk. Not that I was looking for it. I was just cleaning out the desk. I didn't mind. In fact, I preferred it to cleaning out the closets, which Hannah was doing, or cataloging the furniture, the job Heidi had chosen.

It was a small, black, cardboard ring binder with a white label. The printing on the label was definitely Dad's—a small and precise lettering from a hand that seemed to be more comfortable with cuneiform than the English alphabet. It read: "The Matthew Cloud Lexicon of Practical Usage."

Intrigued, I flipped through it. There were tabbed dividers for each letter of the alphabet. Each page appeared to have a single entry consisting of a word and a definition. I flipped back to the beginning. The first entry was:

> *Adolescence:* Insanity; a (hopefully) temporary period of
> emotional and mental imbalance. *Symptoms:* mood swings,
> melancholia, rampant idealism, insolvency. Subject takes
> everything too seriously, especially himself. *Causes:* parents,
> raging hormones. *Known cures:* longevity, homicide. *Antidotes:*
> levity, Valium.

That prompted a chuckle. I had no doubt this entry had been written while Jimmy Carter grinned from the Oval Office. I sat back in the swivel

1

chair for a welcome bit of reflection, which was to be expected, seeing as how we were settling Dad's estate. Nostalgia traps were likely to be rampant in closets and drawers all over the house.

I suppose adolescence is somewhat like insanity. In both cases isolation is sometimes seen as a method for limiting the damage. I suspected that in 1968, when I turned twelve, my parents must have sensed the initial stages of the dreaded malady. I could think of no other reason why they would have moved from metropolitan America to Fred, Texas.

I know you're dying to ask, so I might as well tell you right up front. Fred is located in East Texas, between Spurger and Caney Head. It looks different now, but back then it spanned nine-tenths of a mile between city limit signs and included six buildings of note: a general store, an elementary school, a Baptist church, a hamburger joint, a service station, and a post office. The nearest movie theater was sixteen miles south, in Silsbee. The nearest mall appeared in the early 1970s, forty miles south in Beaumont.

In many ways Fred was idyllic. There was nothing but pine woods and dirt roads to be explored, creeks to be splashed through and swam in, and fresh air to suck into your lungs in an eternal draught. Since I was only twelve and had not yet succumbed to the symptoms of adolescence, I loved it. By the time I hit sixteen, however, Fred's greatest assets had become, for me, its greatest liabilities. There was nothing but pine woods, dirt roads, and creeks.

Still, as a twelve-year-old, I reveled in the unruly semiwildness of the Big Thicket. I delved pine thickets, ferreting out hidden sanctuaries in oil-company tracts, miles from any road. The lust for adventure shared by all young boys provided me with traveling companions.

Swaying one hundred feet in the air at the top of a pine and surveying a green ocean, we were Columbus, devoutly seeking land after months at sea. Cresting the top of a limestone outcrop and finding a bottomless pool in an abandoned quarry, we were Balboa gazing in wonder upon the Pacific. Picking our way through a stagnant bayou, balanced precariously on moss-covered logs and leaping from one knot of ground to another, we were Marion Francis—the Swamp Fox—cleverly eluding the British once again. Following the meandering trail of a dried creek bed, we were Powell winding through the Grand Canyon.

But even in the passion of exploration, caught in the frantic surmise that we were probably the first humans to have ever seen a particular secluded hideout (deduced from the absence of beer cans or other trash), I felt the subtle walls as real as stone between me and my companions.

For example, the names Balboa, Francis, and Powell meant nothing to them. (Of course they knew of Columbus. After all, he had a day named after him to guarantee his immortality.) One of my failings—academic success—didn't endear me to my peers.

Language was yet another plank in the scaffold of my isolation. My parents had taken great pains to weed ungrammatical habits out of their children, with mixed success. In my speech such phrases as "I done did," "I seen him," or "I ain't" were conspicuous by their absence. I discovered that Fredonians didn't trust anyone who talked differently.

But those differences paled against the Great Divider. We had moved to Fred because my father was the new pastor of the Baptist church. I was a preacher's kid (or PK, as we say in the business). Nothing is guaranteed to bring a spicy conversation or a racy joke to a dead halt like the arrival of the preacher's kid. I became as accustomed to seeing conversation die when I approached as a skunk expects the crowd to part when it walks through.

Nonetheless, I tolerated those inconveniences in my preadolescent state, glorying in the remote wilderness like a hermit. It was only when hormonal changes initiated the symptoms of the malady of adolescence that I began to languish rather than glory in my isolation from modern

3

culture. The crude tree house that had served variously as fort, ship, headquarters, prison, hideout, and throne now did duty as a sanctuary of solitude to which I retreated to puzzle out Fred's provincial culture and my place in it.

Many teenage boys would have loved such an environment; indeed, most native Fredonian teens thrived in it. With graceless effort they shot deer, snagged perch, played football, and rattled in pickups down dirt roads. George Jones and Tammy Wynette oozed from their pores like sweat. Under black felt Stetsons they sported haircuts as flat as an aircraft carrier. Pointed boots with taps announced their coming as they approached, and leather belts with names stamped on the back proclaimed their identity as they departed. They dipped snuff, spitting streams like some ambulatory species of archerfish. Their legs fit around a horse as naturally as a catcher's fist nestles in his mitt. They split logs and infinitives, chopped wood and prepositional phrases, dangled fish bait and participles—all with equal skill.

However, in the throes of the teenage condition, I gradually grew dissatisfied with this remote Eden. Although native Texans, our family had spent four years in Ohio. (Since Yankeeland is technically in the same country, no visa or inoculations are required to move there. However, as far as Texans are concerned, Yankeeland is a foreign country and travelers should update their cultural resistance immunization before spending any significant time there.) Nothing can stop the onslaught of adolescence, but perhaps my parents had hoped that my first eight years in Fort Worth were sufficient to inoculate me against Northern influences. Unknown to them, however, I contracted the germs of a companion disease during my four years of Yankee exile.

In the North, I watched in fascination as hippies and "flower power" bloomed around me. Although too young to participate, I was mesmerized by Peter Max, paisley, and psychedelic posters. Still, I arrived in Fred seemingly intact. But as the symptoms of adolescence surfaced, they triggered the dormant 1960s-counterculture virus, which in turn sprouted in that unlikely Texas garden.

Fred was no place for a would-be flower child seeking sympathetic flora. The British Invasion of the seventeenth century took more than one hundred years to reach East Texas. As I surveyed Fred, I suspected it would take the second British Invasion—the Beatles, the Rolling Stones, and Led Zeppelin—at least that long to reach me.

My distinguishing features, combined with my growing detachment, separated me from the culture short of complete social isolation. Consequently, I remained on the outside looking in, spending most of my teenage years observing rather than participating.

But I guess I should start at the beginning.

CHAPTER TWO In 1964, when Mom and Dad returned to Fort Worth with the news that we were moving to a place where snow stayed on the ground until after Easter, I was skeptical. Who did they think they were kidding? At eight years old, even I knew that snow didn't hang around until April, not even in the Panhandle where they always got snow in the winter. The March ice storm that had accompanied my birth had been a fluke, like the lions whelping in the streets and men on fire strolling through Rome the night before Caesar got it in the neck.

Yet my parents insisted they had actually seen the stuff, right there on the ground. Snow, I mean. Not lions and flaming men. And parents are never wrong.

I wasn't particularly anxious to go north. I felt that living on Felix Street gave me a special connection to Felix the Cat and his bag of tricks, and I was loath to abandon that magical location. Plus, there was a cute girl down the street I wanted to look at a few hundred more times. But, alas, it was not to be.

Heidi didn't welcome the idea either. She was two years older than I was and looked more like Dad—brown hair, green eyes, and tending toward plumpness. Unlike Dad, she was shy and didn't make friends easily. The announcement struck her like a prophecy of exile. No sackcloth and ashes were available at J. C. Penney's, so she had to settle for gloomy looks as she moped around the house.

Hannah didn't share Heidi's outlook. At six years old, she had the inverse apportionment—Mom's looks (slim, blond hair, blue eyes) and Dad's disposition. She looked forward to the trip, her only regret that the snow would be melted before we got there.

As seems to be my lot in life, looking backward at what I was leaving behind left me unprepared for what lay ahead—the change in status from obscurity, as son of a graduate student in theology, to prominence as a preacher's kid. PKs, like preachers themselves, seem to have a spotlight perpetually trained on them, highlighting their every success or failure. But there's one minor difference: preachers are, hopefully, prepared to live in the limelight. Given their choice of careers, perhaps they prefer it.

Somewhere in the seminary curriculum must certainly exist a course explaining that as a member of the congregation an open fly might be noticed by twenty or thirty people, but as the pastor a similar lapse in vigilance in the pulpit will result in hundreds of devout Christians discussing it for weeks, if not years. I suspect the students are required to sign a statement absolving the seminary of all blame in the event of dire embarrassment from undue public exposure. They accept it as part of the territory when they take the gig.

PKs get this fringe benefit with or without prior knowledge or consent. Or signing the form. This gives them plausible deniability, but that is little consolation to those who suffer under a weight that proves too great for many. They break under the strain and tumble into a life of dissipation, taking up bad habits such as spitting and scratching in public or leaving their beds unmade, and they eventually run off to join the circus and fraternize with undesirables such as hurdy-gurdy hustlers and actresses, or other people of that sort.

But my immediate future didn't include actresses, hurdy-gurdies, or even spitting.

The long trek to the North culminated in my first moment in the spotlight. Sunday morning arrived and, as per custom, I found myself in a church. But this was not a large brick building of imposing proportions, with pipe organ, white pews, scarlet carpet, and matching seat cushions. Instead, it was a white nineteenth-century frame building on the edge of downtown, all wood and stained glass, and able to accommodate about three hundred souls, penitent or apostate. Instead of sitting in relative obscurity somewhere in the middle, I sat on the first row in the semigloom. The man in front wasn't some imposing silver-haired gentleman; it was Dad, a pale man, short and dumpy, with a crew cut that made no attempt to disguise the receding hairline, and glasses recovered from the estate of Buddy Holly. He called us up to be introduced. Heidi, Hannah, and I stood in stair-step fashion next to Mom and faced a crowd of perhaps one hundred people who got a good look at us, as though to be able to pick us out in the lineup afterward should there be any trouble.

Little old ladies came by and patted my head and held my hand with their withered claws and told me how cute I was and how happy they were to have the chance to say so. I nodded gravely back at them. Buxom matrons wearing too much powder and perfume hugged me messily and told me how much I looked like my mother. I nodded gravely back at them. Deacons, smelling of aftershave or coffee or cigarettes, slapped me on the back and told me what a fine specimen I was, as if I had been captured and placed in a jar in a natural history museum for their amusement. I nodded gravely back at them. They all had one thing in common: age. Not a kid in sight.

The next day I made the first of many grand entrances into a strange classroom. I didn't encounter much difficulty, other than the fact that all the other kids had learned to write cursive in the second grade, something I was expecting to do in third grade. The teacher dealt with this problem by giving me some books and telling me to figure it out.

The house Dad had located on short notice was a two-bedroom farmhouse, which posed problems for a family of five. I muddled through the third grade with cramped quarters and cramped handwriting. The next summer Dad found a more suitable house in the suburbs, and we moved to another school district. My first day in fourth grade caught the teacher shorthanded when it came to desks. Since I was built along the lines of a soda straw (only with larger hands and feet), she found another slender student and we shared a desk. The other student was a cute girl named Sheila. I approved her plan.

When we finished our lesson, we got a book on birds and leafed through it together, snickering when we got to the picture of two lovebirds. I saw this as an omen, but the next summer our family moved yet again, to a white-flight neighborhood. Just as I was getting around to writing a note that said, "Do you like me? Check a box. __ Yes __ No." (OK, I never said I was quick off the line, but I heard somewhere that slow and steady wins the race.)

I had, by this time, learned how to write at least as well as a doctor. I had also learned that classmates are like the dog that follows you home. Better not get too attached. When a little dark-haired cutie named Carolyn batted her eyes at me, I didn't even have time to organize my note-writing materials before she became the stuff of memory. In September, a two-story frame house opened up in town a few blocks from the church. But the distance from the white-bread-America suburb to the inner-city neighborhood was a lot further than the twenty miles we put on the Vauxhall driving in.

By now, Heidi was in a perpetual state of mourning, which helped me understand the reaction of the Israelites to Jeremiah. I refrained from digging a pit for her, sensing that the plan might not meet with universal approval. Hannah bounced from one school to another with the flexibility of a switch-hitter.

Settling into the house was an adventure. It had a full basement and attic. In my bedroom I discovered the door to the attic stairs. I abandoned unpacking to explore, which I did with the thoroughness of a cartographer. I climbed and crawled over rafters and under dormers, blazing a trail through decades of dust and disintegrating newspapers. I noted the grimy window in the hidden alcove that I claimed, silently, as my personal refuge. It overlooked a mass of housetops and trees with the receding leaf-lines of fall. Next, the basement, which yielded little beyond flaking paint, the smell of mildew, and a monstrous beast Dad identified as the furnace.

The backyard was a rectangle of weeds and crabgrass surrounded by a vine-covered chain-link fence. Dead leaves sloped against the garage. I went to the back fence and peered through the vines. A large set of brown eyes peered back from a dark face. I jumped back, tripped, and fell backward. A strange sound emerged from behind the curtain of leaves. I rolled to my knees and looked through the bottom of the fence.

A Negro boy was rolling on the ground, snorting like a pig and kicking up leaves and dust. Evidently he had also been startled and was having a seizure of some kind. I tried to remember what to do, something about making sure he didn't swallow his tongue. I wasn't sure how to do that, but I assumed time was a critical element. I was halfway over the fence, trying to disentangle my shoelace, when the snorting changed to a thin, rising and falling wail. I paused, puzzled. Obviously he wasn't swallowing his tongue. As I stood in frozen indecision, the noise became a sound that left me both relieved and annoyed. Laughter.

I straddled the fence, shoes crammed pigeon-toed into the wire, glaring with impatience and pique. The convulsions of glee subsided into tremors of giggles, like the fading thunder of a passing storm. I waited, looking down from my exalted position with royal disdain. However, each time the boy looked up at me, the sirenlike noise erupted, and he flopped about on the ground, mottled brown and black, dust on skin.

My ankles complained of the impossible angle I had forced on them. I shifted my weight to my hands, but the vines were too insubstantial to support even my meager weight, and I tumbled into the yard onto the laughing boy. This development, while alarming me, only served to increase his amusement. He suffered a relapse of the snorting stage, rolling around and slapping weakly at me as he laughed.

I struggled to my feet and looked down at him with as much amazement as annoyance. How could he sustain such spasms without internal injury? He grabbed at my leg and used me as a support to crawl to his feet, leaning against me and laughing. Odors of grass, dirt, and the musky smell of the boy's sweat mingled in the air. I felt him quivering as he staggered against me. As if it were spread by contact, I began to be infected by his laughter and, against my will, found myself chuckling. The boy looked up from his bent stance and pawed feebly at my chest, trying to catch his breath between barks of delight. This struck me as rather amusing, and I began to laugh in earnest. We spurred each other on to greater heights of hilarity until we both collapsed on the ground and surrendered to an ecstasy of elation. It gradually faded in fits and giggles, replaced by the contented silence of exhaustion.

I sat up. "Mark," I said, holding out my hand.

"Yes?" He looked at my hand. Bits of grass and leaves adorned his close-cropped hair like Christmas ornaments. Now that we had recovered from our convulsions, I was able to get a look at him. He was very dark, like the dark chocolate Mom liked but none of us kids did. He was a little

shorter than I was, and much stockier, which was no great feat. I had seen
walking sticks with more meat on their bones than I had. His head bulged
out in back as if to counterbalance his large nose and lips. He was wearing a brown V-neck T-shirt under a nappy burnt-orange sweater. Black
high-tops protruded from his frayed jeans.

"I'm Mark. What's your name?" My hand hung out between us.

"Marc." He grabbed my hand and shook it as vigorously as he had
laughed earlier.

"Right. And you are?" I vibrated from the energy of his handshake.

"Marc." He continued to shake my hand, smiling hugely.

I began to wonder if I had tumbled into the grounds of a private
lunatic asylum. I looked at him blankly while developing an appreciation
for the rigors of the life of a pump handle.

He finally quit shaking my hand and stood up. "Only youse guys
prob'ly spells yours with a *K,* as in Mark Twain. Mine has a *C,* as in
Marcus. Marcus Malcom Marshall, to be exack, as in Garvey, X, and
Thurgood, respectively. No relation, though. But everybody jus' call me
M." The torrent of words gushed from him with no discernable pauses for
breathing.

I hated to admit I didn't follow any of it. I latched onto the one part I
did understand. "M?"

"Yep. Man, you talk funny. Where you from?"

"*I* talk funny? *Youse* guys talks funny."

"Alabama? I bet it's Alabama," he declared, undeterred by my
comments.

"Alabama?" I snorted in disgust.

"Texas, then."

I was torn between pride at being a Texan and reluctance to admit he
had guessed correctly. "Fort Worth," I countered.

"And Bingo was his name-o!" M declared with a quick pirouette of triumph and a short siren wail of laughter that was suddenly cut off. "Come on," he said, grabbing my arm and dragging me away from the fence.

"Where are we going?"

"You gots to meet Mama."

"I do?"

"Yeah, everybody gots to meet Mama."

I looked back at the fence, catching a glimpse of the moving van above the vines. From a second-story window, Hannah peered out through the film of grime on the glass like the ghost in a Gothic novel. I attempted a shrug, which was difficult while being dragged across M's backyard. I waved as we mounted the back steps, but it probably looked more like a kid reaching back toward the house in distress. Then we disappeared through a screen door.

We maneuvered through a dank laundry room and emerged into an amalgam of potent odors. A very tall, slightly plump and very black woman stood in front of a stove. She was wearing an apron over a nice dress. Without turning around she said, "Go back an' wipe your feet. I jus' mopped this floor." I looked down. The linoleum was a dull yellow, cracked and curling, but clean. I was dragged back through the laundry room to the doormat, where M and I wiped our feet and returned to the kitchen.

"Mama, it's Mark from Texas, but with a *k*, as in Mark Twain." He shoved me forward, and I stumbled to a stop at the foothills of the black mountain towering above me. She turned around, ladle in hand, and smiled down at me with large teeth. "Hello, Mark from Texas." She held out a hand, the pink palm enveloping my puny white hand. "Did you move in back there?" She pointed the ladle toward our house.

I nodded.

"Well thas jus' fine. Careful you don't let M talk your ears off."

I nodded, again.

"Are youse guys hungry?" she asked. I looked apprehensively at the steam rising from the pots on the stove. I had no idea what was in them, but the deep odors didn't call to the deep of my appetite. The aroma verged between a slaughterhouse and a laundry.

M leapt as if he'd been stabbed in the flank with a hat pin. "Yes!" he cried, producing two plates seemingly from thin air. He placed them on the green Formica tabletop. Before I had a chance to say "Pepto-Bismol," I was seated in front of a plate of limp, slimy green leaves and some unidentified meat in a watery brown sauce.

"You comin' from Texas, I'm sure you been havin' some chitlins and collard greens lots of times," Mrs. Marshall said.

"Not that I recall," I replied. I assumed the green stuff was the greens, so the other must be the chitlins.

M looked at me in disbelief, and his mother said, "Well, then, you is in for a real treat!"

I was now on center stage, the audience waiting for my next move. My fork wavered over the plate like a divining rod. I went for the meat. Two sets of eyes followed my fork to my mouth. I chewed quickly and swallowed, and waited for the taste to catch up. Not bad. Pretty good, actually. I enthusiastically went for another bite and made a devoted friend. Mrs. Marshall nodded and turned back to the stove. And not a moment too soon because the greens were another story entirely. I was able to finish them with generous portions of chitlins.

As I was forcing down the last bit of greens, I heard a knock on the back door. Mrs. Marshall disappeared into the laundry room. A familiar voice said, "Good afternoon. I'm Matthew Cloud, just moving in across the way. I was checking up on my son, who I understand might be bothering you folks over here."

Mrs. Marshall laughed. "Oh no, Mr. Cloud, he ain't no trouble. He jus' finishin' up a plate of chitlins and collard greens right now. That boy needs some fattenin' up!"

Dad walked in to see me with a forkful of chitlins suspended between plate and mouth. Hannah, evidently the messenger who had alerted Dad to my abduction, peeked her blond head around the door like a sideways Kilroy.

"Well, I suspect you're right about that point," Dad chuckled, apparently amused at the sight of me tossing down the chitlins like one of the family. "I'm afraid I'm going to have to borrow him back. It's a little matter of a dozen boxes in his room he was supposed to unpack before he took off."

The Amazon clicked her tongue disapprovingly, and I suddenly felt guilty. I gulped down the chitlins and jumped up.

"Thanks." I looked at M. "I guess I have to go back now."

Mrs. Marshall nodded at me. "You're welcome, Mark. And I hope you come back when you done your chores."

I looked at Dad. "Sure, if it's not too late."

Unpacking took until after dark, but Sunday after church I returned. M took me on a tour, starting with a basement much more interesting than mine. Poor lighting, unfinished walls, and exposed rafters gave it the ambiance of a cave. M grabbed a hammer and pounded furiously at a sixteen-penny nail jutting from one of the studs.

"When Papa hits a nail, there's sparks fly," he said with respect, and swung the hammer again. "Hey, I think I saw a spark. Here, you try it, man." I declined, but M wouldn't rest until I had taken a few ineffectual swings at the nail. No sparks.

The rest of the house wasn't much different from mine, albeit in a more advanced stage of disintegration. M's attic view faced the opposite street, so I was able to see how the other half lived as we sat on an old trunk and squinted through the grime. More roofs and trees in their final stages of abandonment.

"That's the school over there." M pointed at a square roof several blocks away. "What grade are you in, man? I bet it's fifth."

"Fifth."

"And Bingo was his name-o!" he cried and attempted a pirouette, but the cramped quarters of the attic made it impossible. He settled for a jig and a chuckle. "Me too. Which class? I bet it's Ma Barker's." He stood poised for another victory dance.

"I haven't been yet."

"Oh, yeah." He sat back down on the trunk. "What's it like in Texas?"

"I don't know. Like here, only no basements. And hotter."

"One day I'll go see. I'm gonna go see everything, like Marcus Garvey."

"Like who?"

"The Right Excellent Marcus Mosiah Garvey." He waited, but I had nothing to say. "Never met the guy," seemed flippant.

"Malcom X?"

I shook my head.

"Thurgood Marshall?"

I shook my head.

M looked at me for a long while with an impassive stare I couldn't interpret, as if he were trying to make up his mind. He suddenly stood up and walked down the attic stairs; I followed him to his room. He pulled a thin paperback book from a cardboard box next to his bed and shoved it at me. I looked at the title: *The Negro Protest: James Baldwin, Malcom X, and Martin Luther King Talk with Kenneth B. Clark.* I looked back up at M, but he just walked past me and down the stairs. We walked through the kitchen to the back door. "I'll see you tomorrow, man," he said and closed the door behind me.

CHAPTER THREE I was indeed in Ma Barker's class, who turned out to be Mrs. Barker, a middle-aged white woman and not, as far as I could tell, the matriarch of a bloodthirsty outlaw gang. But you have to admit, being a fifth-grade teacher would have been a great cover.

After school I found M waiting at the back fence.

"Come on," he said. "It's Meesha and Keesha's birthday."

"Meesha and Keesha?"

"The twins."

"I would have never guessed. What twins?"

"Harriet's twins. Just come on and you'll see."

In the living room a sheet was spread out on the worn wooden floor. In the middle a cake slathered in white icing was graced with a single candle flickering in the drafty room. Two identically dressed babies sat on either side, looking up at the looming adults with that complacent apprehension one sometimes finds in babies.

A girl I took to be Harriet towered over them, and me. She was wearing a purple paisley tube of some kind of stretchy material with a black patent-leather belt. Her large hands and feet left no doubt as to whose daughter she was. She wasn't quite as dark as M, except around her elbows and knees. She hovered over the twins in a half-crouch, her knees together. "Blow out the candle," she said in baby talk. The twins just looked at her.

"Make a wish," Mrs. Marshall said, also in baby talk and also towering. The twins blinked in unison, realigned their sights on her, and picked up where they had left off, doing their best imitation of confused one-year-old babies.

Across the room an older man with close-cropped gray hair sat in a frowzy armchair, a newspaper open in his lap. He watched the babies dispassionately, but I thought I detected a hint of amusement.

M strode forward. "They don't know how to blow out a candle. They're only one!" He leaned over and blew the candle out.

"Now have some cake," Harriet said.

"Yes, eat your birthday cake," Mrs. Marshall said. "It's chocolate. Everybody like chocolate cake."

M looked from his sister to his mother with exasperation, leaned over, scooped icing off the cake with his finger, and shoved some in each baby's mouth. Their expressions changed instantly, and they converged on the cake. Before Mrs. Marshall had time to cut us slices from the other cake set aside in the kitchen, there were three lumpy masses of icing and cake in the middle of the sheet, like an accident scene of a collision with a zebra, a penguin, and a nun. Two of them moved. M and I disappeared into the basement before we were recruited for cleanup duty.

M dug up two claw hammers, turned off the light, and we took turns banging on a nail, trying to make sparks. We labored in shadow, silhouetted by the light from the little rectangular basement window high above us.

I began singing "I've Been Working on the Railroad" but stopped when M threatened to switch his attentions from the nail head to my head.

"Did you read that book I gave you, man?" M asked between strokes.

"Hey, that was only two days ago."

"Do you know who John Brown was?"

I began singing again. "John Brown's body lies a molderin' in the grave . . ." but the silhouette of M's hammer hung over me in the gloom and I quit.

"Why was his body molderin' in a grave?"

"He was dead." That was an easy one!

"Why did he die?"

That was a little tougher. "Uh, chicken pox?"

M rolled his eyes, which was about all I could see of him, and resumed his hammering. "Do you know who George Washington was?"

"Of course."

"George Washington Carver?"

"Yes."

M stopped. "Really?"

"Of course. He invented the peanut." I held the hammer aloft and spun around. "And Bingo was his name-o!"

M didn't laugh. "OK, man, how about W. B. DuBois?"

I stopped and peered at him in the dimness. "Uh, can you spell it?"

"Marcus Garvey?"

"That's the guy you're named after, right?"

"One of them."

"What did he do?"

"Read the book." He slammed the hammer down. "Look, sparks!"

As the weeks passed, M and I eventually bored of banging on nails in the basement and hanging from rafters in the attic. My house offered even less excitement. We had already squeezed the neighborhood dry of every last drop of entertainment. We started making regular Saturday trips to the library, ten blocks downtown.

Sometimes we took detours, exploring sections of downtown. One of our favorite spots was next to the theater, which was in the middle of the block. The parking lot was in the back by the alley, but the entrance was in the front on the street. A long corridor through the building provided a shortcut. It was paved in small, white ceramic tiles, the floor undulating in gentle waves. The sides jutted in and out at sharp angles, with columns against the walls at regular intervals along the way. It was enclosed with a glass door at each end.

The corridor provided a great setting for reenacting episodes of *I Spy*, the old spy show with Robert Culp and Bill Cosby. M thought it was amusing and appropriate that Cosby was the intelligent one in the show. I didn't concur.

We would traverse the corridor, running and ducking behind columns, shooting at imaginary villains or, sometimes, at each other, an inexplicable plot development for which the scriptwriters had not provided. Before long our territory for spying extended down the alley and out several blocks, past the back doors of cleaners, diners, barbershops, and five-and-dimes.

Late one Saturday afternoon, as the shadows were stretching to the horizon, I was eluding M, who stalked me down the corridor. In a bold move I rushed the alley door, almost colliding with a couple on their way to see *Fantastic Voyage*. Their confusion delayed M, allowing me to round the corner before he could see which way I went. I had a plan. I sprinted down a dead-end alley, thinking he would never expect me to trap myself. At the end, I climbed some trash cans and dropped over a dilapidated wooden fence into a neglected area behind an auto shop.

It was the perfect refuge, one I had discovered the week before when I was the hunter instead of the hunted. I planned to crouch along the back fence, watching for M's approach. For cover, I had my choice of a fifty-five-gallon oil drum or a large cardboard box that had once held a washing machine. It lay on its side, old rags spilling out onto the ground. I chose the oil drum, from which I could peek through a knothole in the fence. I checked my surroundings. The asphalt faded a few feet from the shop into dry, cracked, packed dirt broken up with weeds and littered with rusted transmissions, wheels, mufflers, and other detritus. A metal door pad-locked on the outside broke the brick wall of the shop, which had been painted white a long time ago. The only other access to this area was a two-foot gap between the shop and the liquor store that ran the length from the alley to the street.

I watched for M's shadow on the bricks of the alley, the rags in the box rustling in the wind. Then I realized there was no wind. I jerked away from the fence and looked at the rags. From the shadow of the box a raspy voice asked, "What's yer name, boy?"

I couldn't have been more startled if the oil drum had started to spon-taneously play "Wipe Out." I was poised to jump and run when a face materialized among the rags and shadows. A woman's face. Green eyes burned from sunken wells of eye sockets. A wealth of nascent wrinkles was evident on the leathery skin, skin that had seen many a day in the open sun and more than one night under the stars. Short brown hair, matted and tan-gled, disappeared into the tattered brown blanket draped around the woman. But what held my eye captive was the large purple-red birthmark that ran from her left eyebrow to her cheek in a meandering splotch.

"Yer name. What's yer name?"

I said, as if in a trance, "Mark."

"Ah, the Mark. The Mark. It's got the Mark." An emaciated hand flut-tered to her left temple and dropped down like a bird frozen and falling from a branch.

"Well, Mark, do you have anythin' so much as a fiver on yer?" I shook my head slowly. "I could use a bite to eat, yer know. How 'bout some change?" Her eyes burned even brighter. "I got a powerful thirst." She looked at my pants pocket, the one with the dollar in it, as if she could see it through the fabric. Her hand twitched.

As if on its own, my hand dug down and produced the dollar. I held it out, fluttering from my shaking hand in the stillness. Her hand shot out like a cobra and snagged the bill, eyes flaring up and returning to the burning green.

"Thank ye, thank ye. Mighty white of ye, Mark." A low, raspy chortle emerged from the depths of her throat. She unfolded from beneath the blanket like a moth shedding a chrysalis. A worn and dirty cotton print dress flapped a few inches above her ankles and the worn brown brogans on her feet as she shuffled to the gap and disappeared.

I blinked and felt as if I had suddenly awakened. Had I dreamed it? I reached into my pocket. The dollar was gone. I climbed the oil drum and vaulted the fence into the alley, ready to be found by M.

I didn't tell anyone about the Creature, but I couldn't erase her image from my mind. I dreamed about her Saturday night. Her face of creases and splotches haunted me during the Sunday school lesson of the woman at the well. In church I formulated a plan. When the offering plate went by, I held an empty hand low over the plate and thumped the bottom with the other thumb as it passed in front of me, my money still safe in my pocket.

At home that afternoon I hopped the back fence in pretense of visiting M, but passed his house. Downtown I walked through the tile corridor, turned into the blind alley, climbed gingerly over the fence, and dropped quietly to the ground.

The Creature was in the box, but she didn't acknowledge my presence. I crept closer, alert for any movement. As I approached, I heard a steady raspy sound from beneath the bedraggled blanket. Something clinked on the ground—my foot had hit a clear flask. I kicked it over and looked at the label. Gin. I looked at her a little longer, then threaded my way through the gap to the street.

It took me awhile, but I finally found a place I could buy a sandwich and a bottle of Coke with the offering money. I returned to the box, set the food on the ground, and sat down on a wheel in the shade of the fence. After awhile I got tired of waiting and started throwing pebbles at the box. Three minutes and twenty pebbles later, I was rewarded.

The Creature stirred, saw the food, and looked suspiciously out of the box. The purple splotch was dark against the pale skin on the left side of her face. "It's the Mark," she croaked. She crawled out of the box, snatched the food, and sat on the edge of a transmission housing several yards away, her feet straddling a dirty red stream of transmission fluid.

She positioned herself so she was facing the gap in the wall, but could see me from the corner of her right eye. I watched in silence while she devoured the sandwich like a wild animal, eating some of the paper wrapping in her haste. Once the sandwich was gone, she picked up the Coke and drank the entire bottle slowly in one long draught, looking at me obliquely with leaden green eyes like the Atlantic on a cloudy day. She closed her eyes and let out a belch that reverberated through the courtyard.

In a sudden movement she hurled the bottle against the liquor shop wall. It shattered in a shower of glass and I jerked like I'd been slapped.

"The Mark follered me. What's yer game?"

"Game?"

She turned her head slightly in my direction with a jerk, eyes narrowing and darting, sometimes in my direction, sometimes around the littered courtyard, like a bird watching a cat while looking for food. "Meaty, beaty, big and bouncy." She dropped her chin, lowering her coarse voice until it sounded like a man. "He speaks plain cannon fire, and smoke and bounce."

I looked at her blankly.

She raised her head, voice returning to its normal level, and peppered me with questions. "Got the drop on me? Got me bang to rights? Flushed me out, five by five?"

"I just thought you might be hungry. At least, I remember you saying something like that."

The Creature grabbed the frayed hem of her cotton print dress and wrapped it tightly around her calves, bunching it up in her hand. Brown legs covered with black hair extended to the scarred brogans below.

"The Mark was hungry." She rocked forward and backward on the transmission. "In hunger and thirst," she rasped in a throaty whisper, "in nakedness and dire poverty, ye will be a restless wanderer on the earth. But the Mark will foller ye." She twisted the cloth in her hand and turned her head slowly toward me.

"I was also powerful thirsty." Her eyes followed mine to the empty gin bottle. "Fancy a drink?" I shook my head. "Got another dollar on yer?" I shook my head again. "Didn't reckon yer did." She turned her head back and rested her chin on her knees, keeping watch on me from the corner of her eye. We sat in silence for awhile.

I finally got the courage to speak. "What's your name?"

The Creature didn't move, or even blink, but I heard a small growl that seemed to echo from the walls enclosing us. It could have only come from her, since we were completely alone.

"Lilith," she hissed.

"Thilly rabbit," she lisped in falsetto. She jerked upright. "Thufferin' thuckotash, the Mark follered me!" She looked at me suspiciously. "Yer tryin' to make me?"

"Make you what?"

"Stand and deliver," she boomed, jumping up and stomping in the red mud at her feet. "The Mark follered me. Which one are ye? Senoy? Where are yer friends?" She reached into the neckline of her dress and pulled out a chain with some kind of charm or pendant hanging from it. It looked like a cross, but the top was a loop. "Sansenoy, Semangelof, show yerselves!" Holding the charm toward the sky, she turned slowly around, looking at the roofs surrounding us. "Yer can't touch the child. I have the Mark!"

I looked around apprehensively. Who was she talking to?

The Creature completed her circle, scowling at the sky. Then she dropped the chain back into her dress, shuffled to the cardboard box, and crawled in, wrapping the blanket around her and facing out so that I couldn't see the purple splotch on her face. "Who are ye?" she whispered. "What do yer want?"

"You know my name but I don't know yours."

"Naamah," she said, hoarsely. "Just call me Naamah."

"Naamah? What kind of name is that?"

"The kind I hand out fer free. I make yer a present of everythin' I said today." She was silent for a few seconds. "What do yer want?"

"I just wanted to find out about you." I ignored the babble. "After all, I did give you a dollar. And some food," I added, in an attempt to shame her into answering my questions.

"And here I thought ye was doin' yer Christian duty."

"Maybe I was. I can still get something for it, can't I?"

"Oh, no. Yer supposed to do it expectin' nothin' in return." She cleared her throat, which induced a coughing fit that concluded in her spitting phlegm four feet in front of the box. In a deep, throaty voice she intoned, "Cast yer bread on the waters. Don't let yer left hand know what yer right hand is about. Ye ask and receive not because yer ask amiss, fer yer own selfish lusts."

After this last utterance, she arranged the blanket low on her shoulders like a party shawl and tossed a suggestive leer my way. Her green eyes sparkled from beneath the shadow of her brow. I saw the ghost of a younger woman—attractive, carefree, a hint of playful innocence.

Then she turned her face full toward me, and I caught sight of the purple splotch. The ghost was exorcised. Her eyes returned to the dull, leaden green I had seen earlier, and she glowered at me.

"What do yer want, boy?" she demanded in a low, threatening growl.

I glanced around nervously and looked back at her without a word. She turned, crawled into the recesses of the box, and pulled the blanket over her head. I waited for awhile, staring at her brogans, then got up quietly, circumnavigated the box, and squeezed through the gap toward home.

CHAPTER FOUR The next Saturday M and I made our library trip as usual. I let M use my twenty-inch Spyder bike with the chopper handlebars and tiger-skin banana seat; I "borrowed" Heidi's bike. (I would not have normally agreed to be seen in public on a girl's bike, but it had a large basket convenient for transporting the large number of books we always checked out.)

I was quiet as we rode along, which didn't bother M. He chattered, oblivious to my silence. My thoughts were on the Creature and how she was faring. I wanted to check on her, but I didn't know how to ditch M. As we neared the theater, I made a snap decision, turning down the alley instead of taking the street to the library. It took M awhile to realize I wasn't with him. He stopped in midsentence. "Hey, man, where you goin'?"

"This way," I hollered over my shoulder. He caught up with me at the end of the blind alley.

"Hey, what . . . ," he started, but I held up my hand for silence.

"Wait here," I whispered, "I want to check on something." I climbed the trash can by the fence.

"Where are you going?" he asked in a stage whisper.

I jumped over the fence. The courtyard was unchanged. I padded silently to the cardboard box, but the Creature wasn't there. I stood looking into the box's shadows when M dropped over the fence.

He looked around nervously. "What are you doin'?" he demanded in a hoarse whisper. "Are you crazy?"

I could see something in the back recesses of the box, beyond the tattered blanket, and was intrigued by the thought of what the Creature would stash away. I hoped it might give me a clue to who she was and why she lived as she did. I looked around quickly and dropped down, reaching into the box. A miasma of sweat, alcohol, and vomit enveloped my head and I rolled back out, gasping for fresh air.

M said, "Hey," but I took a deep breath and plunged back in, so I didn't hear the rest. My hand reached back and closed on the object. It was a small Bible, bound in limp, black leather with the name Pauline Jordan barely legible in flaking, gold gilt letters. A screeching wail and a startled shout caused me to drop the Bible, and I scuttled backward like a deranged crab.

M was backing toward the fence, his eyes large and fixed on something behind me. I spun around. The Creature shuffled toward me, a large cabbage nestled in the crook of her arm. The other arm stretched out, forefinger extended toward me like an accusation, trembling.

"The man who does not enter the sheep pen by the gate, but climbs in by some other way, is a thief and a robber," she screeched, spittle in the corners of her mouth. Then she saw my face. "The Mark," she breathed. "The Mark follered me."

Her gaze drifted from me to M. "Ham," she said, eyes burning a deep green. "Cursed be Canaan! The lowest of slaves will he be to his brothers." She jumped a menacing step in his direction, and he disappeared over the fence without a word.

The Creature turned to me. "Those who hate me without reason outnumber the hairs of my head," she said with deep venom and threw the cabbage at me. I dodged it and followed M over the fence. It took me a block to catch up with him. He didn't stop until we were on the steps of the library.

"What was that?" he demanded between gasps for air.

"I think it was Pauline." I told him the story of my previous visits.

He shook his head. "Don't mess with her, man. She's crazy."

Once inside the library, M insisted I get something by "my namesake," so I picked up a copy of *Tom Sawyer* to go with *Treasure Island*. M got *Homer Price* and *The Underground Railroad*. We got on the bikes and headed back. I suggested a detour by the church to watch Dad work on the furnace, a recalcitrant coal-burning monstrosity in need of occasional rehabilitation. We were halfway down the hill to the church, zipping along at a good pace, when my shoelace got hung in the chain. I couldn't pedal forward because the lace was wrapping around the center shaft and binding up. I couldn't pedal backward because the bike had coaster brakes. I had finally figured out that I had to hang my foot out to the side and turn the gears to push the lace through when I heard a yell.

While I had been preoccupied with the physics of shoelace-from-gear removal, I had traveled the half block to the corner, gaining speed all the while. A flash of tiger skin, black skin, and large white eyes passed under me as I mowed M down and lurched into the street—just in time, as luck would have it, to bounce off the side of a passing mail truck turning right. The rear bumper of the truck snagged the front tire of Heidi's bike and dragged me back up the half block to the point where my troubles had begun before the driver realized he had a bike attached to him like a lamprey on a shark. He screeched to a halt, jumped out, and ran back to where I sat, dazed. I was still sitting astride the bike, which leaned toward the front of the truck, held up at a forty-five-degree angle by the bumper. I stared at him, my attention riveted to a patch on his shirt that said, "Dotson."

"What's all this, then?" he demanded.

I was roused from my stupor and leaped backward from the bike. "Oh, no! Oh, no! Oh, no!" I shouted.

"What?" Dotson leaped backward too.

"Heidi will kill me! Look at the bike!" The front tire was shaped like a paramecium, the spokes splayed out like cilia.

"Look at you!" he responded.

I looked down and leaped backward again. "Oh, no! Oh, no! Oh, no!"

"Now what?" Dotson asked as he echoed my leap.

"Mom will kill me! Look at my shoe! I just got these yesterday!" My left shoe looked like it did when I left the store. My right shoe looked like Old Glory after a particularly rough night of shelling. It was in a state unlikely to inspire the most ardent patriot when viewed by the dawn's early light. Viewed by the afternoon's light, it was appalling.

A lady, looking like she was constructed entirely of feather pillows cinched up in an apron, scudded from the house behind us. "Oh my goodness! I saw the whole thing. Are you OK?" she screeched in a flurry of agitation, practically running a figure eight around Dotson and me, her hands pressed to her cheeks, fingers splayed like overstuffed sausages in a pan of dough.

If only her voice had been as soft as she appeared to be. Instead, it had much in common with the screeching of metal on metal I had heard while the truck was transforming Heidi's bike into modern art. She could have had the same effect with a lot less effort if she had just pounded nails into my ears. I covered my ears with my hands.

Dotson thrust his hand in my direction. "He's crazy. He keeps raving about his bike and his shoes."

Mrs. Puffy-Screechy looked at me holding my head. "Oh my goodness, oh my goodness! He hit his head! I must call the ambulance." She veered toward the house and screeched, "Heathcliff! Call an ambulance.

He hit his head." Then she spiraled in my general direction, grabbed me, and steered me through the gate to the porch. "Here, you must sit down and don't alarm yourself. No time for hot tea, but I can bring you some lemonade." She disappeared into the house, squeaking, "Oh my goodness, oh my goodness."

I looked around, wondering how I ended up on the porch swing. Dotson produced a little cigar with a white plastic mouthpiece and paced beside the truck, trailing smoke like the Little Engine That Rather Wouldn't. He stopped occasionally to gesticulate toward the bike and ask "Now what?" to nobody in particular.

Mrs. Puffy-Screechy reappeared, thrust a jelly glass into my hand, and disappeared back inside the door like a Frau in a cuckoo clock. I stared at the lemonade. She popped back out again with a wet dishrag and slapped it against my forehead. "Here, hold this on." I was sitting on the swing, lemonade in one hand and a dishrag in the other, when M came running up the sidewalk to the porch, leading Mom, Heidi, and Hannah. I was attempting to explain what had happened, pointing at my shoe with the dishrag–which Mrs. Puffy-Screechy kept pushing back up to my fore-head–when an ambulance appeared. The technicians jumped out, popped open the back door, and pulled out a gurney.

"I'm OK. I can walk," I hollered and jumped up from the swing, spilling the lemonade.

"Oh my goodness, oh my goodness, he's going to faint," the harpy cried and grabbed me. I jerked away and stumbled down the stairs. M caught me. "Whoa, man," he said. "Take it easy. I'll just hang right here with you."

The assembled masses decided I should be x-rayed to make sure I wasn't harboring a fatal wound like a secret grudge with which to accuse them later. As they ushered me toward the ambulance, I heard a familiar voice cry "Hey!" and I looked up. Dad was headed toward us, looking from the ambulance to the mail truck to the bike and to me. He was covered head-to-foot with soot from the furnace, a slightly overdone Pillsbury doughboy.

Dotson paused inside his cloud of cigar smoke and spread his arms, looking up. "Now what?"

"Hey," Dad repeated, gesturing with his glasses toward me in the middle of the crowd. "That's my boy you got there." He looked like Malcom X's brother Y, the short one with the gland problem.

The ambulance driver looked at dark, short, and dumpy Dad and then at M standing next to me, also dark, short, and dumpy. "No, sir, your boy is just fine. It's this one we're taking to x-ray." He took me by the shoulders and lifted me into the front seat of the ambulance. I still held the dishrag in my hand.

"No, no, *that's* my boy," Dad said, following the ambulance along as it pulled away, looking like an escapee from a minstrel show. I could hear Mrs. Puffy-Screechy wailing, "Oh my goodness, oh my goodness" from her yard.

"It's OK, mister. We're just going to give him an x-ray," the driver said, and rolled up his window. He looked over at me. "Was that your dad?"

I looked back and nodded.

He shrugged, looked out the window, and looked back at me. "Do you want to hear the siren?"

I nodded. And we went to the hospital.

––––––––

Later that evening I sat in my room under house arrest, charged with unauthorized removal of Heidi's bike from the premises. Heidi was given exclusive custody of my bike until I could earn enough money to repair or replace hers. I was reading *Tom Sawyer*. A dark, round head appeared around the door.

"You conscious, man?"

"Yes, but grounded."

"That's what I figured." M walked in and pulled a flashlight out of his back pocket. We padded lightly up the attic stairs to the secret alcove and sat next to the window, M pointing the flashlight to the ceiling between us. It cast a soft light with heavy shadows around us. "So, what happened at the hospital? Did you have brain surgery?"

"No, just an x-ray."

"Did they find a brain?"

"Ha. Very funny. They said I have a concussion." I had no idea what a concussion was, but it sounded impressive, so I was glad to have one since I had no bandages to show I'd been to the hospital.

"Wow! A concussion! Does it hurt?"

"Not yet. I'll let you know if I feel anything coming on."

"Just think, man, if I hadn't been there, you'd probably be dead right now."

"What?" I hadn't considered this theme and wasn't particularly pleased with its introduction.

"Think about it. What was the difference between you hittin' the side of the truck or being in front of the truck? Maybe a second? A second and a half?"

I replayed the events in my mind. "Yeah, about that."

"Runnin' over me probably slowed you down just enough to make the difference between concussion and coffin."

I didn't say anything. Dust sifted through the beam of the flashlight in front of M's face.

"Do you believe in God?" M asked.

"Of course," I answered automatically.

"All the time?"

"Of course." I looked at M a little closer. "Don't you?"

"Yeah." M looked away and shone the flashlight to the floor, away from his face. The shadows turned upside down. "But not all the time."

"Why not?"

M turned off the flashlight. The alcove plunged into darkness. We sat in silence. Eventually my eyes adjusted to the thin illumination that penetrated the grimy dormer window from the streetlight. M's face was a black moon in a blacker night, eyes lost in shadow.

"Sometimes, there is no God."

I squinted in the dark, trying to see his eyes. He turned his head away from me and his eyes came out of shadow, shining. He looked out of the window into the night. I said nothing.

"Sometimes you pray for somethin', somethin' good, but it never happens. Sometimes you pray for somethin' bad to quit, but it don't."

I said nothing. I rarely bothered God with my problems. Of course I prayed before meals, at least when Mom and Dad were around. And at church. Just the regulation stuff. I had heard of desperate people pleading with God, but I had never done so, probably because I had never been desperate. What did I have to be desperate about? I was only ten years old, for crying out loud!

M kept his gaze riveted to the window. "But today I saved your life. That should count for somethin'." He looked back at me, his eyes veiled in shadow again. "You owe me one. Or maybe God owes me one. Maybe there is some special thing for you to do, and I kept you alive so you can do it."

This whole thing sounded too hypothetical for me. "Or maybe you just happened to be there. Does it have to be some big reason? Maybe it's just for no reason. Maybe it just is."

M sat still for a long time. "You said you believed in God. All the time." With fierce deliberation he breathed, "There is a reason." He switched the light back on and shined it directly in my face. I squinted at him and shielded my eyes with my hand. M turned and walked down the stairs, leaving me in the darkness.

A long time later, I followed.

CHAPTER FIVE That Christmas something happened that changed my life. I got an AM radio. It was a battery-operated portable, not very big for a milestone, only about the size of a deck of cards. Still, it was an opaque window into another world that didn't have much in common with mine.

Each night, when I was forced to quit reading, I would tune in to WLS AM 890 out of Chicago and put the radio under my pillow. I fell asleep to the world-according-to-pop music in all its eclectic glory—from quirky, weird songs like "Auntie Grezelda" to production masterpieces like "Good Vibrations." I drove my parents crazy by making them turn up the radio whenever Tommy James and the Shondells came on singing "Hanky Panky." Heidi, Hannah, and I sang along without a clue as to what the song was about.

Sometimes strange, disturbing images of another world trickled through in lyrics to songs like "Lucy in the Sky with Diamonds" or "White Rabbit"—images I didn't understand, but were all the more fascinating to me because of their elusiveness.

One weekend we drove down to Kentucky to visit some friends. I was staring out the window as we passed through Cincinnati, looking at all the tall, narrow houses lined up like pastel dominoes waiting for a perverse giant to push the first one. In the downtown traffic we inched past a park. A group of teenagers were hanging around a fountain. They all had long hair, even the guys, and were dressed like they were headed to some kind of psychotic costume party: tie-dyed shirts, hip-hugger bell-bottom jeans, fringed leather vests, headbands, necklaces of various kinds.

"Oh, look," Mom said, pointing out the window.

"Hippies," Dad said, using the same tone of voice he would have used to identify a hippopotamus or giraffe in the zoo.

Hannah giggled. "Hippies!" she repeated.

I was intrigued. "What's a hippie?"

"Young people who live in communes and grow their hair long and wear necklaces they call 'love beads' and take drugs and protest the war," Mom explained. She didn't mention the "free love" thing, which I didn't realize until later, of course.

"That's stupid," Heidi said.

I looked back out the window. "Why are they called hippies?" I expected them to have very large hips.

"I don't know," Mom said.

Dad volunteered some etymology. "It comes from the word *hip,* which came from the word *hep,* which means fashionable or knowledgeable about the latest trends."

"Hippies," I whispered to the window as the park faded from view, certain that these hippies were pieces in the puzzle forming from my AM-radio-sponsored lessons in pop culture.

The reference to drugs fascinated me even more. I had heard of acid, heroin, cocaine, and marijuana, of people hearing colors and seeing smells and smelling music. I was very curious about how the senses could trade places, and I wondered what red sounded like. Was it loud? Soothing? Alarming? Obnoxious? Hypnotic? Stories of bad trips and acid flashbacks added a darker, menacing tone to the magical stories. Why did these hippies risk such dangers for the experience? What was I missing that made the reward worth the risks?

From that day forward I listened hungrily to the evening news whenever I saw a protest march or a love-in, grasping for details that would enlighten me about this new world. My tastes in music shifted from pop hits to music with more edge to it. From the Supremes doing "Keep Me Hanging On" to the Vanilla Fudge version, from the Monkeys to the Stones.

I also started wondering about the Creature again. I periodically peered through the fence, sometimes catching a glimpse of her brogans jutting out of the box. When it got colder, she disappeared like the robins. One January afternoon I ventured through the gap. The box had collapsed into a soggy ruin. I propped it up. The tattered blanket was still inside, now hardly more than a rag. Nothing else of the Creature remained.

The next Saturday M and I walked to the library, bundled in hats, mufflers, mittens, and overcoats. A low gray blanket shut out the sun. Melted snow left behind a mantle of gray slush that mirrored the sky. The world seemed a muted dreariness. We kicked at the slush with our boots as we trudged along. I told M that I thought the Creature had left.

"Don't even mention her, man," he said with feeling. "It's bad luck to talk about witches."

"She wasn't a witch, just a lady hobo."

"Oh, she wasn't? Didn't you hear her put a curse on me? She tried to turn me into a pig!"

I stopped and looked at M. "What?"

M stopped and turned back. "Yeah, man. She said, 'You will be cursed and become a ham,' or somethin' like that!" He shivered, but not from the cold. "And," he added resentfully, his eyes narrowing into slits, "she said somethin' about me being a slave. I missed some of it when I cleared that fence."

I laughed, puffs of breath floating around my head. M was not amused. He walked on.

I ran to catch up, almost slipping in the slush. "M, she wasn't putting a curse on you; she was quoting the Bible." (Sometimes it comes in handy to be a PK. Not very often though.) "Ham was Noah's third son. After the flood and the ark and two of every animal and the seven of some kinds of animal that nobody ever mentions and the rainbow and all that, Noah got drunk and was lying naked in his tent, and Ham made fun of him, but the other two sons walked into the tent backwards and dropped a robe on him or something, so Noah said that stuff about Ham. Cursed him."

"What?" M stopped, again. "Where did you hear that, man?"

I walked back to him. "It's in the Bible."

"Really? There's stuff like that in the Bible?"

"Oh, yeah. All kinds of stuff like that. Even weirder."

"Really?"

"Really. That's not the half of it."

He considered for awhile, shrugged his shoulders, and we resumed our walk to the library.

"I still think she's a witch," he said.

I pushed him and he slipped on the ice, dragging me down with him. We wrestled in the slush and arrived at the library a little soggier for the trip. I got three Hardy Boys mysteries and *Kidnapped*. M picked up *More Homer Price* and *Sounder*.

On the way back, M introduced a topic that had never come up between us.

"I bet I know who you like." M kicked a can exposed by the melting snow.

I immediately kicked the can back and said, "Who?"

"Pam." He kicked the can back to me.

I faltered and missed the can completely. Every boy had some girl he liked, but it was usually a secret he guarded more jealously than his middle name, assuming, of course, he had an embarrassing middle name, like Maurice. (Apologies to any guys out there named Maurice, but at least your middle name isn't Shirley, like one guy I knew! No apologies to any guys named Shirley.)

I liked M, but he was treading a little too close for my comfort. I hesitated to divulge the truth, but to deny it seemed to betray the girl of my secret affection, and my sense of honor shrank from that dastardly deed. I self-consciously admitted to M that I was entranced by the plain but intelligent Pam.

"And Bingo was his name-o!" M cried just before slipping to the ground in a wail of laughter while attempting a pirouette in the slush.

Of course I wasn't giving this information away for free. After he got back up and picked up all his books, I kicked the can back at him and demanded a corresponding disclosure.

"Guess," he said, with a kick.

I mentally ran through the Negro girls in the class and picked a likely name.

"Nope." Kick.

I picked another.

"Nope." Kick.

I named them all.

"Nope." Kick.

I gave up in exasperation. I figured it must be someone in another grade, and I didn't know many kids in other classes. "So, who is it?" I demanded.

"Terri," he said with a grin.

I was stunned. "Terri?"

"Yeah, Terri."

"Oh." There was no denying Terri was cute, but she was also white. The fact was so glaringly obvious I wondered why M hadn't noticed. I walked in silence for awhile, kicking the can when it came into my lane. Because he was my friend, I felt I should say something. But also, because he was my friend, I didn't want to hurt his feelings. I didn't know how to do both.

"Well . . . I don't . . . I mean, it's not . . . well, I'm not sure that would work out," I said lamely.

"Why not?" he asked.

"Well, because . . . you know." I kept my eyes safely on the can.

There was silence for a moment. "Oh, you mean because—"

"Yeah," I said in a rush, feeling vaguely ashamed without knowing why. We walked on in silence for a long time, the can abandoned behind us in the slush.

We finally arrived on our block. Our library visits had developed into a tradition. The ritual was usually concluded with us repairing to an attic, his or mine as the whim took us, to read for awhile, often with refreshment smuggled up the stairs. This time we stopped on the corner, awkwardly not turning toward either house.

The impasse was broken by M. "You know, Moses' wife was black."

"What?"

"Looks like there's some parts of the Bible you don't know that much about, man."

That decided our destination. A few minutes later we were in Dad's study, still in our coats, steaming slightly on a heater grill, waiting to be noticed. He ceased his labors and peered over large black-frame glasses. "Yes?"

M looked at me. I cleared my throat. "We have a question."

"Yes?"

"About the Bible."

Dad raised one eyebrow, wrinkling the forehead that extended into his scalp. "So, thou hast come to the Oracle. Speak and I shall attend thee." He leaned back in his chair, crossing his hands over his stomach. This little speech didn't phase me. Dad always talked like that. If it had any affect on M, he didn't show it.

I hesitated, a little shy about introducing the topic. I decided there was nothing for it but to plunge forward. "M says that Moses married a Negro woman." I couldn't bring myself to say *black* even though M had just used it a few minutes ago. It seemed indelicate. My family always used the term *Negro*. M and I never discussed race, beyond his attempts to educate me about the people he was named after.

Dad nodded his head slowly and looked from me to M and back. "That is certainly one interpretation of Numbers 12."

I raised an eyebrow of my own and stole a glance at M, who was nodding solemnly, vindicated before the authority.

Dad flipped through the Bible on his desk. "The King James Version says, 'And Miriam and Aaron spake against Moses because of the Ethiopian woman whom he had married: for he had married an Ethiopian woman.'" He looked up at me. "Do you remember the Ethiopian missionary who visited our church last year?"

I nodded. The man spoke very strangely, like he hadn't quite mastered the use of his tongue, or like it was slightly too thick for its purpose. He was also the blackest person I had ever seen, much darker than even M, who rarely took second place in the battle of blackness.

"However," Dad continued, "the Revised Standard Version reads a little differently." He pulled another Bible off the shelf behind him. "'Miriam and Aaron spoke against Moses because of the Cushite woman whom he had married, for he had married a Cushite woman.'" He looked up. "Which would mean she was a native of Arabia Chusea, where Saudi Arabia is today. Which would make her race much closer to the Hebrews."

"Does that answer your question?" Dad closed the Bible and returned it to the shelf.

"Yes. Thanks," I said, and we left, climbing to the heights of the attic. M didn't say anything until we were at the top.

"See? What did I tell you?" There was a touch of gloating in his voice.

"Yeah, yeah, so you were right." I sat down and pulled out my book, but didn't open it. I looked out the window for awhile before I spoke again. "I guess the question is, which version does Terri have, King James or Revised Standard?"

M didn't say anything for awhile. He opened a book and held it in his lap, his black thumbs pressed against the white pages. Then, without looking up from the book he was pretending to read, he said, "Yeah, you're probably right."

On a Sunday in March, Heidi received a new bicycle for my eleventh birthday, and my bike was finally restored to its rightful owner. M and I celebrated by riding downtown. We passed the theater, and on a whim I detoured down the alley to perform my periodic check on the Creature's courtyard. When M realized where I was headed, he wasn't happy. I parked my bike and climbed the trash cans. M refused to get off his bike and remained poised to shoot out of the alley at the slightest provocation.

"Relax. She left a long time ago."

"Then why are you checking, man?"

"I don't know. Just habit." I pulled myself over the fence and looked down into the courtyard. The catalog of debris appeared unchanged. God had neither added to its plagues nor taken away from its shares in the tree of life. I was almost back on my bike when I realized that one slight change had indeed occurred. A refrigerator box sat where the washing machine box used to be. I gasped, and M was halfway down the alley before I threw down the bike and returned to the courtyard. I crept to the opening of the box, which faced the gap between the buildings, as before. Inside, a faded red blanket and the familiar stench greeted me. Outside, a few fresh gin bottles were scattered about. The Creature had returned.

CHAPTER SIX The return of the Creature filled me with a sense of excitement and dread. My insatiable curiosity about her life was almost unbearable. I sensed a connection between her and the pharmacological utopia of the flower children, a mystical, magical, and menacing parallel universe intertwined with my world but never touching it—except when I talked with the Creature. She was a looking glass through which I could see darkly an incomprehensible alternate reality. A fascinating but frightening reality.

As is often the case, the same element provided both the fascination and the fear. The world of the flower children and the Creature appeared to be devoid of the boundaries that circumscribed my existence. There was no list of do's and don'ts, no foundation, no absolute. Anything seemed to be possible: incredible flights of fancy, wild deliriums of ecstasy, improbable exchanges of senses and even reality.

With the boundaries removed, one could fly to the zenith of experience. Or plunge to the depths of torment. But who could say which direction the journey would take? The available information indicated that the path one took did indeed make all the difference, but also that it was completely out of one's control. Those who trampled the barriers exchanged their future for a pair of dice.

I avoided the courtyard for weeks but was ultimately unable to stay away. March closed with three days of drizzle and an unexpected freeze.

The Saturday morning of April 1 dawned cold but clear. I resolved to visit the Creature. At first M thought my proposal was an April Fool's joke. When he realized I was serious, he refused to accompany me but agreed to keep my secret.

I walked downtown and approached from the street rather than the alley so I could see into the opening of the box. I peered around the corner and saw a dark shape in the shadow of the interior but nothing more. I walked into the courtyard with bold but quiet deliberation and stopped five yards from the box, waiting. There was no reaction from within. I stepped closer and peered inside.

The Creature was there, twisted inside the red blanket, shaking violently as if she were being electrocuted.

"Hello?" I said, tentatively. There was no reaction. "Hello?" I repeated, louder. Still nothing. I hit the side of the box with no effect. I bent down and touched the blanket. It was cold and damp. The Creature's head was hidden in darkness, too far inside the box for me to see her face. There was no reaction to the pressure of my hand on the blanket other than a slight moan wheezing through the jagged breaths that accompanied the shivering.

I jumped up and ran from the courtyard, almost knocking down M as I emerged onto the sidewalk. He was lurking there, too afraid to come into the courtyard and too afraid to leave me alone. A brief consultation apprised him of events, and we raced back to our respective houses. We procured an old dress his mother used when doing chores, one of Dad's old robes, two faded but serviceable blankets, a jar of Vicks VapoRub, a jar of NyQuil, and a bottle of aspirin—all without attracting attention. These items were placed in two paper bags, and we returned to the courtyard.

M stood guard on the sidewalk while I threaded the gap and approached the Creature. Nothing had changed in the hour we had been gone. I spread a blanket on the ground before the opening of the box and knelt on the edge of the cardboard. Grabbing the bottom of the red blanket, I lifted it and pulled her out like a corpse in a drawer at the morgue.

Even though she was shivering with a vengeance, she appeared to be unconscious of what was happening. Her eyes were closed, her face ashen, the birthmark standing out in relief in the bright sunlight, an angry purple. Her brown hair, longer than last year, was wet and plastered against her head and face. She was surprisingly light, and I had little trouble getting her onto the dry blanket.

It was more difficult to pry the wet blanket from her grasp and pull it from her body. When I pulled the blanket from her fists, the Bible tumbled out. I picked it up. Most of the gold leaf was gone, but the name *Pauline Jordan* was still legible. I opened it up. On the inside an inscription read, "To Pauline on her sixteenth birthday. Love, Mom and Dad." I closed the Bible and threw it into the back corner of the box.

Next came the step I had been dreading from the moment I had realized it would be necessary. I opened M's pocketknife and cut away the damp dress from the Creature, focusing on the knife and cloth. I was relieved to discover she was wearing a slip under the thin, ragged dress. She shivered beneath the point of the blade. It took a lot longer than I expected due to having to cut the length of both sleeves and the extreme care I had to exercise not to cut her skin, which was cold and clammy.

By rolling her first one way, then the other, I was able to completely remove the wet dress and blanket. The task was simple to do single-handedly because she was distressingly light. The slip, though wet, I chose to leave intact. I was shocked at how emaciated she was. The chain with the strange symbol still hung from her neck.

I quickly draped Dad's robe over her. Before I wrapped the dry blanket around her, I rubbed the Vicks on her chest and neck. Then I climbed into the box, grabbed the blanket, and dragged her in after me. Through a delicate bit of straddling I escaped from the box and pushed her the rest of the way in.

I then collapsed on the ground, exhausted from the emotional strain. I sat there for a long time, staring into the gloom of the box and the darker shape in the blanket. For some reason, M's words came back to me: *"Sometimes you pray for something, something good, but it never happens. Sometimes you pray for something bad to quit, but it doesn't."*

I thought about my life. Although I felt like it was filled with events and even crises—the constant bouncing around from one school to another, the aborted friendships, the sudden spotlight of being a PK—nothing had ever happened that moved me to such desperation that I felt the imperative of turning to God for intervention. I had never asked M what things had moved him to that extreme. None of my business, most likely.

I was feeling something. I wondered if it was what M felt when he prayed. I thought about the Creature. She had a name, didn't she? Why did I always think of her as the Creature? I glanced at the sky and then looked back into the depths of the box.

"God," I muttered under my breath. "I think that's Pauline in there. Don't let her die."

I got up and spread the second blanket over Pauline, who seemed to be shivering less than before. I placed the aspirin, the NyQuil, and Mrs. Marshall's dress in the box next to her. I spread the wet blanket over the oil drum and tossed the old dress over the fence.

I joined M in the gap, gave him his knife, and we walked back home in silence.

That night I realized that Pauline needed more than warm clothes and medicine. She needed food. After everyone was in bed, I sneaked down and lifted a can opener and several cans of soup from the pantry, making sure to take only things Mom had two of. Sunday after church I returned to the courtyard without M.

I approached the box as before, stopping just short of the opening. The bottle of NyQuil was lying empty at my feet; the top, a few feet away.

I called out, "Hello?" I saw the blanket jerk. I crouched down and looked into the box. Pauline stared blankly past her shoes at me. I made a mental note to bring socks next time. "Hey, it's me, Mark."

"Mark. I have the Mark." Her voice was an exhausted whisper with no emotion or comprehension, an automatic echo reverberating from her subconscious. Her hand moved slowly up to her face as if on its own and stroked the birthmark.

"I brought you some food," I said, even though I didn't think she realized who I was or even that I was there at all. I grabbed the blanket and pulled her out.

She stared at me without any indication of recognition. "I have the Mark," she whispered hoarsely. "The Mark."

I sat on the transmission housing and opened a can of soup. Then I knelt next to her and tried to get her to drink it right from the can. It ran down the side of her face, but some of it went in her mouth, and I saw her throat pulse as she swallowed. I looked around, found the aspirin, poured out four, and pushed them into her mouth. Then, very slowly, I fed her the entire can of soup and returned to the transmission.

I watched her for awhile, but she seemed to be asleep. She was wearing the robe under the blanket. The dress was crumpled in a back corner of the box. I shoved all the cans of soup except one into the box next to the dress. I then went through the awkward ritual of returning Pauline to the box, opened the remaining can, and placed it with the opener next to her head in the box.

As I was leaving the courtyard, I saw an old milk jug. On an impulse I took it to the front of the shop where I found a water hose. I cleaned out the jug as best I could, filled it with water, and left it next to the box.

"Good-bye, Pauline," I whispered, and left.

———

When I returned Monday afternoon, Pauline was still asleep. An empty soup can lay outside the box, and the jug was half empty. I put socks on her feet, opened another can of soup, and left. I couldn't stay gone long on a weekday. This process was repeated for the rest of the week, supplemented with more soup from M's pantry. Each time I came, Pauline was there, asleep or semiconscious. Sometimes she would repeat my name when I said hello.

Friday I went downtown a little before sunset, Mom under the impression I would be playing with M until after dark. When I emerged from the gap, I saw Pauline sitting on the transmission. She was wearing the dress, the faded red blanket draped over her shoulders. I stopped abruptly, surprised to see her up. At the noise of my feet scraping the gravel, her head jerked toward me. She squinted at me and whispered, "The Mark."

"Hi," I called from the edge of the gap. "You're up." I looked down to see the Bible was in her lap. "You're Pauline Jordan, aren't you?"

She didn't acknowledge my comment. "Yer the Mark." Her green eyes burned weakly, but burned all the same, with the light I had seen the first time we met.

"Well, people usually just call me Mark, not 'The Mark,'" I joked lamely.

"Yer the one what's been bringin' me food," she said, looking at the soup can in my hand. "And this dress," she said, looking down at the skirt.

"Yeah, I guess I am."

"What's yer game?"

It had been months since I had first heard this question. This time I was ready for it. "No game. Don't have one."

"What do yer want?" She jerked her face back up at me, eyes turning hard. Her face had more color, the birthmark no longer as starkly contrasted against it.

I looked directly into her eyes. "At first I wanted to know about you, but now I guess the main thing that I want is to know you're going to be OK."

She dropped her eyes to her hands and said nothing, leaning her head so that her hair hung over the birthmark. Suddenly she grabbed the Bible, pulled the blanket around her, and shuffled to the box, crawling in. "I'm goin' to be OK," she whispered huskily from the darkness of the box.

I came forward and sat on the transmission, facing the box. "I brought you another can of soup," I leaned forward and placed it on the edge of the cardboard. She was sitting cross-legged just inside the opening, looking down, her hair hiding her face.

"What do yer want ta know?"

"Are you Pauline Jordan?"

"Yes," she whispered.

"Why do you live in a box? Sometimes," I added, remembering she had disappeared during the winter.

"I didn't mean to. I mean, I didn't start out meanin' ta live in a box."

I didn't know what to say, so I said nothing.

"I ran out of money. I couldn't stay at the shelter when . . . if . . ." She cleared her throat. "I couldn't stay at the shelter. And the box ain't so bad. Nobody bothers me here. 'Cept you."

"Why do you keep that Bible?"

She made a noise that was either a laugh or a cry, I couldn't tell which. "My parents give it to me. Daddy was . . . is . . . a preacher."

"A preacher?"

"Scandalous, ain't it?" She laughed, but a tear dropped to the Bible in her hands. She wiped it away. "Yeah, he was a welder down in Mansfield.

That's in Texas." She looked up at me, her eyes shining from the darkness in the box. "Yer from Texas, ain't ye?"

"Yeah, but I didn't tell you that."

"Yer didn't have to. Yer got the accent."

I didn't think so, certainly not one like hers, but I didn't interrupt the flow.

"So, he was a welder down in Mansfield, but he got the call, so he sold the house and bought a truck, a trailer, and a tent, and we hit the road, spreadin' the gospel. It was just before the war. I was five. It was a different town ever week, exceptin' when the Spirit fell and there was a revival. Then we might stay a month or two.

"It weren't so bad, really. Got to meet a lot of interestin' people. Daddy always liked to find out who was the toughest guy in town, hunt him down, and challenge him to come to the meetin'. And he'd usually get saved. Daddy sure knew his business. Knows his business," she corrected.

"When I was sixteen, right after I got this," she clutched the Bible, "he got a live one in Tucson, a nice-lookin' feller, about twenty-two. He was a ring-tailed-tooter, this'un. He used to tear up the town; they called him a holy terror. Daddy would always say, 'The bigger they are, the harder they fall.' And this'un fell all right. First he fell in the Spirit and come up saved, all in a flash, like Saul. Then he fell fer me."

She looked up at me, shyly, her head leaning to one side so that her hair hid the mark. It was such a transformation that I almost didn't recognize her. Peering from behind the leathery skin and wrinkles in the warm glow of sunset was an innocent girl of sixteen, overwhelmed by the unexpected attentions of a dynamic man.

"I wasn't used ta bein' looked at the way Vic looked at me. Because of this," she said, tossing back her hair. The mark burned darkly in the shadows.

"Once we saved all the folks worth savin' in Tucson, we moved up to

52

Phoenix, then to Flagstaff, and on up into Nevada. Vic follered along in his truck and begun preachin' along with Daddy. They was a powerful team, and just about ever tough guy west of the Mississippi got saved. He traveled with us fer a long time, all over the country, savin' sinners and courtin' me. This is all before yer was born. What are yer, nine?"

"Eleven," I replied indignantly.

"OK, eleven then. It was still before yer was born. We finally married when I was seventeen. Daddy did the ceremony." She let out a bitter laugh. "Did it himself.

"After a few years, the more Vic preached, the more people got saved, and he thought he should be getting half the offerin'. Daddy didn't see it that way, Vic bein' like his apprentice and all, but Vic said he was better'n Daddy and the only reason the offerin' was so big was because of him. They had a big fight in Nauvoo, Illinois, and Daddy threw him out. I don't think he realized he was throwin' me out too. I guess it never sunk into him that we was married."

She shook her head. "Next mornin', we was gone, Vic and me." She fell into silence. The gloom of the courtyard deepened into twilight. I waited.

"Well, Vic didn't have the wherewithal to get his own trailer and tent. We moved to Chicago, and he went back to construction work. He had a hard time keepin' a job; never met a boss he didn't like to hate. Lost all the religion he had, just like that. And he got mean." Her voice sank to just above a whisper. "He would hit me. With his fists. Told me I had the Mark of Cain. Said the only reason he didn't kill me was he would suffer the vengeance of God seven times over if he did."

She coughed and spat out of the box at my feet. "Yer don't have so much as a fiver on yer, do ye?" I shook my head, but she couldn't see it in the twilight. "I got me a powerful thirst sometimes. Got any change, Mark, boy?"

"No," I croaked. I cleared my throat and repeated, "No."

"Shame." She moved inside the box, changing positions, moving deeper into the shadow.

"That's why I didn't tell him when my time come. Didn't know what he would do. So he didn't know, when he beat me, when he kicked me in the stomach, that he killed his own son. Never knew it. The first time." Her voice was turning raspy, like the first time I met her. "But he found out the second time because the neighbors heard and called the cops. So I was in the hospital when it came."

"Dead," she croaked from the blackness of the box. "He said it was the Mark." She coughed again. "It was the Mark," she whispered.

I regretted the curiosity that had caused me to pursue this woman's story. Nothing in my meager eleven years had prepared me for such a tale of horror. The fascination that had driven me was turned to revulsion, not for Pauline, but for the darkness she had clawed her way through. I felt nauseated.

"While I was in the hospital, he got a job and started preachin' at a storefront mission. The third one made it. Vic named him Enoch. And left." She fell into a coughing fit, leaned out of the box, and spat on the ground.

"He showed up six months later and stayed the night. The next mornin' they was both gone." She breathed heavily, as if she were climbing stairs. "A long time ago," she whispered.

"I'm sorry," I said, not knowing what else to say. It seemed a waste of breath, inadequate and pointless.

"But I found 'im," she said in a voice of triumph and vindication. "I found the creature what stole my boy."

"What?" I said, startled not only by the news but also by the word she had used.

"I looked fer years and I found 'im."

"How? Where?"

"The Mark showed me," she rasped. I heard a clinking sound. I figured she had pulled out the chain and the strange pendant, but I couldn't see it. The sun had set. A streetlight cast a feeble, silvery light but not into the box.

"Is that where you went? Is that why you disappeared?" I was suddenly filled with fear, not for myself, but for whomever she had found. "What did you do?" I demanded.

"The Mark follered me," she whispered. I heard a rustling, and she crawled out of the box, kicking the soup can aside. "I have the Mark!" she said with fierce passion as she stood up. The murky gloom of the streetlight reduced the scene to a black-and-white movie. The blade of a large butcher knife glinted in her left hand.

I jumped up and backed away behind the oil drum, ready to jump the fence if she made the slightest move in my direction. Pauline paid me no mind but instead shuffled into the shadow and through the gap into the street.

CHAPTER SEVEN I took the other way out of the court-yard and watched for ambushes by deranged box-ladies. My return home was a jumble of black-and-white images and disturbing conjectures. Where had she gone during the winter? Had she found Vic and Enoch? What had she done? Why did she still have that knife? Where was she going now?

The last question was the only one I could have answered, but I didn't have the slightest intention of following her. My curiosity was safely dead, no longer a threat to the welfare of any cats in the vicinity.

I entered the house by the back door, just as I would have if I had been with M. I did my best to behave normally, which was difficult for an eleven-year-old recently in fear for his life. The dinner plates were still on the table, but the kitchen was empty. I looked in Dad's study. A book lay open on his desk with some notes. An ink pen lay on the floor by the chair.

As I passed by the downstairs bathroom, I heard the toilet tank filling, but the door was open, the room empty. Somebody had been here not very long ago. I checked the living room. No one. Nobody on the first floor. I went upstairs and checked the bedrooms, also empty. "Heidi? Hannah? Mom? Dad? Hello?" My voice echoed in the old frame house.

I went back downstairs, but the place had not repopulated. It made no sense. I went up to my room and took the flashlight from my sock drawer.

Looking in the attic for my family made no sense, but the house being empty made no sense, either, so it seemed the logical thing to do.

What I found was equally logical. Nothing. Then it hit me. The Rapture! Jesus had come back and they had all been snatched away. One will be taken and the other left. But . . . but . . . I was left! How could this be? Wasn't there supposed to be a Tribulation or something? What about the Mark of the Beast? I didn't remember anybody trying to make me take a mark of any kind in order to get food. "I think I would have remembered something like that," I whispered to myself. "In fact, I remember it not happening."

I looked out the window. The car was gone. My apprehension about the Rapture diminished. They wouldn't take a Vauxhall to heaven, would they? I thought people were supposed to just vanish, or maybe fly up into the clouds. I didn't remember any verses about a road trip to the New Jerusalem. An old folk song flashed randomly through my mind: *"There was two little imps and they was black as tar and they was trying to get to heaven in an electric car."* That was no help. Besides, the Vauxhall had a gasoline engine.

I went down three floors in a calmer frame of mind and tried the basement. There was Dad, changing the plug on the lawn mower. I had no fear of Raptures now. There was no question that if—I mean when—a Rapture happened, Dad would definitely have his ticket punched.

"Where is everybody?" I plopped down on an overturned laundry basket that promptly collapsed and deposited me on the floor.

"They went to see *The Jungle Book*," he said without looking up.

"What? Without me?" This news was worse than almost being murdered in an alley and almost being left behind in the Rapture.

"They intended to take you, but when they went to the Marshalls' to see if you wanted to go . . ." Dad applied a final turn to the new spark plug and looked at me over his glasses.

Uh oh. My mind raced, searching frantically for some plausible lie. I imagined my eyes were blinking on and off like the lights of the computers computing an answer in the movies. But no paper tape rolled out of my mouth with a solution. I was in for it, and no mistake.

"Imagine our surprise when we found out you weren't there." He wrinkled his nose in an attempt to adjust his glasses without using his greasy hands. "A conundrum that stymied even the most astute member of the force. Would you care to venture an explanation before you are sentenced?"

I was afraid the truth would sound more outrageous than a lie, but after the multiple shocks my system had sustained, I had no energy left to formulate even the most rudimentary of lies. It was a fair cop.

"I was taking a can of soup to a hobo lady who lives in a cardboard box downtown. It took awhile because she told me her life story."

Dad nodded. "Excellent." He wiped his hand on his pants and held it out to me. I looked at it in confusion; he grabbed my hand and shook it. "Congratulations. You're grounded for two weeks."

"What?" My arm jiggled up and down.

Dad dropped my hand and began cleaning up his tools. "Excellent because you told the truth. Your story matched with the story Marcus told us. He even told us where the woman lived. Your mother called from the pay phone at the theater to say that she saw you running home and that there was indeed a cardboard box behind the auto shop around the corner, but nobody was there."

"But, but . . ." A thought hit me. What if Pauline had been there, with the butcher knife, when Mom had come looking for me. That was a sobering thought indeed. But I returned to the immediate problem at hand. "But, if I told the truth, and I was doing a good deed, why am I grounded?"

Dad closed the toolbox and smiled. "Oh, that's easy. For lying." He winked at me and walked back upstairs to the study.

I had a lot of time on my hands the next two weeks. No trips to the courtyard, no trips to the library, no banging on nails with M. I got a lot of reading done. I also found an old book called *Oscar on Promotion*. It was five-by-eight inches and two inches thick. I spent an afternoon in the basement gluing the pages together. Then I spent another afternoon cutting out a hollow spot in the middle, just big enough to accommodate a squirt gun. Hey, a boy who's grounded has to do something!

I began reading the newspaper out of boredom. In the middle of the second week I almost choked on my milk and cookies over the Local section.

Middletown, OH–A local man was hospitalized and an unidentified indigent woman is dead after an attempted mugging went wrong last night. Victor Albert Davidson, 47, of 3944 Hazelnut Drive, was treated at Mercy Hospital for bruises and lacerations and released.

Officers responded to calls of a disturbance downtown near the Jesus Lighthouse Mission and heard gunshots as they neared the scene. They arrived to find Davidson unconscious on the sidewalk and the woman dead of gunshot wounds, a knife clutched in her hand.

Davidson is a pastor at the mission. According to police, he closed at midnight and was accosted by a gang of three men who demanded money. When he told them he had no money, they knocked him to the ground and began kicking him. He cried for help before he lost consciousness.

The incident report indicates that the unidentified woman sustained two gunshot wounds to the chest. The knife showed traces of blood, and a trail of blood led to the curb and apparently the getaway car of the assailants. Local hospitals were alerted to watch for emergency room reports of knife wounds.

Davidson was not available for comment, his wife telling reporters that he would be staying home with her and their son for a few weeks. The mission will reopen by May.

The police are looking for help in identifying the woman. She is described as 5'4", 95 lbs., green eyes, brown hair, with a large birthmark on the left side of her face.

I realized I wasn't breathing, so I took a deep breath. It looked like Pauline had found Vic right here in town. I would put a year's allowance on the son having the quaint name of Enoch, son of Cain.

But I didn't understand the police report. I expected a report on the death of Vic, from knife wounds, and the abduction of Enoch. Instead, I found a story of Pauline saving the life of the man who beat her into two miscarriages and stole her child. It made no sense. If ever there was a miscarriage of justice, this seemed a sure thing to win the Oscar! I cut the story from the paper and put it in the Oscar. The book, I mean.

———

At the end of the second week I gained my freedom and showed the clipping to M in the refuge of the attic alcove.

"That's it, man." He punched the newsprint with a blunt finger. "That's it."

"That's what?" It was a news story; that much was clear. But I didn't think that was what M had in mind.

"The special thing, the task you were supposed to do that I saved your life so you could."

"This is it?" I held out the clipping, the fluttering paper reminding me of the fluttering dollar Pauline had snatched from my hand the day we met.

"You saved this Victor guy's life."

"No, that was Pauline. She saved his life. I was grounded at the time, if you will recall."

"Yeah, but you saved the life of the witch, and she saved the life of the Victor, probably so the kid would still have his papa." He presented the chain of logic, if I can use that word, with a flourish. "And I saved your life."

"OK, so where does the chain end? You save my life, I save Pauline's life, she saves Vic's life, then Vic does what? I mean, what's the point?" I put the clipping back in the Oscar. "And she's not a witch. Wasn't, I mean."

"We don't know where the chain ends, just about the link we touched. And you know what, man? I bet most people don't know even that much. But we do. At least I know the 'why' for my link in the chain. So God owes me one."

"OK, so you save my life and now you think God owes you something. What about Pauline? She saved Vic's life and what did she get? Killed, that's what. He lives, she dies. If that's what God is handing out as rewards for saving a life, I wouldn't be standing in line for favors if I was you!"

On Saturday we went to the courtyard. Even though Pauline was dead, M was still reluctant to go in. He guarded the bikes while I threaded the gap one last time. The courtyard was just as I had left it the night Pauline lurched out with a knife in her hand. I doubted if even she knew what her mission was when she left, to kill or to save.

I walked to the box. The red blanket was in there. So were the two blankets I brought, and Dad's robe. I knelt down and pulled them all out. Further back was the can opener; the aspirin bottle, half empty; and the Bible. I picked up the Bible and sat down on the transmission.

It fell open to a page with a piece of cardboard in it. Faded ink awarded the "First Prize in Scripture Memory to Pauline Jordan," dated 1949. It was stuck between the pages at Psalm 51.

Intrigued, I continued flipping through the pages and found an envelope. It was postmarked in Chicago, Illinois, 1957, and unopened. The address and return address were illegibly smeared from moisture. On the front was stamped "Return to Sender." On the back in indelible ink with the broad strokes of a fountain pen was written, "You made your choice."

I put the envelope back into the Bible unopened and walked out of the courtyard for the last time. But not before I got Mom's can opener back.

A month later, school ended. The entire summer lay ahead like a blank slate. But before we could implement our grandiose plans for conquering the world, the camel of reality nosed its unwelcome way into our tent. On the first Sunday of June, Dad got up to deliver his sermon. I got as comfortable as I could on the wooden pew, settling in for a long summer's nap when Dad's words jerked me rudely back to consciousness.

"I have an announcement that may surprise some of you. I have been doing some extensive praying and seeking the Lord, and I feel He has spoken to me and said my work here is done. It is time for us to move on."

What?!? Move on! Like, move? Again?

I looked at Heidi and Hannah and saw an echo of my own shock and dismay. It had been a well-guarded secret.

I couldn't believe what I was hearing. We had finally stayed in one house longer than a year. I had been lulled into an illusion of permanence and stability. I had violated my own personal rules of engagement, ignored my instinct for self-preservation, committed the irreversible act of getting attached to the dog that had followed me home. I wasn't leaning on my elbows now. I was sitting up, staring at the doleful, albeit dumpy, prophet in sackcloth and ashes announcing woe and doom.

Move on to where? My mind quit screaming long enough to let my ears return to what Dad was saying.

". . . was in debt, and attendance had dwindled to double digits. As of January of this year, we are debt free and attendance has more than tripled. But even more importantly," he took off his glasses and looked out myopically over the congregation with moist eyes, "we have made many dear friends and have been honored that so many of you have opened up your homes and your hearts to us."

Right, so don't ditch them! Isn't that the right thing to do? Don't ditch your friends? You stick with them, hovering on the perimeter if that's all you have the strength to do, so you will be there if they need you.

". . . that the excitement of a new horizon is mingled with the sorrow of leaving behind so many we have come to know and love. But we won't be leaving immediately. We are just now starting to see what opportunities God will bring, and we will be here to assist in your transition to whomever God has for this place."

It wasn't much consolation, but one must cling to whatever small joys can be salvaged from catastrophe. I felt like an Israelite trudging in chains toward Babylon thinking, *But, hey, at least I get to see those funky hanging gardens! I wonder who's playing at the Palace?*

Down in the dungeon of M's basement I told him the news. There was little to say. We both drew sparks from the spike in the rafters. That summer we savored every moment, but it was difficult to ignore the sword hanging above our heads on a thread, never knowing when the blade would fall that would cut us apart forever.

When autumn and school arrived with no change in status, we were cautiously optimistic, or maybe guardedly hopeful. We took our status as sixth-graders seriously, particularly because we were both members of the Safety Patrol. This dubious honor meant we must arrive at school thirty minutes before it opened, don a belt/sash rig with a badge, and stand on a corner, fighting against natural selection by preventing stupid third-graders from running across the street against the light.

In preparation for our exalted status as Safety Patrol members, we upgraded our wardrobe. We felt that sixth-graders had a responsibility to take a leadership role not only in traffic safety but also in fashion, as dictated by "American Bandstand." We pulled out the stops, went for broke, grabbed the brass ring, jumped in with all four feet, and took the bull by the horns. By the end of our shopping orgy we had a pile of stylish togs that would have humbled the Mod Squad. Bell-bottom jeans, turtleneck sweaters, Nehru jackets, taper-cut shirts with no pockets, French sleeves, patent leather shoes, ankle-high brown boots—we had it all. Paisley, neon pastels, electric pink, tie-dye. I'm not sure about this, but I think M bought the horse of a different color. (It was on special.) We even picked up some love beads. I convinced Dad to let me skip a few trips to the barbershop so my hair would match my new style, and M started a long-term project—growing an afro.

All was copacetic, even while standing on the corner in November at 7:00 A.M., holding shivering arms parallel to the ice-coated sidewalks in a crosswalk-turned-arctic-wind-tunnel. We were truly cool, both within and without. Then the thread broke.

CHAPTER EIGHT

The trip down was a lot like our trips to Grandma's house for Christmas—a one-thousand-mile, nineteen-hour marathon. We left the interstate at Texarkana and crawled down the eastern edge of Texas on state highways. By that time I had exhausted every Hardy Boys book in my collection and was looking out the window at an endless procession of pine trees. I saw signs pointing off the highway to winding, two-lane roads that disappeared into the trees. Red Lick—17 miles. Bleakwood—6 miles.

Having spent my meager eleven years living in cities, I wondered what life was like in these one-blink towns we breezed past on those trips. This time, we stopped at one of them and not just for a tank of gas. Before I knew it, I was looking from the other side of the glass at cars breezing through with noses curiously pressed to the back windows.

We arrived in the Greater Fred Metropolitan Area on a Wednesday afternoon, passing by the church on the way to the house. It faced the highway on the corner of a fourteen-acre lot. Through a pine wood and across a creek (or, in the local vernacular, a branch), the parsonage occupied the opposite corner facing a dirt road. It was a rambling ranch-style brick house with dogwoods out front, a gigantic magnolia on the side, and a sweet gum in the back. There were, of course, numerous pines scattered about, but to say so would be to say there was grass on the lawn. There were pine trees everywhere, depositing cones indiscriminately like super-powers in an arms race and laying down a carpet of dead needles that would flare up like gasoline at the drop of a match. And there was grass on the lawn. Saint Augustine, to be precise.

The house had a two-car garage and a guestroom/study at one end. The kitchen, dining room, living room, and den came next, followed by three bedrooms at the far end. There was, regrettably, no basement or attic suitable for service as a refuge from reality.

As the lone man-child in a land without promise, I was awarded the customary private room, in contrast to the semiprivate enjoyed by Heidi and Hannah. As an added bonus, my room had a sliding glass door. With such easy access and a wood so handy, I had no doubt that I would be subject to fits of nocturnal perambulations.

Contrary to my expectations, I began to suspect that my life might not have come to a horrid and dismal end. I had landed in the middle of what was the next thing to a jungle just waiting to be explored. From my room I could see at least a half-dozen trees waving at me, practically begging me to climb them. And then there was the branch.

I abandoned my unpacking to take a brief tour of the environs, the wood at the top of my list. It was sufficiently overgrown and tangled to sat-isfy even the most fastidious adventurer. As I slogged down the branch, I came upon desideratum. A tree house loomed before me, jutting out over the water.

It wasn't very impressive as tree houses go, but I saw El Dorado. Based on carvings in the tree, I deduced it had been built by the previous PKs. The floor was fairly solid, although the boards had gaps between them and tended to wobble as you walked. There were walls on the two sides facing civilization (the house) and a half roof. A few improvised shelves and benches finished out the interior. I returned to my unpacking reconciled to my fate.

Wednesday evening we had the dry run of introductions at church, standing in regulation stair-step fashion at the front of the sanctuary, looking back at white pews, red cushions, faux stained glass, and a bunch of old people. Other than the accents, it didn't differ significantly from similar events in Ohio.

Thursday was a new day and a new school. Being an old hand as the new kid, I expected to adapt and thrive in short order. I selected my favorite outfit from the shopping spree with M: black-and-white patent leather shoes, an olive-green shirt with French cuffs, white hip-hugger bell-bottoms, and a two-inch black belt sporting a square silver buckle that could have served as a counterweight for an elevator.

I'm afraid the care I had taken in shoe selection remained unappreciated, however. Subtleties such as loafer vs. lace-up were lost on my audience. The room was a sea of plaid western-style shirts with pearl-inlay snap buttons, jeans with brown leather belts, and cowboy boots. Obviously I had misjudged my audience. But fate provided compensation in the form of a loose shoelace, and before the collective mind had a chance to process the strange image imprinted on the collective retina, I was sprawled on the worn floorboards. Judging by the laughter, I was a hit.

Not that it was much of a consolation. As I brushed the dust from my bell-bottoms, the red in my face definitely clashed with the outfit.

A hush fell on the room as the dust I had raised drifted lazily through the beams of sunlight streaming through the ten-foot windows toward the fifteen-foot ceiling. The teacher directed me to a seat in the back.

I walked through bands of dark and light and the smell of dust, pencil shavings, hair oil, grass stains on denim, and sweat. The shoes chosen for their aesthetic qualities creaked ominously in the silence as every eye followed The-Creature-from-the-North-at-Large-in-Fred-Texas. In an attempt to mitigate the interminable walk, I feigned indifference. I flipped the perennially troublesome shock of hair from my eyes with a toss of my head and glanced impassively around the room at the regulation crew cuts. The scarred wooden desk I slid into had a hole in the upper-right corner for an inkwell. I felt like I had stepped through a time warp.

Evidently everyone else felt the same way. They peered at me as if I were Buck Rogers from the twenty-fifth century. Turning heads rippled through the room like wind through a cornfield. I didn't meet the gazes; I was too busy in a mental comparison with the Ohio schoolroom I had left behind—visions of metal, Formica, and tile contrasted with wood, wood, and . . . wood. Snow-covered skeletons of trees loomed outside the window in my mind's eye; the green of pine that had yet to know a coating of snow towered outside the windows of my new world.

It appeared that I was the advance guard of the Cultural Revolution. Or more like a lone scout lost deep in enemy territory. The indigenous population eyed me with the same mixture of fear, curiosity, and distrust as I did them. On the surface I wasn't that remarkable. Granted, the dishwater-blond hair that hung over my collar and into my eyes didn't conform to the prevailing tonsorial whim. Granted, my skeletal frame made me seem a walking science project. The true source of their morbid fascination was clear: one didn't see olive-green shirts and white bell-bottoms every day in Fred. Or ever, until my arrival.

I was startled from my reflections on the vagaries of fate by the kid sitting to my right.

"Hey."

I flinched and jerked my head toward him. He had a burr haircut, round eyes, and a curved nose. If imitation be the sincerest form of flattery, somewhere in these piney woods lumbered a very proud turtle. "Yeah?"

"Hey," he repeated, slightly confused.

"Hey, what?"

He looked at me, seeming to search for a sign of something. "Just hey, that's all." He turned back to face the front of the room.

I shrugged. "OK."

I suddenly had an image of Andy Griffith saying, "Hey, Barney," and a response of, "Hey, Andy." It had always struck me as odd because everybody I knew greeted each other with "Hi" or "Hello." So Turtle-Head was just trying to be nice. So much for first impressions. Or maybe third or fourth impressions by this stage.

During recess, while the other boys stood around eyeing me like I was just visiting this planet, Turtle-Head walked up.

"Hey."

I was granted a second chance. I used it wisely. "Hey."

Turtle-Head took in the totality of my ensemble, an expression of confused wonderment on his face, as if he were looking at a sequence of hieroglyphics on the wall of a pyramid, trying to cipher the story. He glanced at my eyes and looked away, his expression changing instantly to studied indifference. He spat in the dirt.

"So, this is yer first day."

"Yeah."

"What wuz your name again?"

"Mark."

"Yeah, that's right—Mark. I knowed the other preacher's kids, the Pricharts. Did you know 'em?"

"No, I've never met them."

"Oh, that's right. You're from Ohio, ain't ya?" When he said "Ohio," his eyes got harder and his voice changed slightly. Kind of like the way it does in a Western where someone says, "Not from around these here parts, are ye, boy?" and the next thing you know, they're looking for a rope.

"Well, not really," I corrected hastily. "I'm from Fort Worth, but we lived in Ohio for a few years."

"Oh."

"Yeah." We lapsed into an awkward silence, the noise from the playground suddenly seeming very loud. "You're from here, aren't you?"

"Yeah."

"Yeah, I thought so."

"Yeah."

Silence, again. I looked past Turtle-Head to the school, a redbrick building built on a hill. A wide set of concrete steps descended from the middle toward the highway. On the left a circular driveway met a door at ground level. The hill sloped down to the right, leaving the windows ten feet above the ground at the other end, where a covered walkway led to a white frame building at the edge of a pine wood. Fifty yards into the woods, a creek marked the bottom of the hill. The woods continued up the other side toward the church, redbrick and white steeple barely visible between the trees.

I tried to jump-start the conversation. "So, what's your name?"

"Ralph."

"Ralph."

"Yeah."

"Oh."

The silence seemed to be relentless. It was finally broken by Ralph.

"Want some Red Man?" He dug in a pocket.

"What?"

"Red Man." He held out a crumpled red-and-white pouch.

"I don't know. What is it?"

Ralph froze for a second and looked to see if I was serious. "Chewin' tobacco."

"Oh." I stared at the brown shreds dangling from his fingertips. "No, I don't think so."

70

He shrugged and crammed the tobacco in his mouth. "Suit yerself." He rolled up the pouch, crammed it back into his pocket, and looked around.

Three kids were bouncing a red ball against the wall to the right of the steps, the metallic whang sounding like the ricochet of a bullet. Further up the hill, a circle of boys huddled around a circle of marbles. I looked toward the trees between the school and the highway. Playground equipment was scattered on a bed of pine needles and sand.

On the monkey bars a girl hung upside down, chunky thighs and calves hooked over a bar. Her brown ponytail dragged in the dirt, and two pudgy hands gripped her plaid skirt in a halfhearted attempt at modesty. Large pink panties were plainly visible fore and aft. She was staring directly at me; her inverted smile, filled with crooked teeth the size of piano keys, hung over her large nose like a bad moon rising over Stone Mountain. A Milky Way of freckles blazed a trail across the sky of her face. Even upside down it was evident that this was a girl who had taken homeliness to a level I had never considered possible. The mind boggled. Or at least mine did, as an involuntary shudder ran through my frame.

Ralph followed my gaze. "That's Thelma Perkins. Don't pay her no mind." He spat carelessly into the dirt. "I done kissed her last year."

I looked at her mouth, teeth pointed crazily like vandalized headstones in a neglected graveyard.

"Where?" I asked in fascinated horror.

"Behind the lunch room. Twict." He offered the information in such a matter-of-fact tone that I was at a loss as to how to interpret it. Was he bragging? Warning me to stay away from his property? Giving me a hot tip straight from the stable? Or compulsively cleansing his soul of foul deeds committed in a moment of passion via confession to a stranger?

I felt obliged to offer some response. Gagging, while appropriate, seemed inadvisable. The best I could muster was a vague, "Ah."

"Now that one," he said, spitting in the direction of a scrawny black-haired girl on the top of the monkey bars, "I wouldn't mess with her. She'll punch you right in the gut."

"Right." I took note of her features, adding her to the list of girls to avoid on the off chance I were to launch a kissing rampage in this strange land. She didn't seem to be much more than hair and bones covered with a flower-print dress. And she was tying together Thelma's shoelaces around one of the bars.

"Then there's that one." I followed his gaze to a swing set. A girl hung at the top of the arc, red hair and skirt temporarily in free fall. As we watched, she whisked away from us, hair and skirt following in a blur of red. "Main problem is keeping her quiet."

"Ah." I wasn't sure if I was supposed to be taking notes. We seemed to be moving through the roster of the gentler sex, identifying those characteristics most notable to Ralph. "Talks a lot, does she?"

"No, she squeaks ever' time you try ta grab her." He turned his head to one side to spit but caught sight of the teacher not far away. Checking himself in mid-expectoration, he walked toward the trees, muttering a quick "Come on" between clenched teeth. I followed. Safely behind a large pine, he discharged a large quantity of saliva, which overwhelmed a troop of ants and settled into a clear, brownish pool between the roots. Ralph looked around the tree at the teacher, who was looking elsewhere. With a nod of satisfaction he turned back around. Noting my puzzled expression, he said, "Tobacca ain't allowed at school."

"I see." I couldn't imagine why anyone would want to chew tobacco, at school or anywhere else, much less risk punishment for it, but declined to share my perspective with Ralph. My clothes already marked me as an outsider. Why exacerbate the issue by sharing radical viewpoints on smokeless tobacco? A voice from behind me interrupted my reflections on controversial opinions.

"Hey!" This time I could tell this wasn't a greeting; it was an attempt to get my attention. I turned around. The scrawny black-haired girl stood looking at my belt. She was taller than I had expected. "Did that belt come with a pair of holsters and a six-shooter? Where's the star?"

"Star?" I stepped back defensively. She had a pale face and large eyebrows that gave the impression that two caterpillars were line-dancing on her forehead. Her eyes were as black and shiny as a hamster's. Strands of pine straw jutted from her tousled jet-black hair.

"Star. Sheriff's star. Ta go with the belt. And the six-shooters." Her eyes sparkled. She took a step back, spread her feet into a wide stance, and bent her knees slightly. I took another step back, wondering if this was some kind of hillbilly kung fu. I glanced over at Ralph, noting that he also seemed wary. I looked back at the girl, alert for any sudden motion. She held her hands out from her scrawny hips, bony elbows poking out to either side. "Draw," she hollered.

The penny dropped. She was comparing my belt to a play cowboy outfit. Her ignorance of stylish '60s dress was lamentable, of course. However, her attempt at ridicule only highlighted her own naïveté, and I felt it my duty to defend myself by pointing this out. I tossed the hair out of my eyes. "This isn't a . . . obviously you don't know . . . I mean . . ." My voice trailed off into second thoughts. What if she interpreted my correcting her as "messing with her?" She might feel moved to punch me in the gut.

"Oh, don't pay her no mind," Ralph muttered. He turned to my accuser. "Jolene, don't be so ignernt. This is how Yankees dress. Ain't you ever seen pictures of the Pilgrims?"

I felt the need to correct the record on one particular issue. I didn't see the value in pursuing the slight 350-year gap between Plymouth Rock and acid rock, but my point of origin was an important distinction. "Uh, I'm not a Yankee."

"Oh, yeah," Ralph said. "I fergot."

"Yer not?" Jolene asked.

"No. I was born in Fort Worth," I replied with a touch more asperity in my voice than is customary for such an admission.

"Then why do you dress like one?" Jolene asked.

It was a good question, but I didn't have an answer. At least, not one I could relate before the bell signaled the end of recess. As I stood under the pines in all my sartorial splendor, Jolene facing me in a gunslinger's stance, I began to get an inkling that things might prove a little more difficult this time out.

CHAPTER NINE

The following Sunday I discovered that, contrary to the impression formed on Wednesday night, humans younger than thirty attended the church. The fifth- and sixth-grade Sunday school class had a handful of kids in it, including Ralph, Jolene, and her twin brother, Bubba. The predictable routine of lesson and crafts was followed by the church service, where we were all introduced, again, and then a dinner in our honor in the fellowship hall.

As the guests of honor, our family went through the line first. I bypassed the pimento cheese sandwiches and piled my plate with fried chicken, potato salad, pork and beans, and corn bread. Heidi, Hannah, and I sat down and sampled the goods. We were joined by inmates from our respective classes. Ralph, Jolene, and Bubba plopped down near me. I realized I had neglected to pick up a drink. I left to get a plastic cup of sweetened tea and was joined by Ralph. We returned together and sat down to enjoy the home cooking of Fred's finest kitchens.

The chicken was of the first water, a crispy batter drained of the taint of excessive grease. The potato salad featured mustard, which suited my palate more than mayonnaise. And I strongly suspected that one would not taste finer corn bread until we all gathered at the Marriage Feast of the Lamb, where even the chitlins would be heavenly. I tended toward optimism about the possibilities of life in this wilderness, filled with the warm glow of beneficence engendered by good cooking.

I was talking to Ralph as I sampled the pork and beans, intent on my story about crashing into a mail truck, when he grabbed my wrist, stopping the fork en route to my mouth. I looked at him, annoyed, and jerked my arm away.

"Stop!" he yelled with an inexplicable urgency.

I froze, my mouth open, fork poised inches from my expectant taste buds.

Ralph pointed at my fork. "Look."

I looked. The beans were restless. Closer inspection revealed a stinkbug covered with juice. It circumnavigated the mound of beans, searching for an escape from this island suspended in the air. I followed Ralph's gaze to Jolene, who seemed unusually interested in the Lottie Moon missions poster on the wall next to her. I looked back at Ralph and raised my eyebrows. He nodded. I flicked the bug off my beans in her direction, but she didn't acknowledge it as it sailed past her and bounced off the poster, leaving a smudge of pork and beans in the middle of China.

"Thanks."

"No problem." Ralph began salting his lima beans, but the lid dropped off the shaker and his plate took on the look of the bottom half of an hourglass. He bit off his exclamation in midsyllable. We looked back at Jolene, who was intently evaluating the thermometer on the poster that gauged the donations given to date. I looked at Bubba. He gave me a sympathetic smile. I looked at Ralph. We exchanged knowing nods.

I dumped the tainted beans to the side and took a healthy bite from the opposite side of the pile of beans. Just before my head exploded. At least, that was the impression I got. It didn't actually explode, but it was several minutes before I had the spare time to confirm this fact. I had the distinct impression that Mount Fuji had relocated operations in the general vicinity of my mouth and was open for business. If that wasn't fresh lava pouring down my throat, I didn't know what it was. Three glasses of tea later, I found the empty bottle of Tabasco sauce at the end of the table. I looked for Jolene, but her place was vacant. I saw her peering from the door to the hall, a gleeful smile of satisfaction on her impish face, and then she disappeared.

I still felt a warm glow, but it wasn't the same warm glow of human kindness I had felt before. Obviously, I wasn't out of the woods yet. My instincts had been correct. This transition was not to be like those that had gone before. The weeks and months that followed confirmed my suspicions.

Conversations with my classmates were rare. When I joined a group, I would get noncommittal nods acknowledging my presence or, sometimes, frank stares. All I knew of these kids was what I could learn from a distance, like an astronomer studying a star.

Seating for lunch was predictable. At the far end of the table the three Furies that Ralph cataloged on day one—Squeaky, Jolene, and Thelma—sat huddled together, whispering like a convention of sprinklers and self-consciously ignoring the boys, who sat as far away as possible.

I usually sat next to Ralph Mull. Since his family went to my church, I saw him on weekends. His older sister, Janet, was in high school, wore short dresses and plenty of makeup, and sometimes smoked cigarettes behind the church. I knew him better than anyone else at the table, which wasn't saying much.

There was Darnell Ray. He had straight, blond hair cut in a style reminiscent of Adolph Hitler and wore thick glasses that always seemed to be as greasy as his hair. His lunch conversation consisted primarily of details about his latest project. The son of a trucker, he had an entire stable of go-carts and motor bikes in various stages of disassembly.

Bubba Culpepper had short, dark hair and a cautious demeanor, always checking the salt shaker before using it. His apprehension was due to a lifetime of anticipating and enduring the assaults of his twin sister, Jolene. His real name was Bodean, an unfortunate by-product of his twinness, but only his family was allowed to call him that. I always wanted to call him String Bean Bodean because he was long and lanky, but I didn't run fast enough.

Thelma's brother, Jimbo, with his round head perched atop an equally round body, only lacked a scarf and carrot nose to be mistaken for a snowman. His pie-face was completely devoid of expression. Department store mannequins had more personality than Jimbo, also known as Jumbo Perkins. He rarely talked at all, but when he did, he specialized in one-syllable words, particularly of the four-letter variety. Jimbo was the only kid who openly chewed tobacco at school, undeterred by official censure. Down on the river bottom he lived a life of fierce independence like his misanthropic ancestors, an embodiment of the legacy they passed on–an existence of voluntary isolation interspersed with violent encounters with civilization.

Late in the school year Darnell amazed the entire populace by riding a go-cart to school. The surprise was that he actually had one in working order long enough to ride it anywhere. He parked it under a corner of the school building, and during lunch he let some of us ride it in the field until the principal appeared and impounded it. We spent our time clustered around it in admiration until the bell rang and we reluctantly returned to the classroom.

The warm May afternoon was not improved by a spelling test. I struggled to stay awake in the long pauses while everyone labored to spell "mischievous" and "conscience." Flies buzzed through the windows, and the ceiling fans spun ineffectually in the heights above us. Suddenly a raucous din echoing in the hall broke the silence. We looked up to see Jimbo

Perkins flash past the door in the go-cart, his normally expressionless face suffused with a look of fiendish delight.

How the teacher failed to miss Jimbo was a mystery, but Darnell didn't pause to contemplate this particular conundrum. He leapt from his desk with a cry of dismay, the matter of the number of *m*'s in "immediate" temporarily tabled to pursue new business. He bolted to save his treasure from certain destruction.

The class crowded to the door and spilled into the hall as Jimbo careened with abandon down the hall and Darnell, hampered by his cowboy boots, tried vainly to stop him. Jimbo skidded around a corner. Darnell plunged after him. We heard the screeching of tires and Darnell emerged seconds later, Jimbo following close behind like the Hound of Heaven with deliberate speed, majestic instancy.

The chase ended when Darnell bolted back toward the great cloud of witnesses in the hallway and Jimbo failed to negotiate the turn. The go-cart slid through the open doors of the library, past a startled librarian, and slammed into a shelf, bringing down a rain of books. One of them hit the throttle and killed the engine. Silence washed through the school.

Then, from the sea of silence, a wailing, inarticulate ululation emerged. It gradually resolved into a litany of curses emanating from Darnell as he dug his way through the mound of books, disinterring the object of his fury. The breadth of his vocabulary was impressive—informed, as it was, by his dad, the trucker. The principal pulled Darnell aside, revealing the figure of Jimbo sitting motionless, like a lawn jockey in a pile of leaves, transcendent joy shining from his face. Not even the principal in all his administrative glory could fail to be taken aback by the ecstatic bliss newly awakened on that perpetually impassive face. It was as though Jimbo heard the distant trumpet sounds from the hid battlements of Eternity.

Then the mists closed round the half-glimpsed turrets and Fred, Texas, reasserted itself. I blinked as if awakening from a dream. The hand of authority that was not restraining Darnell delved into the fallen chaos of literature, drew Jimbo forth, and delivered him unto the halls of justice for a proper reckoning. But even the administration of the dreaded paddle failed to remove the glow from Jimbo's countenance. It took several days for the fading glory of his mountaintop experience to completely dissipate, and by that time, school was out.

CHAPTER TEN When summer arrived, I found myself isolated at the parsonage. I would see Ralph and the Culpeppers at church, but there were six long days between, and I might go the entire week without seeing anyone under thirty. Except for my sisters, who didn't count.

I used my spare time, an item I had in shameful abundance, to upgrade the tree house. I added some embellishments, most notably a secret compartment where I hid a waterproof metal can I had picked up at the Army surplus store in Beaumont. In it I stored the AM radio, my journal, and the Oscar book, which still held Pauline's Bible and the newspaper clipping.

The only two stations I could pick up on my cheap radio were almost at the same frequency. One was a country station; the other, a college station that played just about anything known to man, and some that weren't. The radio tended to vacillate between them. It made for strange and unintended medleys.

I spent much of the summer in the tree house, which I christened the Fortress of Solitude, after the Arctic refuge of Doc Savage, Man of Bronze. (This must be spoken with a deep, masculine, ringing voice. It's a rule.) I pondered life's imponderables while sequestered in my Fredonian equivalent of an attic hideaway. Half a year had passed, and I still felt like a poster boy for a carnival sideshow.

Then I discovered *Grit,* the newspaper—a weekly publication of human interest stories, jokes, recipes, and puzzles. The ad described how I could amass wealth beyond my wildest dreams at twenty-five cents a whack. Before you could say "Horatio Alger," I was cutting the string from a bundle of *Grit* papers and foisting them on unsuspecting Fredonians. I hoped that the pen was mightier than the hammer and would crack the adamantine surface of this alien culture.

I began by hitting the few dozen houses actually between the city limit signs on the highway and made several sales. Encouraged by my initial success, I ventured south past the city limits and came upon a mailbox that looked like a miniature house, complete with shingle roof. It bore the name Culpepper. I turned down the dirt driveway and eventually found a house one hundred yards from the highway.

It was a rambling hodgepodge of logs, rough vertical planks, smooth tongue-and-groove slats, aluminum siding, asphalt siding, bricks, stone, and cedar shingles. Bay windows and huge sliding doors were scattered indiscriminately along the exterior. I later discovered that the inside was as varied as the outside, finished with paneling, Sheetrock, fabric, Formica, logs, and brick. The startling appearance was due to the fact that Mr. Culpepper was a construction contractor and used whatever he had left over from a job to remodel his own house.

Jolene answered the door with a dangerous look in her eyes, in my estimation, but when she learned of my mission, she deferred to her mother and disappeared. I made a sale and a hasty exit, uneasy about where Jolene might have gone and what she might be planning.

Continuing down the highway, I saw plenty of pines but a distinct shortage of houses. At last I discovered a large dirt road heading east. I took it toward the river, which was five miles back as the crow flies and an eternity as the bike rides. I figured where there was a road, there were people. And there were, just not many. I went a mile before I hit the first house, brick with a large carport and a bass boat next to it. The mailbox revealed that the Walkers lived there. A set of legs jutting from under a fairly new F-150 pickup revealed that at least one Walker was present.

I paused, unsure whether to address the legs or ignore them and knock on the door, when my dilemma was solved for me. The door opened and a short slender man in jeans and sport shirt came out carrying a large glass of iced tea and a can of beer. I recognized him from church, where he taught the high school Sunday school class along with his wife, Peggy. Heidi gave them good reviews, especially the cookouts they held for the youth group at the pond on their farm. I sometimes played with their one-year-old daughter, Kristen, when Heidi was baby-sitting. She smiled for everyone else, but usually just looked at me with a blank expression. I have that effect on kids.

"Hey, Mark."

"Hey, Mr. MacDonald."

"Just call me Mac. Everybody else does." Everybody I knew called him "Old MacDonald," which was hardly surprising given his name and the fact that he ran the family truck farm. I decided to keep this information to myself for the moment.

Mac placed the drinks on the hood and kicked the boots protruding from the shade of the truck. "Wake up, Parker, looks like you got company."

A few cuss words came from under the truck, and Mac looked at me, shrugging his shoulders. Parker slid out from under the truck, holding an oil pan, and then saw who I was.

"Uh, sorry about that." He pulled himself to his feet on the front grill of the truck. His jeans and white T-shirt were a montage of dirt and grease. He towered over Mac, stocky and sunburned, thick black hair pushed back in a cowlick over his dirty forehead.

"That's OK." I held out a *Grit*. "Would you like to buy a newspaper, Mr. Walker?"

"Mr. Walker? Geez, kid, just call me Parker. This ain't no finishin' school." He shifted the oil pan to his left hand and drank half of the beer, leaving black prints on the can as he set it down.

"OK, Parker. Want to buy a paper? Only twenty-five cents!"

"Well, now, that is a bargain. You got two bits on yer, Mac?"

Mac fished out a dollar. "Here, give me two and keep the change."

"Thanks!" As I turned to leave, a car arrived, two women and a baby in the front seat and a large number of paper grocery sacks in the backseat. I nodded politely at the new arrivals and, while waiting for the dust to settle, saw Parker grab a few sheets of the newspaper, drop them on the grass, and lay the oil pan on top of them. I suspected other patrons might find even more creative uses for their reading material, but in the interest of propriety left the thought unexplored.

Two more miles yielded five houses and one sale. By now I had turned left and was riding north. I found a rambling, ranch-style house with a new truck parked in front. The lady invited me into the air-conditioning for a drink. I shuffled across olive-green shag carpet into a paneled den where a huge console color television blared the *Dialing for Dollars* movie. I watched a few minutes while she dug around in her purse. She gave me fifty cents and told me to keep the change.

Half a mile down the road I came upon a decaying shack flanked by a dirt yard in which skeletal dogs scratched indifferently. A rusted-out Depression-era pickup jutted from the waist-high weeds in the backyard. With shaking hands, a frowzy man in overalls fumbled a quarter from an ancient coffee tin to buy a paper I suspected he couldn't even read. I thanked him as he absently scratched at the gray stubble on his chin, his smile resembling a rotting picket fence in front of a haunted house. I recognized a couple of scrawny girls from school peeking around the porch, their ears poking through stringy hair. In the backyard a kid was perched in a rusted metal lawn chair, amusing himself by shooting flies off the table with a BB gun.

This incongruous juxtaposition of affluence and poverty repeated itself as I inched through the sand in search of customers. After what seemed like an eternity of pedaling through the Sahara, interspersed by few houses and even fewer sales, I discovered a branch of the road headed back toward the highway. I entered it cautiously, fearful it might be a mirage, but the sand on it was as real as the *Grit* in my pouch and my teeth.

About a half-mile before the highway I discovered a mobile home surrounded by numerous vehicles in varying stages of assembly and degrees of rust. A carport of impressive height housed a tractor rig with "Ray's Trucking" painted on the side. I hardly needed the sight of Darnell up to his elbows in the hood of a mottled 1952 Ford pickup to realize where I was.

"Hey," I called. Darnell looked up, squinting through greasy hair and greasier glasses. "Think your mom wants to buy a paper?"

"Sure, doll, why not?" He nodded toward the trailer. His mom was a short, wide, genial woman who bought a paper and then talked to me for thirty minutes. Since Darnell's dad occupied himself driving, sleeping, or working on the truck, she was starved for conversation and would use any ruse to trap a victim. I noticed Darnell stayed well out of range, working on the motley collection of rust and grease that comprised his truck. I didn't mind. I was practically dehydrated, and the cookies and Cokes flowed along with the monologue. However, after the first year of my route, I avoided selling her papers around Christmas because she insisted I have a piece of her fruitcake. It had a half-life of five thousand years, inside or outside the stomach.

I left the Ray estate rested and well provisioned for the final miles to my house. Being highway miles, they were inconsequential compared to my ordeal by baking on the sandy back roads, and I sailed along, glorying in the higher density of houses and greater cold-call-to-sale ratio that seemed to be directly proportional in proximity to the highway. In no time I was lounging in the Fortress of Solitude with a keg of iced tea, listening in quiet reflection to a poignant blend of "The Marriage of Figaro" and "Your Cheatin' Heart."

After paying for the stock, my take came out to $2.75, including tips, and I estimated I had traveled seven miles in four hours, mostly on dirt roads. This worked out to about seventy cents an hour, or forty cents per mile. While the experience had afforded me an excellent lesson in capitalism, it was hardly a resounding success, even by my modest standards. The situation called for reflection. I sipped iced tea and listened to the continuation of "Figaro" coupled with "D-I-V-O-R-C-E."

Perhaps I could take in the backwoods loop west of the highway, which was more populated. There were the unexplored forks on the eastern route to consider. And there was always the captive audience on Sunday mornings. No need to abandon the enterprise yet.

As the medley morphed to "Figaro" and "Funny Face," my mind wandered back to my other dilemma, my social ostracization. Many times in the past I had made this transition with much less pain. It occurred to me that my previous moves had always been in urban areas where other products of a mobile society had learned to establish and dissolve relationships as circumstances dictated. Fred was a gift horse of a different color with its shoe on the other foot.

I placed my hopes on the paper route to span the great divide. In my youthful exuberance and optimism, I took up the banner with the strange device and with a cry of "Grit" pursued my lofty goal. I covered plenty of ground and gathered an encyclopedia of information. I discovered that most Fredonians had never been out of Texas, even though Fred is thirty miles from Louisiana as the geese fly. Unlike those geese, I met people who had never traveled more than thirty miles from the house where they were born. Down in the Neches River bottomland were creatures who would have failed a casting call for *Deliverance* due to laying it on a bit thick. People of the land educated with axioms passed down for generations—how to hunt, fish, work the land. And squeeze the corn.

On my cycling tours I became aware of the primary attraction of Fred, one I came to appreciate more through the years—the beauty of the Big Thicket. Lush pine trees towered everywhere, providing a wealth of green even in the winter. On those rare occasions when it snowed, the country-side was transformed into a breathtaking Currier-and-Ives panorama.

Every road seemed a tunnel cut in the earth as I rode my bike through the thicket, dwarfed by the ubiquitous pines. In long treks through pastures and woods, I constantly found beautiful scenes hidden from the view of the casual passerby. I had secret hideaways scattered all over Fred—under dwarf magnolia trees with branches pressed to the ground in a wall of waxy green, or in shallow caves dug out of a steep bank by a rain-swollen creek, or in a sudden clearing in the middle of a dense profusion of undergrowth, or on an isolated knoll deep within a bog of stagnant water and fallen pines. I saw all types of animals—rabbits, foxes, raccoons, opossums, armadillos, and sometimes even deer.

At the end of summer I reviewed my situation. I had a detailed knowledge of practically every twist in every dirt road in a two-mile radius of Fred. I knew dozens of people by sight. I had a greater understanding of the diversity of lifestyles in Fred. I averaged about $3.50 per week income from the sales. But I had not made a single friend. In fact, my classmates viewed me with greater suspicion because I was selling reading material. I was forced to conclude that the project had been a financial and relational failure.

In the Fortress of Solitude I wondered what other factors could be leading to my isolation. The most obvious culprit was my wardrobe. I fit in like a Vegas cocktail waitress at an Amish house-raising.

Months of *Grit* tour-duty gave me ample evidence that hip-huggers were in drastic contrast to local custom. It was time to downgrade the wardrobe. It was a thought that weighed on me heavily, considering how painstakingly M and I had established our position as the forerunners of fashion. But the need for assimilation joined forces with pragmatism. There were no sources of fashionable clothes, as I defined fashion, within a one-hundred-mile radius. Not a single Nehru jacket to be found in Silsbee or Beaumont. I couldn't bring myself to capitulate to the point of jeans, but I did acquire more subdued slacks, in brown and blue.

CHAPTER ELEVEN

However, the new school year brought a change much more significant than my wardrobe. Fred was too small to support anything more than an elementary school. Everyone over sixth grade was shipped seventeen miles to Warren.

For me, commuting to Warren had an unforeseen benefit. Because all Fredonians were outsiders in Warren, they tended to stick together. If there were only a few other Fredonians in a class, they would cluster around me instead of avoiding me. Some of them actually spoke to me for the first time.

But after a few months I discovered that the other Fredonians assimilated into the class quite easily, leaving me the lone molecule incapable of seeping through that invisible, semi-permeable membrane. It took most of the school year before I finally realized what it was. I talked funny.

Meaning, I used proper grammar, and my Texas accent was slight. A person who spoke correctly was an outsider. I could have proper grammar or friends, but not both.

I didn't labor long over this dilemma. To my parent's dismay, I cultivated the "ain't" as assiduously as a violinist perfects her vibrato. I dropped *g*'s from *ing*'s. I was even "fixin' to" in no time. I probably sounded like a white guy singing Negro spirituals for awhile, but I worked on my accent too.

However, there were some things that I couldn't bring myself to do. Mixing verb tenses seemed pushing it a bit far. I was never able to "seen" him do it. I always "saw" him do it. But eventually my speech ceased to be a marker of my alien origins.

───────

Junior high also brought another unexpected development. I sat behind Jolene Culpepper in several classes, and we became friends. She found the sarcastic remarks I muttered under my breath amusing. During band we had time to talk while standing around waiting for the drum section to learn how to play a cadence and march straight at the same time. At first I kept a cautious distance, but soon we were chatting like old school chums. Which I guess we were. Except the "old" part. I gained an intimate knowledge of Jolene's infinite capacity for pulling legs.

Jolene's obsession with pranks started early. In elementary school she collected the merchandise advertised in comic books: whoopie cushions, joy buzzers, red-hot chewing gum, disappearing ink, ice cubes with bugs in them, fake doggie-doo. Bubba didn't share her love of practical jokes, especially because he was the usual target. By the time they were in sixth grade he wouldn't even bother to bend over if he saw a quarter on the floor. He'd found too many glued down or attached to a rubber band or a twelve-volt battery. He developed a cautious, cynical demeanor. He never just walked into a room. He pushed the door open and paused, looking before he walked in. He intuitively checked the lids on salt and pepper shakers before he used them. And he tended to flinch at loud noises.

At first Jolene's jokes were just a kid enjoying life, even if she didn't allow that luxury to anyone else in the continental U.S. But during junior high she slowly transformed from a bratty little kid who annoyed everyone within the international fishing limits to a cute girl who annoyed everyone within the international fishing limits. She had a fresh-scrubbed, natural country-girl aura that New York models spent hours to achieve and that air of simplicity that is sometimes mistaken for naïveté. A fatal mistake in Jolene's case.

As the boys started paying attention, the jokes became a defense mechanism. Because she was very attractive, every boy in the county noticed her. Short, tall, fat, skinny, cross-eyed, buck-toothed, pigeon-toed, freckle-faced, acne-ravaged—they all took their shot. Oh, yeah, good-looking ones too. But there weren't many of those in Fred.

I suspect C. S. Lewis was thinking of Jolene when he wrote that men project their own feelings on women. (I know there is no record of C. S. Lewis visiting Fred, but how else can you explain the remarkable coincidence?) He said a man views a woman as voluptuous, not because she feels that way but because he feels that way when he looks at her. Jolene's mama, recognizing that her beauty would draw suitors like flies, warned her that those boys all had one thing on their minds. Before Jolene even got out of junior high, she was convinced her mama was right. In fact, it seemed as if every boy in the school was doing his best to prove it.

One night during a church fellowship, we sat side by side, our chairs perched on two legs on the tile while leaning against an institutional green wall. We swilled punch, and watched the grown-ups talking, waiting to be liberated from our boredom. Jolene turned philosophical.

"Why do you think it is God made boys like He did?"

"Perhaps He was feeling at the top of His form that day." I had long since learned that one must be aggressive when dealing with Jolene.

"In yer dreams, monkey face."

One learned to endure such things if one was to enjoy Ms. Culpepper's company. If *enjoy* is the right word. I let the comment pass, took another sip of punch, and swung my legs. A trifle too exuberantly.

My quick reflexes saved me from collapsing with the chair, but cost me some red stains on my shirt.

Jolene snorted, as if vindicated in her assessment. I reestablished my position at a less acute angle and resumed my silent observation of the human drama unfolding in the church fellowship hall. Such as it was.

"I mean, what is it about boys?"

"You know, I have often wondered the same thing about girls."

Jolene seemed to take this as a personal affront. "Do girls come up ta you, lookin' at you like yer a car on the lot they want ta take out for a test drive?"

I didn't like the personal turn the conversation had taken. And I didn't understand the tone she was using. I would place a full-page ad in the *Silsbee Bee* if a girl displayed that kind of interest in me. I declined to answer the question directly. "And your point is?"

"Boys just see the outside. Don't they know there's a inside too? Like that lady in the sermon."

"What?" They were coming across the plate too fast for me.

"The lady who poured perfume on Jesus' feet and washed 'em with her tears."

"Mary Magdalene. What about her?"

"The guys just saw the outside, some lady makin' problems. Why are guys like that?"

It seemed like a good time to take another sip of punch. I did.

"Girls have a inside and a outside. Can't boys figure that out? Don't they have a inside?"

I didn't have an answer. I thought I had an inside. The problem was, when I saw a girl that looked like Jolene, my inside performed acrobatics that would have passed muster for the Ringling Brothers.

The situation was not improved when she became a twirler, a position with a wardrobe designed to accent her more compelling features. But since I had a self-image a few points above plant life, I didn't attempt to move our interaction beyond the jousting companions we had become. As a result, she came to view me as "safe." No teenage boy wants to be considered safe, especially by an attractive girl, but since I was more likely to be struck by lightning than become the object of Jolene's affection, the point was moot. In the bus on long band trips or when church fellowships got boring, Jolene would entertain me with stories of tricks she had pulled on her dates.

I was constantly amazed by her creativity. One particularly obnoxious suitor came by her house, intent on landing a date and refusing to take no for an answer. Somehow she managed to spill bacon grease on his boots, which may have been sufficient to cool the ardor of a less-determined cowboy, but not this one. She finally told him if he would go hide in her father's deer stand, she would come meet him after supper. He left, convinced his persistence had won. However, Jolene knew her father had plans to fill the deer feeder that evening, and he always took a dog or two in the back of the truck. As she had anticipated, the bacon grease drew the dogs, and their barking drew Mr. Culpepper. The suitor got such an interrogation in his tryst-turned-trial that he didn't speak to Jolene for a week.

Jolene became my primary source of entertainment and conversation during junior high. I did develop some level of friendship with the guys, but it remained far from intimate. Try as I might, I couldn't find someone to replace M as confidant and coconspirator in my private universe. But with such amusements as Jolene and the rest of the populace could provide, I survived until junior high graduation and spent much of the following summer cultivating the family newspaper business. One Saturday afternoon I set out to hustle a few old copies of *Grit*.

I'd had a glutton's diet of dust when a low rumble growled in the distance. I saw a cloud on the horizon with a dark dot marking its source, a dot that was growing much faster than usual. By the ferocity of the cyclone trailing it, I knew I should take cover or be covered.

I scanned the roadside frantically for a break in the barbed wire. Before I could ditch the bike and vault the fence, the cloud was upon me. Pulling the newspaper bag over my head, I heard a *whoosh* punctuated with staccato rattles. When the pinpricks of sand pelting my arms abated and I could feel the cloud settling on me like a blanket, I peered from under the bag.

A truck that looked vaguely familiar had come to a stop and was now careening toward me in reverse. I jumped to a fence post as the truck ground to a halt, one wheel in the ditch. When the dust cleared, I saw Darnell Ray leering from the window. In defiance of all known laws of physics, he had managed to get the '52 Ford running.

"Hey, doll. Whatcha up to?" he barked from the cab.

I tossed the hair back from my eyes. "Citizen's driving safety patrol. You lose your license."

"What license?"

"Right." I began gathering the newspapers I had dumped in my haste to protect myself, slapping the sand from them before I carefully slid them into the bag.

"Whatcha doin' on that bike?"

"Trying to sell papers. You wouldn't want one. They're things you read." I dragged the bike from the ditch, shook off as much dirt as possible, and swung my leg over it.

"Say, doll, throw that bike in the back 'n' I'll take ya 'round."

I considered his offer. It would be a faster way to sell papers, but given the manner of his arrival, it might be a faster route to the emergency room as well.

He spat into the ditch. "I got a extry Coke in the cooler."

That cinched it. "Sure." I slung the bike into the back and climbed into the cab, where the radio was alternately playing "The Impossible Dream" and an explanation of how to worm cows, with an appreciable amount of static in between. Stretching my legs, I groaned, "That's a lot of miles for a twenty-inch bike."

Darnell popped the clutch and lurched from the ditch, spraying sand across the road in a feathery arc. "Why don't ya drive it?"

"Hey, I'm only fourteen!" I looked at him indignantly.

"Yeah, me too." He looked back at me with a faint air of confusion. "So?"

I was immediately self-conscious. "Well, I mean, I don't have my license yet."

"Me neither."

"Oh. Well, we don't have insurance on me yet."

"Me neither."

I became desperate and frantically groped for any excuse at all. "My dad took the car to Silsbee."

"That's a bum deal."

"Yeah," I mused, relieved I had finally found an answer to satisfy him. However, I nearly drowned in Coke as Darnell gunned the truck into second to take a curve sideways.

Suddenly a log truck loomed in front of us. Of all the hazards to be found on the dirt roads of Fred, log trucks ranked at the top of the list. Being paid by the trip, they came tearing down those turtleback roads with little regard for other traffic. Since they were considerably larger than anything else on the road, they commanded a grudging respect. Few things are more intimidating than rounding a corner on a bicycle to see several tons of fresh-cut timber bearing down on you, trailing a dusty cyclone. In those unfortunate cases where I encountered one, I would hit the ditch as if dodging mortar rounds and try to protect my face from the dust cloud that trailed any vehicle moving faster than five miles per hour.

Encountering a log truck in Darnell's truck instead of on my bike wasn't a source of consolation or confidence. My exclamation of dismay became a shower of Coke, which sprayed the dash and windshield. As gutsy as he was, even Darnell knew he was no match for a log truck, the undisputed monarchs of East Texas roads. He straightened out the wheels, and since we were already sideways in the road, we shot through the ditch, out of the path of the truck and into a field of corn, which choked our momentum to a halt. The log truck roared by like a Tyrannosaurus Rex in search of meatier prey.

"Did ya see that truck hoggin' the road?" Darnell demanded. "The nerve of that guy!"

I sat speechless, an admittedly rare condition.

Darnell reached down to the ignition. "There oughta be a law against folks drivin' like that!"

He started the truck, which had died when we cleared the ditch. I didn't blame it. I had almost done the same thing myself. I opened the door and slid to the ground on shaky legs.

Darnell tossed his greasy hair from his eyes with a jerk of his head. "Hey, doll. Whatcha doin'?"

I stared back at him vacantly. "Look. I just remembered I'm going the other way. See you later." I slammed the door.

Darnell ground the gears into reverse and shrugged. "OK, doll. It's yer nickel." He bounced the truck back on the road and barreled off, drowning out my cries about my bike in the back. Fortunately I was far enough off the road that I wasn't enveloped in the cloud. However, I had a long walk ahead of me. I occupied my time by fashioning new names for Darnell Ray, the mildest of which was Darn ElRay.

CHAPTER TWELVE
The end of summer opened the door into high school and the beginning of my ongoing battle with the school librarian.

Fred was the first place I had ever lived where there was no library. (Not counting the library in the elementary school, which barely had enough books to bury a rotund misanthrope on a go-cart.) Nobody else seemed to feel the lack of a ready source of fresh reading material as keenly as I did. I was certain that M also would have been appalled. Every time I scanned the meager shelves I thought of M and our reading sessions in the attic, and the library began to feel like a lonely wasteland. I avoided it altogether and instead turned to buying books in used bookstores. However, the high school library afforded a greater selection.

Strangely enough, given my love of reading, I had an adversarial relationship with the school librarian, Miss Thermopolis. I viewed her as a manuscript miser, a hoarder of books who was loath to let even one volume escape the confines of her domain. Perhaps my perception was influenced by the fact that I kept trying to check out books by British authors, which were reserved for the senior reading list.

I would skim through the stacks for interesting titles. When I finally found one that sounded promising, I would take it to the desk only to discover that the author was British. One reason I read so much Ray Bradbury, besides the fact that he was an excellent writer, was because he wasn't British, so I was allowed to check out his books.

I tried several times to check out *Animal Farm,* but George Orwell was British. (It wasn't his fault. Unfortunately for me, that's just where his parents lived when he was born.) Even when I buried it under other books, the gimlet-eyed librarian, jealously guarding her reading lists, would snatch it from the stack with a withered claw. Actually, although she was an old maid, she didn't really have a withered claw. I just came to visualize her in terms of the Wicked Witch of the West, so all my interactions assumed Ozian flavors.

"You can't check that out. You're a freshman and this is a British author," she would say for the bzillionth time. However, I heard a nasal screech say, "Oh, no, my little pretty. Thought you could sneak it by me, did you? Well you can just die of boredom. And that goes for your little dog too!"

But my determination could not be thwarted by a mere librarian. Or even an exalted librarian. I orchestrated a daring mission to appropriate *Animal Farm* from her evil clutches. Actually, all I did was sneak a look at the schedule, come in during her lunch hour, and check it out from a library assistant who was less assiduous in guarding the rights of senior class readers. I was feeling pretty cocky until I took the book to one-act-play auditions. I was in the process of regaling a fellow thespian with the tale of how I had finally outwitted Miss Thermopolis when his face assumed a strangely desperate expression. I followed his gaze over my shoulder to find the W. W. of the W. herself standing behind me, staring at the copy of *Animal Farm* on top of my books. I had forgotten that she was also the one-act-play director.

"Did you check that out?" I heard a "my sweet" echo in the cold gloom of the auditorium.

Realizing my mistake, I gulped and nodded slowly, "Yes, ma'am." I longed for a bucket of water with which to melt her.

She peered at me through her trifocals. I was afraid she was going to blast me in a shower of sparks, or at least impound the book, but instead she said, "It's not about animals, you know. It's a political satire."

"Yes, I know," I replied, a bit miffed at the slight to my intelligence. I guess it wasn't her fault. I was probably the first freshman from Fred to stalk Orwell so vigorously.

Ultimately, in my efforts to satisfy an insatiable appetite for literature, I swallowed the bitter pill that began its diabolical work in my vitals—the seed of skepticism that splintered my foundation even more soundly than the AM radio.

Deep within the bowels of the stacks perched on edge between shelves in a back corner, I unearthed an ancient copy of *The Mysterious Stranger and Other Stories* by Mark Twain. It was fifty years old and looked as if it had not been touched in almost that long. It had lain dormant for half a century, as virulent as the day it had been penned at the turn of the century. In my efforts to read everything by my namesake—a quest inspired by M on the historic day he met the Creature and preserved me from destruction by mail truck—I thought I had exhausted the meager resources of the school library. This book wasn't even listed in the card catalog.

I carried it to the desk with barely suppressed exhilaration. The W. W. of the W. seemed to sense my mood. She scrutinized the book suspiciously but was forced to allow me to check it out. Twain was undeniably not British. I repaired to the Fortress, half expecting flying monkeys to appear and confiscate the book. Getting as comfortable as I could, I settled in for a good read to the strains of "Sympathy for the Devil" mixed with much static and "Poke Salad Annie." The book opened tamely enough with the jumping frog story that I had read many times in literature anthologies for school. As it progressed, however, it became darker and more disturbing, until I at last came to the title story.

It was about a kid and his companions in the sixteenth century who met an angel named Satan. No, not *the* Satan, but his nephew, who was named for his famous uncle before he became the black sheep of the celestial family, as it were. The angel dazzled the kids with miracles, such as animating the clay figures they had made, but then dismayed them by "murdering" the miniscule creatures with careless ease as if he were killing an ant. The boys, and I, became more bewildered as the angel conferred a confusing mixture of blessings on villagers that resulted sometimes in wealth and happiness, sometimes in imprisonment and death. By the time I got to the last chapter I had become suspicious that this Satan was more than a namesake—he was the genuine article, incognito. I expected the last chapter to unmask the impostor for who he was and have him banished to his rightful reward in the place prepared for him. Instead, he told the boy that there is no God and that life is only a bad dream. The final page of the book left me aghast:

> "Strange! that you should not have suspected years ago—
> centuries, ages, eons, ago!—for you have existed, companion-
> less, through all the eternities. Strange, indeed, that you
> should not have suspected that your universe and its contents
> were only dreams, visions, fiction! Strange, because they are
> so frankly and hysterically insane—like all dreams: a God who
> could make good children as easily as bad, yet preferred to
> make bad ones; who could have made every one of them
> happy, yet never made a single happy one; who made them
> prize their bitter life, yet stingily cut it short; who gave his

angels eternal happiness unearned, yet required his other children to earn it; who gave his angels painless lives, yet cursed his other children with biting miseries and maladies of mind and body; who mouths justice and invented hell—mouths mercy and invented hell—mouths Golden Rules, and forgiveness multiplied by seventy times seven, and invented hell; who mouths morals to other people and has none himself; who frowns upon crimes, yet commits them all; who created man without invitation, then tries to shuffle the responsibility for man's acts upon man, instead of honorably placing it where it belongs, upon himself; and finally, with altogether divine obtuseness, invites this poor, abused slave to worship him! . . .

"You perceive, *now,* that these things are all impossible except in a dream. You perceive that they are pure and puerile insanities, the silly creations of an imagination that is not conscious of its freaks—in a word, that they are a dream, and you the maker of it. The dream-marks are all present; you should have recognized them earlier.

"It is true, that which I have revealed to you; there is no God, no universe, no human race, no earthly life, no heaven, no hell. It is all a dream—a grotesque and foolish dream. Nothing exists but you. And you are but a *thought*—a vagrant thought, a useless thought, a homeless thought, wandering forlorn among the empty eternities!"

He vanished, and left me appalled; for I knew, and realized, that all he had said was true.

I turned the page to see an empty blankness. I flung the book from me as if it had burned my hands; it tumbled through the branches to the ground. We were a long way from Tom Sawyer now! I was ill-prepared for such vitriol from such a powerful writer. For all my devouring of his works, I knew nothing of his mercurial life, which had been filled with pain and had ended in solitude and bitterness. And, of course, I had never read any philosophy or apologetics, which would have enabled me to see the fallacies rampant in this tirade.

Despite the warmth of the afternoon, I shuddered as if a chill finger had traced a line down my backbone. What if it were all true? Dad, Mom, Heidi, Hannah, all nothing more than a dream? Did I dream Pauline Jordan? How could I have invented in my own mind something as foreign to me as Fred, Texas?

But then again, I was also just a part of the vagrant, useless thought. Something else was thinking it. What could that be? And how can an object of a thought be able to think about itself and the thinker? Trying to follow that paradox made my head feel like it was full of cotton wool. I abandoned the attempt, retrieved the book, and secured it in the ammunition case, sealing it as if it were toxic waste. When I got the overdue notice, I dipped into my *Grit* proceeds to pay the fine. For reasons unknown even to myself, I couldn't part with the book. I kept it hidden in the Fortress of Solitude, stashed in the ammo case with Pauline's Bible, like a worm hidden in the apple, or a snake lurking in the garden.

The disturbing thoughts plagued me in moments of doubt and weakness, but I didn't speak of them to anyone. Certainly not to Dad. I felt as if I had already committed some kind of blasphemy just by reading the book. Not to Mom, Heidi, or Hannah. It wasn't the kind of conversations we had. Not even to Old MacDonald, my Sunday school teacher, since I was now in high school. How would it look if the preacher's kid started questioning the existence of God and everybody else in the room? I could only imagine what would happen if that got back to the deacons.

Not that Old MacDonald ever raised such weighty questions on Sunday mornings, which were typically exercises in tedium and self-amusement. There was a reassuring ritual to the Sunday school classes that Mac and Peggy taught. We typically self-segregated according to gender, goofing around until we were called to order with a perfunctory prayer, our lesson booklets and Bibles in our laps as we sat in the metal folding chairs. The beginning of the lesson consisted of a text read by some hapless designee, followed by a skit read from the booklet by cast members selected at random by Peggy. The theme of the lesson firmly established by these two didactic devices, the gender segregation was reinforced by the girls and boys separating to opposite ends of the room, a collapsible divider snapped firmly into place.

In the private sessions, we took turns reading verses of the Scripture and paragraphs of the accompanying commentary printed in the booklet. Questions followed, read by Mac and answered under compulsion by various laconic teenage boys. Sarcasm and non sequitur, offered sparingly by the PK, served to lighten the ennui. For the PK, at least.

Peggy may have led a much more stimulating experience behind the vinyl partition, but the venue simply didn't lend itself to Mac's personality. In spite of the torture we occasionally visited on him, we gave him an *E* for effort (does anybody know what that means?) because he made up for it in the various extracurricular events that were the real substance behind the show. These included swimming trips to Honey Island, fishing trips to Uncle Herbert's camp house on the Neches River, and cookouts at the MacDonald family farm.

Mac and Peggy poured their hearts and lives into our frantic, confused, and often miserable teenage existences, celebrating with our infrequent victories and commiserating with our too frequent failures. They seemed to actually care about the outcome of those things that were so monumental to us but inconsequential to most of those around us, sometimes even to our families. It was as if they infused significance into our lives when we felt woefully insignificant.

Mac wasn't much at preaching the gospel, but he was a pretty good hand at living it.

CHAPTER THIRTEEN
After a few weeks of high school, I decided that the time had come for drastic measures. In a bold move, I modified my wardrobe in one clean sweep to nothing but Levi's. And, in a stroke of brilliance that I later regretted, I went directly to the office before first period, canceled my business class and transferred to Ag!

In band I was telling Jolene about my schedule change when I stopped in midsentence, unable to speak. Jolene followed my gaze across the room to a girl with short brown hair, green eyes, and a halo hovering over her head. Well, maybe Jolene didn't see the halo, but I did.

"Hello?" Jolene looked at me. I didn't say anything. "Is this the Warren Stare-Down Open? What's yer handicap?"

"Wha . . ."

"That's Becky Tuttle. Don't you know her?"

I shook my head. The rest of the hour was a blur. In the hall I stood nonchalantly next to her and gauged her size. I thought my arm would fit very nicely around her shoulders. The very thought gave it spasms and I dropped my books.

Becky was a year younger, which meant we didn't have any other classes together. A lesser man might have been daunted and abandoned the enterprise right there, but I was consumed with a passion that laughed at such petty obstacles. I made another trip to the office to change my art class to typing. This strategy ultimately proved to be a good one. Although it didn't help me get to first base with Becky, I did learn how to type.

Actually, it's amazing that I learned to type at all, considering the fact that I spent more time looking at Becky than the Gregg typing chart on the wall. The keys on the typewriter had no letters on them. We had to look at the chart on the wall to find out where the letters were. I never did memorize the keyboard, but I memorized every detail of every visible feature Becky possessed. When she wasn't looking, I stared at her with such intensity that I'm surprised it didn't change her hair color.

I studied her like I had discovered a new element on the periodic table. I memorized her full name, address, phone number, class schedule, birthday, social security number, favorite color, favorite perfume, shoe size, everything. I would have memorized her boiling point, melting point, specific gravity, and density, but the information wasn't available. Through the journal entries I made while sequestered in the Fortress of Solitude, I practically kept a notebook on her. She was as documented as an endangered species.

But not all fools rush in where angels fear to tread. Some more cautious fools like myself simply tiptoe around the perimeter and stare through the fence.

Coward that I was, the thought of revealing my affection terrified me. Why would this beautiful girl who dated football players want to spend time with me, a pale, skinny nerd who couldn't keep his hair out of his eyes? So, each day I sat across the aisle in class, burning with such passion that I began to wonder why my desk wasn't reduced to a pile of ashes, with me sitting atop the smoldering heap like a Buddhist monk.

I got most of my ideas about love from the same source that I got my ideas about everything else, from literature. I gleaned examples of romance from tales of chivalry and unrequited love, noble deeds done in the name of fair maidens who only heard confessions of love from the dying lips of a chaste and pure knight. I was at least chaste, if not pure, since I had no other choice, but I couldn't envision any noble deed to be done on Becky's behalf. There were no dragons in the halls of Warren High (except for maybe the librarian), no black knights to capture her and prompt me to a heroic rescue. And if there were, what would I oppose them with, my slide rule? Plus, I hoped to experience the affections of the fair maiden in some context other than while dying. When it came to love, I preferred the requited variety.

I dismissed chivalry as unrealistic and turned to the Romantic poets for source material. Here was passion with a vengeance and in a context more suited to my personal style—effusive script. In the afternoon sanctuary of the Fortress of Solitude, I flooded my journal with freshets of sentimental scribbling. Fortunately, none of this material has survived or I might be tempted to include samples, which would get my poetic license revoked. It was maudlin beyond belief. I wouldn't dream of boring you with it. You would be amazed and disgusted by it. Absolutely out of the question. Well, I guess a short, little sample wouldn't hurt.

> Dare I bid compare thee to a rosebud?
> It would be a slight to thy fair beauty.
> Though the bud would mayhap bloom and flower
> And its beauty far exceed the former,
> One day it must fain decay and wither,
> Falling from the zenith of its glory.
>
> Thy fair countenance by contrast only
> May increase, more fair than flower living,

As thy bud unfolds into a blossom
And from glory unto glory further
Rise above the plane of earthly beauty
'Til thou rival all of heaven's angels.

Pretty disgusting stuff. But, eventually, the Romantic poets also failed to meet the test of reality. The excessive hyperbole made me wince. No human female could match the standards they set in their verse. Or if one could, I would never have the nerve to ask her out. In their world, no girl ever burped or suffered from zits or had an accent so thick you could grease wheel bearings with it or went through half a day of school with an ink mark on her nose or stepped on her shoelace and tumbled in a cascade of textbooks down the bleachers. How could I write syrupy verse if I was in love with such a girl?

I moved on to '60s psychedelic.

ykceb becky echo ohce
molten passion dripping into
outside flawlessness inside transcendence
contour quintessent form
embodiment archetype
echo ohce ykceb becky

I had serious doubts that Becky would understand how this expressed my strong feelings for her. I wasn't sure I understood it myself.

I experimented with an alternative, '70s realism.

Though I know all of that rouge and powder
Hides from human view a zit still growing.
Though I've seen you pick your nose with vigor
When you thought that no one else was watching.

Though your mother's short and fat and ugly
And so one day you will surely follow.
Though your hair is straight and thin and greasy
And you supplement your form with padding.

Still I love you as I love no other.
Love has blinded me to every blemish.
I can only pray that in full fairness
It will do the same to you for my sake.

I shrank from offering such frank confessions of love as well. Somehow, I didn't think it would have the desired effect. Evidently, in love, honesty wasn't always the best policy. Which would I have to sacrifice, my integrity or my passion?

I finally resorted to Hollywood for my images. I would lay back in the Fortress and daydream soft-focus, slow-motion scenes of rolling meadows and flower-saturated fields where Becky romped through glistening brooks in rustling white lace and an enormous floppy straw hat. The radio provided an unlikely sound track of Doc Watson and "Dr. Zhivago." Although these fantasies were as impractical as chivalry, they were contemporary and therefore seemed more attainable. These were the meditations I practiced in my tree-house shrine to romance. Then, each day I returned to school and slowly burned down the stew of my passion into a thick, dark rue, strong and potent.

As the year wore on, I became more desperate to declare my devotion. When Valentine's Day drew near, I searched for a relatively risk-free method of expression and finally decided on the old secret-admirer ploy. The first step was to find the right card: a perfect combination of wit and affection. I had to dig through quite a stack before I found the winner. In the reject heap were such jewels as:

- Picture of a hillbilly on the front. Inside: "If you was grits, I'd go back for seconds."

- Picture of redneck with tools on front saying, "Could you help me study for my TV repair class?" Inside: "I need to practice my horizontal hold."

- Picture of bluetick hound on front and "You kiss a lot better than old Blue." Inside: "But how fast can you tree a coon?"

Finally, I came across the card that was unmistakably right. On the front was a drawing of a dumpy old woman with her hair in a bandanna, Aunt Jemima style, sitting at a kitchen table with a shy, goofy expression of infatuation. Striding seductively through the doorway was an archetypical, dumpy plumber serenading her on a tuba. In the corner sat a wide-eyed dog with claws extended and ears pointing straight up. Inside it read, "Weave your magic spell, my darling, for I am a slave of your love."

I withdrew to the Fortress of Solitude to compose an irresistibly romantic inscription. After several false starts, during which I endured a medley of Farin Young and Caruso, I finally settled on, "You are the music of my soul. Love, your secret admirer." I sealed the envelope, slapped a stamp on it, and put it in the mail.

I waited days for some sign that Becky had received an unexpected valentine. Finally, when I had all but given up, I saw her walking down the hall with the envelope. Her expression did little to inspire hope, because it was a picture of confusion. She came up to my locker and looked at me for a second. Then she opened up the envelope. "Did you send me an empty envelope in the mail?"

I looked down through the screen of hair that fell between us and, sure enough, it was empty. "Uh . . . no. Why would I do that?"

"But this looks like yer handwritin'." She flipped it over and, sure enough, she was right again.

I decided total denial was the only way out. "No, that's not my handwriting. Well, it looks a little like mine, but I didn't send it." I eyed her closely for signs of a prank. "Why would somebody send an empty envelope? Are you sure nothing was in it?"

"Yeah. I opened it myself, and it was empty."

"Huh. Go figure," I said weakly. What else was there to say? I endured the rest of the day and the long bus ride home in agony. I raced out to the Fortress of Solitude and dug out the ammo case. There it was, sitting right on top. I couldn't send it now or she would know for sure that I was the fool who had sent the first envelope. I tore up the card in frustration and burnt it—a sacrifice on the altar of unrequited love.

I now despaired of finding a way to reveal my devotion to Becky without risking a humiliating rejection. In desperation I decided on a last attempt at the secret-admirer approach. I chose the typing class as the most anonymous route.

Following the form in my Gregg typing book, I composed a simple letter of recommendation as follows.

March 2, 1971

Becky Tuttle
Row 2, Thord Third Desk form the Leftt
Room 122
Warren High School

Dear Miss Tuttle;:

I am writin gthis letter in refereence to a certaing admirer who is seeking a position currrently available as the center of yor affection.I have known this admirerer intimately for 15 years and can perosnally vouch fpr his character. heHe is dedicated and loyal and showzs a commemdable attention to

detial, particularlly where you are concernd. he would be willing to spend overtime perforing his duties as youer ardent
suitor .

if you have nor not filled this positino yet,, I hpoe you
will give seruios consideratoin to this admirer. If you are inter-
sted in my recommendation, leave a not to that affect in yuor
type-writer and I will contaact you in hte newar futur.e

Yours truely,

Anonymous

We had typing immediately after lunch, so the next day I sneaked
down the hall during lunch and put the note in Becky's typewriter. When
the bell rang, I hurried to class and was the first one in the room. I glanced
at the note when I passed by Becky's desk. It wasn't there! I went to my
own desk, dropped my books in a heap, and scurried over to Becky's desk.
The note was nowhere to be seen. Students began arriving, and I was
forced to abandon my search.

It wasn't until I was leaving the class that I discovered its fate. I was
walking out and glanced at the bulletin board. There it was—with a D– in
red at the top. All the mistakes were marked and at the bottom it read:

Originality	B+
Typing	F–
————————	
Grade	D–

I abandoned it as a lost cause and merged with the crowd.

CHAPTER FOURTEEN
But I was not the only one destined to be among the walking wounded in the war between the sexes. There were others who walked willingly into the incoming mortars at the front lines.

Ralph, Bubba, and I were hanging out in the pool hall in Fred, wasting quarters. Or more specifically, wasting *my* quarters. Ralph looked up at the sign next to the jukebox, which offered the observation: "Good kissin' don't last. Good cookin' do."

"You know," he said as he chalked his cue, "speakin' of kissin', I have a feelin' Jolene could finish in the top three." I looked around to see if Bubba was back with the ice cream. After all, it isn't exactly the best form to discuss a girl's kissing skills with her brother. One would hope he wouldn't be able to offer much firsthand advice.

"I wouldn't know, personally." I completely missed one of my balls and knocked in two of Ralph's.

"Thanks." He lined up his next shot. "Well, I aim ta find out." He made a nice bank shot.

"Find out what?" Bubba walked up with a handful of ice-cream cones.

"Ralph here has decided to try to kiss your sister."

"Good luck," Bubba replied and handed out the cones. Perhaps a surprising sentiment from a brother, but Bubba had his reasons for thinking that the only way Ralph would discover the flavor of Jolene's lipstick would be by stealing her purse.

I couldn't blame Ralph, even if I did think he was insane to attempt it. Jolene had turned from gawky to cute in junior high. But when she returned from summer to start high school, the world discovered that she had upped the ante considerably. She was just the right height to fit comfortably under an embracing arm and had a figure that was eminently embraceable. Wavy locks of raven hair surrounded a complexion as fresh and smooth as a glass of milk. Her eyebrows, which she had the good sense not to pluck, were thick and full. They accented eyes that seemed all pupils they were so dark. She was such a study in contrasts, you might have thought you were looking at a black-and-white picture had it not been for a hint of strawberry highlights on the cheeks and full, red lips with a slight pout.

Yes, Jolene was a first-rate candidate for kisser of the year, and lots of guys were hankering to help her win the contest. However, few got the chance because the contrasts weren't limited to her looks; they extended to her personality as well. A guy might take her out expecting a dream date but was more likely to have a nightmare.

Jolene had never lost her penchant for practical jokes. When the lights went down and the mood music came up, Jolene and her date started getting ideas, but the two sets of ideas bore no resemblance to each other except for the cast of characters who would be featured in the coming attractions. Inevitably, a conflict of ideas would arise before the night was through. A conflict in which Jolene would prevail.

Practically every guy in Tyler County tried to woo her. Each in turn took her to football games, dances, and movies—even gushy movies like *Love Story*. The most astute planners included a romantic dinner at Pizza Inn, where the lights were low and, if you asked him, the waiter would light the candle in the red tea glass with his Bic turned up to high. The jukebox even had Johnny Mathis tunes.

Toward the end of the evening, the most persistent would creep his pickup under a secluded oil rig romantically nestled in a wilderness of pines, kill the engine, and roll down the window to better hear the pulsing descant of crickets and frogs calling to their mates mixed with the seductive throb of the oil pump. Then he would turn expectantly for a kiss. Unfortunately, he was likely as not to be greeted by a pair of Groucho glasses. Or maybe a set of Dracula fangs. Either way, whatever he saw was guaranteed to cool the ardor of any would-be Don Juan.

Actually, Jolene may have liked kissing. All that anyone knew for sure was that she liked practical jokes more.

Even Old MacDonald noticed Jolene's transformation. He brought it up one day when we were out on the river annoying the loggerhead turtles by drowning worms in front of their noses. Fishing was not my leisure activity of choice, but as a member of the Sunday school class, I found myself obliged to submit to a gamut of tortures in the name of social conformity. On this particular outing I found myself marooned on a rowboat in the middle of the Neches River under the unblinking gaze of the Texas sun. Gnats swarmed around my head like my personal asteroid belt; horseflies slammed into me like meteors; mosquitoes touched down like a lunar lander taking core samples. It looked like things had gone from bad to worse for the center of my universe. The rest of the class was scattered at other fishing holes, probably all in the shade.

Behind me Old MacDonald was contentedly extracting another *Ictalurus punctatus* from its natural habitat. All the fish seemed to prefer his end of the boat. "So, Mark, don't Jolene have a steady boyfriend?" He tossed the fish into the wire-mesh basket hanging from the side of the boat.

"Uh, I don't think so." I terminated the short life of another mosquito, wiping the blood on my jeans.

"You should ask her out. You'd make a nice pair, you two."

"Me?" I considered the suggestion infinitely more ludicrous than an invitation to go fishing.

"Sure, why not?" His line plunked back into the water.

"You want a summary or a detailed list?"

"Might as well make it the detailed list. We got plenty of time."

That was not a pleasant thought. I was hoping for an early reprieve and a swim. "Well, for starters, I'm not suicidal."

Mac twisted around to look at me. "What?"

I glanced at him over my shoulder. "Asking Jolene out on a date is like walking across the highway dressed as an armadillo."

"Yeah?"

"Yeah, and Jolene is the log truck."

Mac turned back to his fishing. "I see," he said, and then under his breath, "I think." He didn't talk again until he was pulling up another fish and I was killing another mosquito. It wasn't a long wait. "So, where's the detailed list?"

I was mystified by his persistence. How could he not see that Jolene was pitching a no-hitter in the majors, and I was water boy for the farm team. I searched for a choice of words that wasn't completely self-demeaning. "Well, she's probably half a foot taller than I am."

"And . . ."

"Well, you know, that would look kind of funny."

"But I see you two together all the time, and it don't look funny."

"Well, that's different. We're just friends."

"Back when I was in high school, Peggy was the head cheerleader. Best lookin' girl in school."

I twisted around to look at him. Perhaps the heat was getting to him. I was on the verge of offering to row us ashore when he continued.

"I didn't think there would be any reason she would take notice of me. Too small to play football, not very popular. Not long after I broke up with another girl, there was a Sadie Hawkins dance. Peggy asked me to it."

"Yeah?"

"Yeah." He set his pole down. "You ready to head back in?"

The boat was too small for an ecstatic dance of celebration, so I just said, "Sure," and grabbed the oars.

"So, just think: what if Peggy had never asked me? I wouldn't have known how wrong I was about her not noticin' me. Think about it."

I thought about it. And about Becky. Mac looked back at me. "Now, what exactly did you mean with that part about the log truck?"

The next week, evidently acting on subliminal communications from the Old MacDonald Psychic Friends Network, Ralph asked Jolene out. To his great satisfaction, she accepted immediately. I awaited the event with as much expectation as he did. Perhaps more. The day after the date, I cornered him between Sunday school and church.

Ralph spat on the ground and said, "Shucks," or something to that effect.

"Is that all you have to say?" I demanded. "You took the hottest fox in Fred to a drive-in last night, for Pete's sake!"

Ralph snorted.

"What? Tell me what happened."

"I took her all the way down ta Beaumont and the drive-in. She made me get her a corny dog and mustard." He looked at me with the deadliest expression I had seen since *Billy Jack*. "You'll never guess what she did with it."

"What?"

"When she tried ta squirt mustard on it, she soaked my jeans." I suppressed a chuckle. I remembered the old mustard trick. It was one of her best because she seemed to be genuinely sorry after she did it. "So," Ralph continued, "I went ta the bathroom ta wash it off, and when I got back, the car was gone."

That was too much for me. I let a laugh slip out.

Ralph squelched it with a burning glare. "Yeah, go ahead, laugh. I hunted all over that dang drive-in before I found the car behind the concession stand." He spat on the ground again. "Then it wouldn't start. Took me thirty minutes ta find out she had pulled out the distributor cap and another thirty minutes ta find it in the glove compartment. The whole time she was sittin' in another car with Squeaky, watching the whole thang and laughin'. That's the last time I waste any money on her."

Ralph didn't know how easy he had gotten off. After all, he took her to a drive-in.

A drive-in has certain connotations to the typical teenage guy, who is usually nothing more than a seething mass of hormones precariously packaged in a container with the approximate shape of a human body. When Jolene suggested they go to the drive-in, Ralph had his expectations raised to critical levels. Visions of sugarplums danced in his head. The winged shaft of Cupid, or at least Eros, was lodged in his heart. So it was from a lofty height that she sent his hopes tumbling down into the ruins of his ego.

The truth was that, in spite of the East Texas macho facade, the self-image of these cowboys was as delicately balanced as my own. They needed a girl with an equally fragile self-image to accommodate them. Dating was little more than a group-therapy session of two (and sometimes grope-therapy as well) where the patients mutually validated each other's identities.

Ralph focused his attentions elsewhere, and before I knew it, he had a girlfriend. Ralph Mull, for crying out loud! Granted, the girlfriend was Squeaky, but still, a main squeeze is a main squeeze, and he had one. I pondered asking him for advice.

Darnell Ray had a girlfriend, but there was no use asking him how they hooked up. Everybody knew she had asked him. They were a matched set, anyway, both with greasy, Coke-bottle glasses and stringy hair. I didn't figure any of Darnell's advice for the lovelorn would apply to Becky.

My opportunity to pump Ralph for advice came when he was helping me build a fence for my pigs, an unfortunate side effect of having signed up for Ag. Unsurprisingly, even in Ag I found myself diverging from the norm. Everyone else made gun cases; I made a bookcase. But, then reality set in—I discovered a requirement of the class was to raise some type of farm animal, ostensibly with the purpose of making a profit. I took the cheapest and most unusual route—raising pigs.

While Ralph and I were building the pigpen, he handed me an eight-track tape. "Here. Put this on while we work."

I popped it in the tape deck and was immediately assaulted with a nasal female voice whining through the speaker. "Whoa." I hit the eject button. "What's that?"

Ralph eyed me with suspicion. "You never heard Tammy Wynette?"

"Thankfully, no."

"What tapes do you have?"

I opened my tape box. "How about Alice Cooper?"

"Never heard of her."

"Him."

"Oh, I thought you said Alice."

"I did. How about Steely Dan?"

"Never heard of him either."

"Them."

We finally compromised on Creedence Clearwater Revival. When I accidentally hit Ralph's left foot with a hammer, I figured the time was ripe for a change of subject.

"Say, Ralph."

"Yeah."

"How did you and Squeaky get together anyway?"

A pause followed of such duration that I began to wonder if he had forgotten the question. As I was about to ask again, he cleared his throat. "You remember that coon dog that used ta sleep on the yellow stripe on the Warren highway?"

"Yeah."

"That was her dog."

I waited for awhile, but that was all he said. It may have explained all as far as he was concerned, but I was shaky on the details. "Yeah, so?"

"So, it bit me."

"Yeah?"

"Yeah."

Another spell of silence left me wondering. Was a coon-dog bite some kind of aphrodisiac? I gave up and asked again, "Yeah, so?"

"So, I came limpin' up ta her house, and Squeaky felt sorry for me and doctored my leg, and then she started lookin' at me like, well, you know, and then I was lookin' at her the same way, and the next thang I knowed she was wearin' my rang."

He paused his hammering for a moment and looked off. "It just sorta happened. I wasn't aimin' ta get a girl, but all of a sudden I had one." He glanced at me, spat in the mud, and went back to hammering.

It didn't sound like much of a plan to me. I didn't even know if Becky had a dog. If she did, with my luck it would be a Doberman.

CHAPTER FIFTEEN
One week before school let out, Ralph broke through my morning fog as he boarded the bus.

"Say, doll, did you hear about last night?"

"No." It was an ambiguous question. I did know that last night had occurred, much like the many nights preceding it, but that was hardly news. The only difference I was aware of was that Dad received a phone call and left. I went to bed before he returned.

"You didn't hear about the wreck?"

"What wreck?"

"Old MacDonald had a flat tire on the road about a mile from his house. You know, that curve just past the oil rig?"

"Yeah." It was one of the hazards on my *Grit* route. It was a sharp turn at the bottom of a hill that was as close to a sandpit as you can get and still be a road.

"Well, he had his car jacked up and was changin' the back tire. Peggy and the baby was in the front seat. Parker came round the corner and plowed right into 'em. Killed Peggy and Kristen outright. Parker went through the windshield. Mac was trapped under the car for hours until they finally got 'im out. They both is in the hospital."

"Wow." That explained why Dad was called. He was probably at the hospital in Silsbee. "How did you hear about it?"

"Uncle Hurst was on call, so he was the first one there. He called Mama when he got home." Hurst was a sheriff's deputy and Ralph's mother's brother.

"Oh." We rode along in silence. I thought about the news and my reaction to it. It was like hearing something on TV, something happening in Bangladesh. These were people I knew. Mac and Peggy were my Sunday school teachers. Kristen frequently stared at me, in that solemn way babies do, over Peggy's shoulder from the pew in front. I tried to make her smile without attracting attention from Dad, and had succeeded a few times. I thought I should feel something more, some kind of sorrow, but it was just news, nothing to do with me.

"Kinda makes ya think, don't it?" Ralph mused.

"Yeah." It certainly made me think. I had no idea what it made Ralph think about. I wouldn't be kept in suspense for long.

"Ya know, this bus could blow out a tire and go off this bridge right now," he observed, looking out the window into Toodlum Creek as we blew past at sixty miles per hour. "We could all be dead in a second." He switched his gaze from the creek to my face. "You and me. Just like that."

"Yeah." The speculation seemed about as real to me as the possibility that the Berlin Wall would be torn down. It was nothing more than an intellectual exercise. Yes, the laws of probability could roll the dice and off we could go, over the bridge into the creek. People lived; people died. That's how it worked.

"The funeral is Saturday. Mac is in intensive care and probably won't be out by then. Parker is doing OK. He was cut up somethin' fierce and lost a lot of blood, but he's not in too bad shape. Don't know if he will be out or not."

I didn't relish the thought of going to a funeral, but I didn't see how I could get out of it. They were members of the church, taught Sunday school, and I was the preacher's kid. How would that look?

I floated the idea of skipping the funeral to Mom as the easier touch, but she nixed it without the you-have-to-ask-your-dad stay of execution. Not that I had much hope.

Dad did the service. Mom played the organ. Heidi, Hannah, and I sat on the fifth row—far enough back not to intrude on the family but close enough to show respect. I sat there quietly in my suit, looking at two caskets, one very small. Both were closed, to my great relief.

Peggy's mother, father, and two sisters sat at the front on the right. The father sat rigid and expressionless, eyes red but dry. The sisters, both in their twenties, were crying quietly. Between them the mother stared vacantly ahead as if she had no idea where she was or what was happening. Or perhaps as if she had no idea how this could have happened to her baby. Other members of the family sat around them, some loudly expressing their grief.

Sonia Walker, Parker's wife and Peggy's best friend, sat alone on a pew, looking as helpless as a five-year-old lost in a department store. Under the too hasty and too thick makeup, her face showed she had been crying, probably for three days, but now the mascara clotted on her lashes was dry. She clutched a twisted and knotted handkerchief that seemed in danger of ripping from the stress of her slender fingers and thick red fingernails. No other member of her family was present. Parker, like Mac, was still in the hospital, and her family held a deep-seated animosity toward the church. Nothing could move them to step across the threshold, not even the agony of one of their own.

Ralph sat across the aisle with his family. He seemed shaken, as if still contemplating the possibility of his own sudden death. The Culpeppers were in the next row back, both Jolene and Bubba shiny-eyed. Heidi and Hannah, to either side of me, were sniffling. I felt as if I alone sat unfeeling and untouchable, a victim of a rare strain of leprosy of the soul.

Judy Graham got up and sang "In the Sweet Bye and Bye." Then Dad stood in front, quietly looking out over the congregation. He seemed moved but in control.

"'Eli, Eli, lama sabachthani? My God, my God, why hast thou forsaken me?'" A gasp arose from the front row, followed by a sob. Peggy's mother suddenly seemed focused and in great pain. One of the sisters put her arm around her.

"That's how we feel when a tragedy like this happens. 'God, why have You forsaken me? How could You let this happen?' And we don't hear an answer. We don't hear anything but the sound of our own hearts breaking." Dad stopped for a long pause. I could see the muscles in his jaw bulging out and his eyes grow hard and fixed. He took off his glasses, wiped them with a handkerchief, but didn't put them back on. The mother was crying quietly but steadily; the father still resolute but eyes no longer dry.

"Peggy Harmon MacDonald was a beautiful young woman. Beautiful to the eyes of man, but more importantly, beautiful in the eyes of God. She loved God and sought to please Him with her life. She honored her father and mother. She married a godly man. She bore a daughter and dedicated her to the Lord. She gave her energy to the Lord's work, investing it in the life of her family and her community.

"Today we have all come here to honor the lives and memories of Peggy and Kristen. Yes, our hearts are broken and we can't imagine what life will be without them. But for a few moments, let us honor them by recalling what life was like with them. Let us take some time to share memories of how they touched our lives."

Dad looked at a row of people sitting on the front pew to the left. Janet Mull, Ralph's sister, stood up and walked unsteadily to the front.

"When I heard Pastor Cloud wanted people to tell stories about Miss Peggy, I called and asked him if I could help." She swallowed and continued. "Miss Peggy was very special to us high school girls. Not like a mother, not like a sister, not like a best friend, but somethin' that was like the best of all three. There was times when I was on the verge of doin' some things that weren't too good, and if she hadn't been there to talk to, I'm not so sure I wouldn't of done 'em." She shot a nervous glance at her parents. "I know that my life would be different right now if Miss Peggy hadn't been there for me. Thank God she was."

Janet nodded quickly and darted back to her seat. Dad looked to the next person, a young woman in her twenties.

"What I remember best about Peggy was how she treated Kristen like she was a special gift from God. She kept her in line, but she did it with such a gentle way. I know I have a time with my own, and sometimes they exasperates me. But they has the benefit of a mother that has learned how to nurture them by watching the example of Peggy Harmon. MacDonald, I mean. And there ain't no better example."

One after another, people came up and talked about the impact Peggy had had on their lives, some calmly, some very emotionally. Then, as the last person on the front row sat down, Sonia Walker stood up.

"I was Peggy's best friend," she said loudly. "She was all those things to me and more. I think I loved her even more than Mac did, and that's saying a lot!" Her eyes flared from behind the clumps of mascara. "So, what kind of God would kill her?" She choked out the last words and closed her eyes, gripping the pew in front of her until her knuckles turned white. "And her baby!" she blurted out. "A baby! He killed a baby," she cried.

Everyone stared in stunned silence. Sonia looked at Peggy's mother. "I'm sorry. I wish it would of been me." She turned and jerked her purse from the pew. "She was the good one. It shoulda been me," she pinched out in a shaky voice as she rushed out of the church.

"Let's pray for a second." Dad's voice echoed in the silence following the slam of the church door. "Heavenly Father, we ask that You surround

Sonia with Your Holy Spirit. Comfort her in this time of grief, and protect her from harm. Amen." All eyes were on Dad as he looked up from his prayer.

"We have heard from many people whose lives were touched by Peggy MacDonald. Even Sonia, in the passion of her grief, has shown us how special Peggy was. And Sonia has shown us something else: that it hurts when someone is taken from us, especially someone as special as Peggy. Of course we feel betrayed. Death was brought into this world by the Enemy. It is natural, it is right, for us to feel pain, grief, anger, and even betrayal. It is right for us to feel outrage at the insult of death.

"Even God knows the pain of losing a child, the righteous anger of seeing a good person suffering the ultimate injustice of a wrongful death. Even an innocent person, as Kristen was completely innocent. He knows how we feel, for He has felt it Himself." He paused and looked at Peggy's family. "So, none of us should be ashamed to let our feelings out like Sonia has. No one need feel guilty for feeling or expressing anger. Let God know how you feel, even if it is against Him that you want to cry and rage. He is a big God; He can take it."

Dad sat down heavily, and Judy Graham sang "Precious Memories." I sat between my weeping sisters, my head bowed, hiding behind a screen of dirty blond hair as I wondered if I had a heart of stone. All I could think about was the parting words of Twain's Mysterious Stranger and wonder at all the pain that washed across the room like the tide coming in.

———

A month later I stopped at the Walker house on my *Grit* route. Once again a pair of legs protruded from an F-150 pickup, but it was a different truck, an older one, and this time Old MacDonald didn't come out of the house with tea. Parker had been out of the hospital for awhile, but it was the first time I had stopped at this house since the funeral, the first time I had seen any indication of life. I stopped next to the truck.

"Hey, Mr. Walker. Did you want a paper?"

The legs jerked and a curse came from under the truck. "Didn't I tell you to call me Parker?"

"Yes, sir." Calling adults by their first names was difficult for me to do. "Did you want a *Grit,* Parker?"

"What would I want with a paper?"

"Uh, I don't know. You could read it, I guess."

Parker crawled out from under the truck and to his feet. A large, jagged, red scar ran from the middle of his forehead across his left eye, which was covered with a black patch, down his cheek to the corner of his mouth. I flinched. It was the first time I had seen him since the wreck.

"Kinda takes ya by surprise, don't it, kid?" He leaned toward me. I could smell alcohol. "Give me your paper."

He held out a hand black with grease and oil. I gave him a *Grit.* He took a few sheets off the top, smearing them with grime as he cleaned his hands on them, dug out a billfold, and extracted a dollar.

He shoved it in my hand and crawled back under the truck without another word. I looked toward the house and saw Sonia peering timidly from the door of the carport. I waved, but she didn't wave back.

———

The next time I hesitated about stopping at Parker's, but the 300 percent tip was hard to pass up. The pickup was gone, so I knocked. Sonia pulled back the curtain and peeked at me, then opened the door. She had on the kind of thick makeup that always made me want to scrape it off with a putty knife just to see how much I would get. It ended at her jaw line, her natural skin a little lighter. Her lashes were fat with mascara around her brown eyes. Brown roots showed from beneath her shoulder-length, bleached hair.

"Would you like a paper, Mrs. Walker?"

She glanced apprehensively at the road, then back at me. "Sure, come in, I'll get my purse."

I stepped into the cool dark cave, closing the door behind me. Sonia fumbled around inside her purse nervously.

"You're the preacher's kid, ain't ya?" She looked up. "The brick church in town. What was your name again?"

"Mark."

"Right, Mark." She pulled out a coin purse. "How much is it?"

"Twenty-five cents." She gave me a quarter. "Thank you." I turned to go.

"Do you live up next to the church, on that hill?"

I stopped and turned back. "No, ma'am. We live on that dirt road back behind the elementary school. First house. Brick."

"Right, that road."

"Yes, ma'am." I turned to go, again.

"Hey . . ."

I stopped and turned back, waiting. She looked nervously around, avoiding my eyes.

"Uh . . . so, I hear Mac teaches a Sunday school class there." She glanced at me and quickly away.

"Yes, ma'am. The high school class."

"Is he, uh . . . is he back?"

"No, ma'am, he hasn't come back yet. I don't know if he's out of the hospital or not." I waited, but no other questions came. "Bye. Thanks." I turned, and this time I got out of the door.

"Bye. You're welcome," I heard her say quietly as it closed behind me.

CHAPTER SIXTEEN When school started up the next fall, Jolene's assault on the Fredonian male ego continued unabated. However, by now all the available males had made their ardent assault on the Culpepper fortress. Each in turn had retreated, pieced together his shattered ego, and focused his attentions on more receptive targets. By the time the homecoming dance rolled around, nobody even bothered to ask Jolene. Why volunteer to be the straight man with the whole class watching?

If the thought had occurred to me, I might have asked her, but by then I had become accustomed to my role as Jolene's personal eunuch. Old MacDonald's advice notwithstanding, I didn't relish the thought of walking in front of an oncoming log truck, even if it was an incredibly beautiful log truck. So it looked like Jolene wouldn't be going to the homecoming dance that year, and none of the other girls were too heartbroken about it either. They were tired of watching every guy in the school flutter mindlessly around her like moths around the back porch light, getting zapped, and then limping in search of lesser lights.

When things looked hopeless, a miracle happened. A new family moved in—a family with a male teenager who had no date to the homecoming dance. The new guy, Turner McCullough, was surprised to discover that the prettiest girl in school was still available, but he didn't question fate. None of the other guys warned him, feeling that a date with Jolene was a rite of passage in Fred.

Jolene did what most of the girls had done weeks before; she sewed her dress. The light in the Culpepper den could be seen late into the night as Jolene worked feverishly. In band each morning she dragged her haggard frame around the practice field. She told me of her progress while we waited for the woodwinds to get within a halftone of the same pitch while moving their feet. Of course, nothing Jolene did could be completely free from slapstick. Some of the details of what ensued eventually entered into the public domain, due to unexpected developments that Jolene didn't orchestrate, but also didn't fail to exploit. As Jolene's au pair, I was privy to the more salacious details of the backstory denied to the hoi polloi.

When the dress began to take shape, she attempted to enlist Bubba as a clotheshorse. "Fergit it!" he bellowed. He had felt the brunt of too many jokes not to suspect her motives. Besides, no self-respecting Fredonian male of sixteen could possibly consider wearing a dress, even to enable his twin sister to attend the homecoming dance.

The battle raged for days, and time was running out when Jolene discovered his weakness. Romance lurks in the most unlikely places, and it seems Bubba was hopelessly smitten with Turner's younger sister, Marianne. Jolene deduced his secret when she walked into his room one night without knocking and found him enhancing his fledgling mustache with mascara.

He was staring intently into the mirror. "Marianne," he said in an unnatural baritone voice, "would you like to go out with me Friday? No, that's no good." He assumed what he evidently felt was a sophisticated expression, one eyebrow suavely raised. "Marianne, how 'bout takin' in a movie Friday night?"

Then he saw Jolene in the mirror. "Hey! Didn't you ever learn ta knock?" he demanded.

"Didn't you ever learn ta ask before you borrow my makeup?" Jolene retorted, waving the mascara in his face. Bubba flushed a glowing scarlet and leaned on his elbow, casually covering his mouth with his hand. "Don't try ta hide it, now. It's too late."

"Dang it, Jolene." He slammed his hand on the dresser. "There's such a thang as privacy."

"Calm down, Bubba. This is your lucky day."

He eyed her suspiciously. "How's that?"

"Obviously you're sweet on Marianne McCullough, right?"

"So?"

"So, I'm going with Turner to the homecoming dance. You can take Marianne, and we can double."

"You're forgettin' one very important fact. I'm takin' Judy to the homecoming dance."

"Oh, that's right." Jolene thought for a moment. "But you'd like ta take Marianne out, wouldn't you?"

"Sure, who wouldn't?"

"OK. How about if I get a double date set up with the Culpeppers and the McColloughs?"

"Why?"

"Oh, quit being so cautious, Bodean. Would you like for me ta do it or not?"

"Sure, as long as you don't screw the whole thang up by embarrassin' one of us."

"You worry about the silliest things, Bubba. Look, if you'll help me finish my dress, I'll set you up with Marianne."

"I don't know . . ."

"On a single date, just you and Marianne."

"What are you gonna do? Ask her yourself?"

"OK. I'll invite her over and arrange for you ta be alone with her fer a few minutes. How's that?"

Bubba relented, his passion overwhelming his ego. Jolene led him to the den and the sewing machine. He locked the door and closed all the curtains. Then, with second, third, and fourth thoughts and protests too numerous to relate, he gingerly donned the formal and stood on a telephone cable spool while Jolene pinned and taped and stitched. As she worked, he complained bitterly about the indignities he was forced to suffer in the name of love until Jolene flung the curtains open wide. Bubba shrieked and disappeared into the closet. The fitting session proceeded thereafter with only minor grumbling.

The next day at school Bubba was very quiet. Thoughts of the dress haunted him. He couldn't shake the feeling that people could tell just by looking that he had been wearing it. They didn't actually say anything, but he felt like somehow they knew. Normal events took on sinister aspects. Every smile seemed like a veiled taunting. Every huddle of whispering, giggling girls was a cauldron of rumors threatening to overflow and destroy his reputation. He was certain even the workers in the cafeteria knew. He saw the way the cook looked at him. There was no mistaking that!

That evening it took Jolene an hour to convince him to endure a final fitting. Anxious to get it just right, she gave him a pair of her shorts and had him fill out the hips with extra fabric. She wanted him to wear her bra stuffed with socks to fit the top, but Bubba drew the line at that. Wearing a dress was bad enough, but he absolutely wasn't going to wear girl's underwear! She finally settled for simulating the curves by hanging two squashes around his neck with a length of twine.

Standing on the spool in padded shorts, a formal, and two squashes, Bubba felt he had sunk as low as a man could go. His face was hot, no doubt burning with shame. The longer he stood, the hotter it seemed to get. Then he realized his head was only a foot from the ceiling. Naturally it would be hotter up there. He sniffed suspiciously. "Hey! Somethin's burnin.'"

Suddenly Mr. Culpepper burst into the room. The sight of Bubba in drag on a pedestal stopped him dead in his tracks with his mouth open. Black smoke rolled in along the ceiling above him.

"I told you somethin' was burnin'," Bubba hollered, jumping down from the spool.

The noise broke Mr. Culpepper's trance. "Hurry! Climb out the window! The house is full of smoke!"

Bubba kicked out the screen and helped Jolene climb out as Mr. Culpepper pulled the phone to the floor and called the constable. Bubba followed Jolene out of the window and ran to the side of the house. The pine trees seemed to jerk fitfully with a flickering light. The flames had already eaten through the roof.

"I think it started in the attic," he hollered to his dad, who was running around the corner. Bubba twisted on the faucet, grabbed the water hose, and ran, but it caught on a bush and jerked him flat on his back. Water spurted up like a geyser, soaking him. It was then that he realized he was still wearing the dress.

He jumped up and turned one way and then the other, in a quandary about which disaster was greater, the fire or the dress. The urgency of the fire finally won. He pulled the hose to the side of the house and did his best to discourage the flames, the dress soon forgotten. Jolene looked in dismay at her formal, now streaked with mud, soot, and water.

The glow of flames in the trees attracted the neighbors and folks passing on the highway. Before long a crowd stood watching the spectacle. Bubba stood his post resolutely, his back to the masses. An old F-150 rolled to a stop just out of the light cast by the fire, and Parker stepped out, walking past the onlookers to stop next to Bubba.

"Lady, that hose ain't doin' a bit a good," he said. "Is there anybody in there?" The flames dancing on the roof reflected from his good eye, which was bloodshot.

"Nope," Bubba muttered through clenched teeth.

Parker jumped back, took a closer look at Bubba, and whistled, the smell of alcohol strong on his breath. "It don't look like it spread that quick. Didn't you have time ta find somethin' besides a dress?" Bubba didn't answer. Parker considered the contour of the two squashes, the dress soaked and clinging to them like a wet T-shirt contest. He let it pass.

"Kinda makes ya think a hellfire, don't it?" If it did, Bubba didn't say so. "Sure feels hotter'n hell." He swayed gently in silence for awhile. "You may as well turn off that piddlin' hose. You can't save this house with that anymore'n you can stop the fires a hell. Devil's gonna take it just like he's gonna take them that's his own. Nothin' you can do about it now." He gave Bubba one last distracted glance. "Nothin' you can do about it now," he muttered and slouched back to his truck as the volunteer fire department arrived.

Harlan Johnson, Harmon's boy from the gas station, came running up, dragging a hose. "Watch out, miss," he hollered, "we're comin' through with the hose."

Bubba glared at him but didn't move. Harlan had been devoting his attention to the hose, but when Bubba didn't move, he looked up. "Excuse me, miss . . ." His voice trailed off as he caught sight of Bubba's face. It was as blank and masklike as Bubba could make it, but from the depths of its neutrality two eyes burned like twin coals ignited by the very fire they were fighting. And it was obviously masculine.

"Well, I'll be durned," Harlan said, or something to that effect. That's all he had a chance to say because that was the moment water came shooting out of his own hose and he lost control of it. It just about beat him silly before they got it turned off and tried again.

134

Compared to the fire hose, Bubba may as well have been spitting on the fire, but still he stood his ground with the garden hose. Eventually Jolene grabbed his hand and pulled him across the lawn.

"Come here, Mr. Hero. You've done enough already."

He was soaked from the runaway fire hose. His hair was plastered to his head. The dress clung to the squashes at the top and slapped against his legs at the bottom as he walked. He was definitely a sorry sight and felt every inch of it. Jolene pulled him to a stop in front of a girl on the edge of the crowd.

"Bubba, I'd like you ta meet Marianne McCullough. Marianne, this is my brother, the fireman." She joined their hands and walked away with a grin, delighted to keep her promise. Bubba spluttered out a confused greeting to an obviously amused but discretely quiet Marianne and tore off after Jolene.

That weekend Ralph, Bubba, and I hiked out to our hideout, a campsite we created in the middle of a swamp out near Ralph's place, although we never spent the night there. The mosquitoes were too fierce. Ralph broached the subject of the dress, and I declared the ensuing wrestling match a draw. We were walking in a strained silence when I slipped from a moss-covered log and splashed waist deep into a stagnant pool of algae and weeds. I muttered a few choice words preferred by Jimbo Perkins and pushed the hair from my face with a slimy hand.

"Hey," Ralph said indignantly. "Yer the preacher's kid!"

"Yeah, so?"

"So, you shouldn't swear." A frown creased his freckled face. "Right, Bubba?"

"Right."

"Wait a minute." I clawed my way out of the water and got into Ralph's face, my hair the only thing that screened him from the full force of my fury. "What did you say back there when I let go of that branch and it whacked you in the face?"

"Yeah, so?"

"So, you shouldn't swear either." I delivered the point with an air of finality.

"But I'm not the preacher's kid."

"What difference does that make? You go to church, don't you? You consider yourself a Christian, don't you?"

"Of course, but my dad's not the preacher. Right, Bubba?"

"Right."

I don't know which drove me to greater distraction, Ralph's relentless but irrelevant logic or Bubba's monosyllabic echo. I stormed off the path and kicked at a rotted branch. It crumbled silently in a cloud of fungi. The fact that it made so little noise frustrated me further.

"So what?" My voice cracked like a yodeler. "A Christian is a Christian. What difference does it make what your dad does for a living?" I wanted my words to echo through the woods with the ring of truth. Instead they fell flat like a feeble excuse, hushed by the cloak of pine needles, moss, and algae that covered everything. I turned on Ralph, shrieking. "Why is it any more wrong for me to swear than it is for you?"

Ralph winced. "It just is. I don't know why."

I would have poured forth a fountain of profanity, but I didn't know enough cuss words to make up more than a trickle. Words failing me, I sputtered an inarticulate retort, stomped off in a rage, and promptly fell from another log. Ralph declared this a sign from God that he was right. And perhaps it was.

At the camp I sat on a stump in my underwear, my pants hanging from a branch in a futile attempt to dry them out in the humid air. The excuse for a fire that we built with damp rotting wood produced a vile smoke that hung around the camp in the still air. We rolled up baloney slices, impaled them on sticks, and attempted to roast them over the smoldering mound.

Ralph pulled out his Red Man and offered it around. I declined, Bubba accepted. "I seen Parker the other day at the gas station." He put away the pouch. "That scar is wicked lookin'. And that patch don't help none."

"Makes him look like a regular pirate," Bubba said. "He looked pretty scary at the fi–" He cleared his throat and changed directions. "I'd hate ta meet that in a dark alley some night." We sat in silence for awhile. Smoke curled around the baloney slices.

"He was drunker'n Cooter Brown too," Ralph said. "Not sure how he drives that pickup, but he seems ta do it OK anyhow."

"Yep, it's kinda amazin'," Bubba agreed. "But I think I'd hate ta meet that even more on a dark alley."

"Ain't seen Sonia much. Since the funeral, that is. I think ever'body saw her there."

I decided to join the conversation, having recovered from my fit. "I've seen her." Bubba and Ralph looked at me expectantly. "Just sell her papers, that's all." We stared at the baloney for awhile; the only sounds were Bubba and Ralph spitting and the mosquitoes buzzing. "Seems kind of nervous though."

"Janet says she heard that Sonia showed up at the beauty shop with a black eye. Or at least what looked like might be a black eye under all that makeup," Ralph said. "That would explain it."

Bubba nodded. "Yep, Jolene heard the same thing, plus somethin' about bruises." He pulled his baloney slice up to his nose, sniffed it, and slapped it into a hot dog bun. "I don't think this sucker's gonna get any warmer."

Ralph followed his example. "Probably could get it warmer just by rubbin' on yer pants leg."

"There's no accounting for taste," I said, and ate the baloney right off the stick, like a corny dog.

CHAPTER SEVENTEEN
After my four years' hard labor in the cultural assimilation chain gang, another inmate with the unlikely name of C. J. Hecker was transferred to the Big Thicket Unit. He arrived from Houston wearing a paisley shirt, bell-bottom jeans, and boots that looked like they had been stolen from Van Morrison's hotel room on his last tour. Before the end of the day he was informed his collar-length, dark-brown hair was in violation of the dress code. He returned the next day with a haircut that required a micrometer to measure compliance.

With the innate caution of the outsider, I maintained a polite distance, both intrigued and amused by the discontinuity Hecker must have been experiencing. It was an echo of the cultural whiplash I had experienced back in the time when Nixon was hounding Johnson out of office, but now amplified by adolescence and the fact that this was the first move of C. J.'s life.

During those four years, Tricky Dick had slowly schemed his way toward Watergate, and I had slowly accommodated my wardrobe to local custom. As a result, I was not immediately identifiable as the outsider I really was. But it didn't take more than a few weeks in algebra and English classes for me to realize that C. J. was as close as I was likely to come to finding a replacement for M. We eventually joined forces in our shared fate as outsiders.

C. J. had an air of confidence about him, as if there were no question in his mind that the environment in which he found himself was the anomaly and he was the norm. He had a dark complexion that was more Latin than the name *Hecker* allowed, and his left eye had a silver-gray fleck that ran vertically across the iris. It made me wonder if he could see out of it at all, but I was too timid to ask.

He lived in Warren, so getting together meant twenty minutes if I was driving or fifteen minutes if he was driving. Of course, there was nothing to do at either his house or mine, so we usually followed prevailing custom and haunted Beaumont, which meant another hour on the road. Our relationship was formed in the cocoonlike security of a car ripping through the piney woods at seventy-five miles per hour. We probed each other's minds and souls, our faces illuminated by the green glow of the dash lights.

Both being addicts to music, our deep and searching discussions were carried out at the top of our lungs, shouting over the eight-track as it blared out the Stones, the Beatles, Guess Who, Grand Funk Railroad, or, when I couldn't hide the tape before he got in the car, the Doors. We tunneled through the towering pines with the windows down, headlights shooting into the darkness and ZZ Top's "La Grange" echoing through the woods.

In those hours of traversing the cultural wasteland of the Big Thicket in search of diversion, I found a confidant for my dilemma with Becky. I cautiously divulged the outlines of my obsession. C. J. had a solution at the ready.

"What you have to do is act like you're not interested in her. Then she'll get interested in you."

"But I am." I tried to hold my hand steady. The washboard dirt road we were bounding down made the car rattle like a kid dragging a stick down a picket fence. It not only had the effect of setting up standing waves in my bottle of Dr Pepper, it also made Bob Dylan sound like he was auditioning for the Bee Gees. "Interested in her, I mean."

"I know that and you know that, but she doesn't have to know that. You pretend like you're not."

I paused to listen to the closing bars of "All Along the Watchtower." "Why would she become interested in me if I ignore her?" I asked before the next song started.

"Because that's how it works," C. J. hollered over the stereo. "Look, I didn't make up the rules. That's the way girls work. Hormones and all that stuff."

"But why should I play all those games?" I hollered back. "Why not just be honest?"

"Major mistake. Remember Hecker's Rule of Romance #1: Never tell the truth. It's too boring." He took a sharp curve in a four-wheel skid and whipped the car back straight. I held my breath but didn't panic. C. J.'s driving may have been aggressive, but it was nothing to a person who had been privileged to ride with Darnell Ray.

"Besides, you know how you start talking for no apparent reason and continue with no apparent motive for an indefinite period of time?" He squinted through his aviator glasses in my direction.

"I beg your pardon," I replied with asperity, tossing my head from habit, even though my hair wasn't in my eyes.

"Well, that doesn't go over with icons of beauty anymore than it does with mere mortals. Better to appear unattainable. Then they'll kill themselves trying to get your attention."

"It doesn't make any sense," I complained, deciding in the interest of romance to ignore the insult to my conversational skills.

"Since when do girls make sense?" I had to admit he had a point there. "Girls aren't supposed to make sense. Remember Hecker's Rule of Romance #1: Women should be obscene and not heard."

"I thought Rule #1 was 'Never tell the truth.' And I thought Groucho said that."

"OK, so there's two rules numbered one. Forget the numbers! Just trust me; I've seen it happen lots of times. You play hard-to-get and it'll drive her crazy."

Well, that only seemed fair. After all, she had been unwittingly driving me crazy for months. For the next three weeks I remained cool and aloof. By the end of the month even C. J. had to admit it wasn't working. Neither of us realized that from outward appearances there was little difference between playing hard-to-get and being scared into inaction by the fear of rejection.

C. J. fell back on plan B. "Write her a song," he suggested as we were returning from the mall in Beaumont where we had picked up an eight-track of Neil Young's "Harvest." "That'll do it." While I had been playing hard-to-get, he had been teaching me to play guitar. I had almost reached the point where I could change chords without inadvertently changing the time signature of the song. "I've never seen a girl yet who could resist a love song written especially for her. They tend to throw themselves on the floor in abject submission to your every whim."

I never thought to ask C. J. how many girls had flung themselves at his feet upon hearing a song written for them. Instead, I was petrified at the thought of addressing the matter so directly. This approach seemed to smack too much of the danger of rejection.

"Right. How subtle is playing a song to her?" I grabbed the dash as we rounded a curve thirty miles per hour faster than recommended by the Department of Public Safety. "I might as well just walk up in the hall and kiss her between classes."

"Hey, there's an approach I hadn't considered!" He squinted at the reflectors. "It just might work."

"Don't be ridiculous! I can't just walk up out of the blue and kiss Becky in the hall."

"What? No. Of course not!" He looked at me like I'd suggested we turn off Neil Young and listen to Perry Como instead. The silver fleck in his eye glinted in the dark as he appraised me by the dashboard light. "You couldn't pull it off, being a PK and all. Isn't there a talent show next week?"

"Yeah."

"You could write Becky a song and play it at the talent show."

"Right! I might as well write her a valentine and read it over the P.A. during announcements!" I cupped my hands around my mouth. "The FHA is having a bake sale. The girls will be selling hot buns in the hall during lunch. Let's all get behind our girls and give them our support. And now this announcement from Mark Cloud. Dear Becky Tuttle: I am hopelessly in love with you and will wither away if you don't reciprocate. Please respond by carrier pigeon within the hour."

"Well, you don't have to make it that blunt! You don't even have to use her name."

"Then how will she know it's for her?"

"You can do something like . . ." He ejected the tape and cleared his throat.

> She might have braces and short brown hair
> She could have a harelip for all I care; she's mine
> People don't you see what she's doing to me
> Hanging around this town looking up and down for her
>
> She won't have braces all her life
> But even if she does I've found me a wife; she's mine . . .

I pushed the tape back in and turned it up. "That's OK. I'll come up with my own."

I spent the rest of the weekend struggling over a song. By Sunday night I had come up with something I thought was a proper blend of candor and subtlety. It went something like this.

There's something in you that I like
And I think you know it
There's something about you I like
And I think I show it
Your eyes or your hair? I couldn't swear
Maybe it's your personality
The way that you stay when everyone else goes away
The way that you set me free

I'm not quite sure how but I think you know by now
That I'd like to tell you how I feel
The feeling is so real and it's one that I can't conceal
And it's mine and nobody can steal it
I love you and I think you know it
I love you and I think I show it

I played it for C. J. the next day. He sat in silence for a long time and then cleared his throat.

"Well. Hmm. Yes, that certainly will work. Yup."

I looked at him uncertainly. "Do you think it's too corny?"

"Oh, no," he answered too quickly. "It's got a certain character about it. Very . . . original."

I took his words at face value and entered the talent show. C. J. was also in the show, playing "Old Man" from the Neil Young tape we had bought the week before. He did a great job as usual and received a respectable amount of applause from a room full of George Jones fans.

The next thing I knew the emcee was announcing that Mark Cloud was going to perform an original song. I trembled my way out on the stage and set the music on the stand. I let my hair fall down over my eyes as a protective screen, buffering me from the intimidation of the audience, did a little last minute tuning, and then started playing. Just as I got out the first line, the paper slipped off the stand and into the orchestra pit. With a silent cry of despair I watched it flutter into the abyss. I squinted at the crowd through my hair and my mind went as blank as the music stand. I played the same chord for a few seconds and then started improvising.

> And I think you know it because I show it
> Is it your hair? I swear I don't care
> But she's got a good personality
> It's how you stay out of the way
> With the bare necessities
>
> This feeling is real and I can't conceal
> How much you steal from my heart
> Don't you know that I got to go
> And I'm through before I start

I jumped up and stumbled off stage to stunned silence, followed by a trickle of applause mixed with laughter and coughing.

At lunch I was informed that Thelma Perkins had interpreted my song as a secret confession of love for her. Thelma—sister of Jimbo; the sarcastic write-in for homecoming queen; the forged signatory on hundreds of practical-joke love letters; the one girl in the school who, like me, had yet to experience a date. In Fred, if you want to win awards at being ugly, you have to really be ugly. Merely homely girls need not apply. The years had done nothing to soften Thelma's harsher features. She still had a face as wide and flat as Jimbo's, teeth like a set of ivory dominoes yellowed with age, and short hair as stiff and coarse as a broom.

I was horrified beyond words to receive this bulletin, particularly as Becky was the one to bring the tidings from the uncharacteristically shy Thelma. Becky delivered Thelma's professions of love with poorly concealed amusement and waited for my response with a smile that, for once, didn't seem quite so angelic.

Attempting my utmost to wear the mask of indifference, I couldn't help being reminded of John Alden delivering a similar message to Priscilla Mullens in behalf of the love-stricken but shy Miles Standish. As you no doubt remember (although it doesn't matter if you don't because I'm going to tell you now), the task was all the more difficult for John because he, too, was in love with Priscilla.

Like Priscilla I wanted to say, "Why don't you speak for yourself, John?" but it would have only confused Becky for two reasons. One, she wasn't harboring a hidden passion for me and, two, her name wasn't John.

This development marked the end of C. J.'s career as advisor to the lovelorn. I returned to my daily routine of pining away for Becky while flunking typing.

The night of the homecoming dance I was home early. I had plenty of excuses for being there instead of the school dance. After all, wasn't my dad the Baptist preacher? Where was I going to learn to dance? And if I did somehow clandestinely learn how to dance, why would I think I would be allowed to go to a dance? After all, we don't dance, drink, or chew, or go with girls that do. But the main reason was that a guy who doesn't have the nerve to tell a girl he likes her certainly isn't going to have the nerve to ask her to a dance, particularly when he doesn't even know how to dance. So, lay off, will ya? I was at home soon after we lost the football game, and that's all I have to say about it.

I was sitting in the garage trying to figure out how to play "Honky-tonk Woman" when an old F-150 pickup truck rolled to a stop in the drive-way. I was in the middle of singing "She blew my nose" when Sonia climbed out. The words died, leaving the sound of the guitar amp buzzing loudly in the night. I almost didn't recognize her. She wasn't wearing any makeup, and she had a black eye that would have been visible even on Cassius Clay. A large bruise covered half of her forehead.

"I did it. I did it," she said in a rush, running to me and handing me the truck keys and a set of cowboy boots. I had no idea what she had done and was too stunned to ask as I stood there, keys in one hand, boots in the other, and a beat-up pawnshop Silvertone hanging from my shoulder.

Sonia looked around distractedly and then seemed to realize all at once where she was. Her face crumpled from frenetic animation to hopeless despair, and she began to cry with such a piercing wail that I dropped the boots and keys. The garage door opened and Dad appeared. He took in the truck, the boots on the floor, and the weeping Sonia in an instant. He stepped into the garage in his stocking feet, something I had never seen him do, and guided her into the house by the shoulders.

I discarded the guitar, pocketed the keys, and took the boots to the truck. In the back I found a pile of shoes and boots, all evidently belonging to Parker. I threw the boots in with them and went into the house to see what was going on. Dad was in the wingback chair, leaning forward, elbows on his legs, hands clasped between his knees. Sonia was sitting in the middle of the couch on the edge of the seat, as if about to jump up and run off. Her orange dress was extremely short. There was barely enough of it available for her to sit on. She was in the process of giving a halting explanation, her shoulders shaking when she paused between phrases.

"He's passed out. He'll be out for a good while." Mom walked in with a plastic bag of ice wrapped in a thin dishtowel. "Thanks," Sonia said distractedly, and held the ice to her black eye gingerly.

"So, this isn't the first time he's done this?" Dad asked.

"No." She suddenly stood up, dropping the ice and looking around like a hunted animal. "What will he do when he wakes up? What if he finds me here?" Then she noticed the bag of ice at her feet. "Oh, I'm sorry." She crouched down to pick up the ice and wrap it in the towel again. She sat back down and pulled at her dress self-consciously, trying to cover at least some of her thighs. "I shouldn't of come here."

"Of course you should have come here," Dad said. "The first thing we have to do is make sure you're OK. Do you need to go to the hospital?"

"Oh, no." She put the ice back up to her face. "It's not that bad."

"Good. Now, the next thing is, do you have a place to stay? You obviously can't go back home. Can you go to your parent's house?"

"My parents?" She seemed confused. "I don't think so. They wouldn't be any happier than him to find out I come here."

"How about the Harmons'? You know them well, don't you?"

At this suggestion Sonia became frantic. "Oh, no! I couldn't go there!" She jumped up again, dropping the ice, and headed toward the door.

"Sonia," Dad called as she rushed through the garage.

"Don't worry." I held up the keys. "She's not going anywhere in that truck."

Dad nodded at me, followed Sonia outside, and convinced her to come back in. She sat down on the arm of the couch, pulling at her skirt.

Dad stood next to her. "Sonia, I'm going to pray for you. You don't have to do anything but just sit there." He put his hand on her head. "Father," he said in a quiet voice, "I ask you to surround Sonia with Your Holy Spirit, clear her mind of anxiety, and give her the peace that only comes from You."

He took his hand off her head and smiled at her. "Why don't you sit down in this chair?" he said, pointing to the wingback chair. She sat down in the chair; Dad sat on the couch.

"Have you talked to the Harmons since the wreck?" Dad asked. Sonia shook her head slowly, staring at him. Dad continued, "I have. You and Peggy grew up together, and they always thought of you as their fourth daughter." Sonia nodded slowly, saying nothing. "They still do."

Sonia never took her eyes from Dad. Tears welled up, coursing down her bruised face. Not wild, hysterical tears, but quiet, calm tears of some other kind. Pain? Sorrow? Relief? I wasn't sure.

Dad stood and held the bag of ice out to Sonia. She took it.

"Why don't you sit there and relax while I make a phone call." Sonia nodded and Dad left the room. I stood there, still processing the transformation.

When he came back it had all been arranged. The Harmons picked up Sonia. Dad and I drove the F-150 to Fred Grocery and parked it on the side in plain view of the highway. Brown Watkins, the proprietor, agreed to hold the keys. We walked back home. I was a little curious.

"So, what happens when Parker wakes up?"

"He either calls somebody to give him a ride, or he walks barefoot in search of his truck. Either way, he's bound to pass the grocery store."

"And what happens when he finds out where Sonia is?"

"Nothing."

"Nothing?"

"There are two places in this world that Parker will never go. One is Peggy's parents' house."

He didn't have to tell me the other. The image of Mac, now in a wheelchair, was vivid in my mind. "So, is that the reason you picked the Harmons?"

He looked at me speculatively. "It's one reason," he said quietly.

CHAPTER EIGHTEEN The next night was the first

party at Mac's house since the wreck. During his extended absence another couple had taken on the duties of the high school Sunday school class. They were better than Mac at the classroom part, actually making it interesting, something I thought was impossible. But Mac was irreplaceable as confidant to the confused.

When we arrived at the farm, Mac greeted us on the large porch that spanned three sides of the house. As I walked through the rooms, I was intrigued to see countertops lowered and ramps spanning the split levels between the sunken living room and the rest of the house. It was a little unnerving to see the pictures of Peggy and Kristen in their accustomed places. A few rectangles of the original wall color revealed that some pictures had been removed. I tried to remember what pictures had been there, but couldn't place them. I looked around to see Mac watching me examine the gaps. Our eyes met for a brief but electrifying second, and then he wheeled away to the kitchen to direct the logistics of the cookout.

The unmistakable intensity of that look caused me to scan the room a second time. There were no pictures of Parker or Sonia anywhere. I seemed to recall some shots from fishing trips, vacations, even high school football shots. All gone. But my reflections were swallowed in all the activity of Frisbee, football and volleyball games, cooking, eating, and the languorous aftermath.

Somebody lit the bonfire and we sat around singing "Kumbaya" and "Pass It On." Eventually the big group splintered into smaller conversations, and the singing disintegrated into Ralph trying to figure out the chords to "Stairway to Heaven" while Bubba tried to play "In-a-Gadda-Da-Vida" on a series of feed buckets, gas cans, and oil drums.

I sat on a telephone cable spool at the edge of the circle of light cast by the bonfire. Mac sat nearby, silently gazing into the ever-morphing shapes of the flames. We both chuckled as Ralph emitted an eerie laugh and Bubba joined him in screeching "Wipe Out." We continued in silence as they attempted to cover the song on a cheap mail-order guitar and an assortment of farm implements.

Mac was the first to speak. "I hear tell Sonia has moved in with the Harmons."

"Yeah." I wasn't surprised, even though the news was only twenty-four hours old. After all, he was close to his in-laws. Or were they former in-laws?

"I also hear she was beat up pretty bad."

"Yeah, she had a black eye and some bruises." We both continued to look into the fire.

Mac cleared his throat. "You know, I dated Sonia before I dated Peggy. I told her I loved her. I thought I was goin' to marry her."

Not only was this news to me, I couldn't imagine why he was telling it to me. It was usually the other way around, us confiding the details of our lives to Mac. "No, I didn't know that."

"Yeah, but she dumped me and started datin' . . . him."

"Ah." I didn't know where this was going, but the role-reversal made me uncomfortable.

"Just before the Sadie Hawkins dance that year. Best thing that ever happened to me," Mac said. We both sat in silence for a long time, then he turned his wheelchair and disappeared into the darkness toward the house.

On Sunday I asked Jolene about the dance. After Bubba's debut as a fireman in drag, there was some question as to whether Jolene would survive long enough to go to the dance. Marianne loaned Jolene a dress and even ended up going with Bubba after all. It seems that Judy made so many jokes about him fighting the fire with a dress on that he broke the date. He asked Marianne, who accepted with surprising but gratifying enthusiasm. And, somehow, Bubba convinced Jolene to call a cease-fire for one date, so to everyone's surprise, Turner was spared the trial-by-ordeal on his first date with Jolene.

Emboldened by his success, Turner asked Jolene out again, and she accepted. She told me the details between Sunday school and church.

"So, are you getting soft on this guy? I mean, you didn't even spill punch on him or anything."

"That was Bubba's fault!" She tossed her long, black hair back in irritation. "I don't want Turner ta get any ideas. I need ta come up with somethin' big, somethin' really dramatic, ta make up for the first date."

"What about the trick where you disconnect the distributor, and when he opens the hood to check it out, you honk the horn? That's a good one."

"No, it's not enough. I mean somethin' big. Somethin' new." She concentrated, staring across the branch at the elementary school, and then shook her head. "Can you think of anythin'?"

"Me? I don't want to get mixed up in this. Turner seems like a nice enough guy. This is your war against the opposite sex, not mine."

"Oh, come on. It's not a war. It's just a joke. Where's yer sense of humor?"

"Hiding behind my loyalty to my own sex." In the end I was powerless in the face of her appreciable charm. I racked my brain for ideas and struck pay dirt in the pages of Damon Runyon.

"It's called 'The Brakeman's Daughter.' You get this guy worked up on asking out a girl, but you tell him terrible stories about how jealous the old man is and how he shoots at the guys who try to take her out. You tell him he can only come when the old man is gone. Then you set up a time for him to come, and when he shows up, somebody comes roaring from the back of the house shooting a gun in the air, and you holler, 'Oh, no, he found out!' and the guy loses it."

"Great! He hasn't ever met Daddy. We can do it this Friday when he comes ta pick me up."

"We?! No, siree, Bob. I just supply the ideas. You'll have to find somebody else to do your dirty work." I grasped desperately for a way out. "Get Bubba to do it."

"Oh, don't be silly. You know Bubba has no sense of humor." She shook her head. "And we're twins. How could that be?"

"I can't imagine. Maybe you got both doses by mistake."

"Anyway, you'll have ta do it. Bubba would never go along with it, and I don't know any other guys who would do me any favors."

The following Friday night found me crouched in the shadows on the side of the Culpepper house behind a pallet of roofing shingles. The damage from the fire had been primarily to the roof, and with the help of all his crews Mr. Culpepper had made rapid progress in restoring the house to its former glory. I was wearing an oversized coat and a big, black cowboy hat. I cradled a shotgun loaded with rock salt in my lap and was sandwiched between two very smelly hound dogs. Jolene had arranged every detail. Bubba was playing in a softball league and her parents were with him at the game, so there was nobody to get disturbed about the gun-shots. Except our intended victim, of course. And we expected him to get very disturbed.

I checked my watch for the sixth time in half as many minutes. "Where is that boy?" I muttered to the hounds. They were lying in the dirt, ears making an *L* on either side of their heads like bookends. One of them rolled his eyes up in my direction and whacked his tail on the ground a few times. I shook my finger in his face. "If I had a date with a girl that looked like Jolene, you can bet I wouldn't be late. I might come a few days early, just to make sure she didn't forget." The dog snorted, blowing up a little cloud of dust.

As if in answer to my question, a pair of headlights veered off the high-way one hundred yards away and wound through the trees toward the house. "Uh, oh. Looks like we're on." My pulse quickened.

The dogs perked up. When the car pulled up in front of the house, they started growling. The car door slamming set them both to barking, and I had to grab their collars to keep them from bolting to the front of the house. When Turner started up the walk, they pulled me off balance. The gun fell to the ground, and I was dragged a few feet. "Come on, Jolene!" I muttered through clenched teeth.

I heard the screen door slam, and Jolene's voice exclaiming with unex-pectedly convincing agitation, "Watch out! Daddy came back!" So con-vincing that I looked behind me to make sure he wasn't there. Then I realized she was talking to Turner.

With a sigh of relief I released the dogs. They tore around the corner, baying like they'd treed a coon. I fumbled for the shotgun, scrambled to my feet, and came staggering around the corner, shooting and hollering.

BOOM! "Where is that no-good, mealymouthed, son of a motherless flea-bitten, egg-suckin' cur?" BOOM!

Turner stood frozen in terror, his eyes open almost as big as his mouth, his eyebrows disappearing under his cowboy hat. I lowered the gun in his direction. He turned and ran faster than I thought was possible in boots, the dogs trailing him like clouds of glory. I fired at the space where he had been. He dove through the passenger window and had the car started before he was even behind the wheel. In less time than it takes to tell you, he was burning rubber on the highway, his presence no more than a memory and a cloud of dust.

Jolene and I burst out in laughter, the deep, exhausting laughter that leaves you weak and helpless. She fell against me and we hugged each other to keep from falling over, which was the closest I ever got to embracing Jolene. After several minutes we regained a semblance of composure and staggered into the house.

I collapsed on the couch and had a relapse for several minutes. Eventually the gale of laughter passed, and we were blown by occasional gusts as we recalled the look on Turner's face when I came around the corner. It was the most intense sensation of euphoria I had ever experienced, exceeding the fit of laughter M and I had shared on our meeting. I looked across the coffee table at Jolene and studied her for a minute or so through the hair that hung in my eyes, too tired and contented to bother clearing my line of vision.

"What?" she asked reflexively at my stare.

"Does it always feel this way?"

"Does what always feel this way?"

"You know. When you pull tricks on your dates. Does it always feel like this?"

She considered the question for awhile. "Not really, because I usually can't laugh at the time. Sometimes it gets close." She chuckled. "But this was really the best. It tops them all."

"Now I think I have some idea of why you do it. I always wondered how you could keep it up. You know, after awhile I figured you'd get tired of it." A grin crept across my face. "Shoot, this could be habit-forming."

"Yeah, you're right."

We basked in the glory of it for a little while longer, telling each other the details and reliving it once again. Then I put up the hat, coat, and gun, extracted the car from its hiding place behind the barn, and went home. The worst part about it was that I couldn't tell anyone. The only person who could share that moment with me was Jolene. It somehow made me feel even closer to her, more intimate, which was frustrating.

That feeling served to accentuate my own lack of romantic success. Unable to bear it any longer, upon my return to the house, in a rare fit of vulnerability, I told Heidi of my abiding obsession with Becky. To my amazement, instead of laughing me out of the room, she welcomed this sign that her bookoholic brother was perhaps turning human.

"So, when are you going to tell her?"

"What?!" I stared at her in amazement. "Tell her?"

You know how some people talk to foreigners, as if by just talking slower and louder the foreigner will suddenly understand English? That's how she started talking to me, like I was a little slow on the uptake.

"You have to tell her. How else will she know?"

"But what if she laughs or gets sick?"

"Tell her," she repeated. "No girl can resist the idea that someone has such a passionate devotion." I expressed my doubts that any girl would find me difficult to resist. "Don't be silly. Any girl would die to have an admirer who wrote poems about her."

At last her insistence won out. I resolved to bare my soul to Becky the next day. I stayed up half the night composing a poem worthy of the occasion.

> Becky, how it beckons to my soul and
> Summons forth a yearning for your kisses

Tuttle, aye now that name I would rather,
With your heart, transform into my own

I left for the bus early that morning and stopped by a rosebush to arm myself for the quest. To my dismay it was empty. Looking around in panic, I spotted a dogwood tree. I stowed several blossoms in my notebook. On the bus I tried to memorize the poem, being careful not to let anyone else see it.

I endured each class in agony and rehearsed my confession of love until the words rolled off my tongue as emotionlessly as the Pledge of Allegiance. When lunch arrived, I trudged to the cafeteria, my trancelike appearance belying the raging pulse pounding in my veins. I mechanically bought a lunch and shoveled the contents in my mouth, ignoring everyone around me. Then I went in search of Becky, clutching my notebook like a life preserver.

I found her kneeling in front of her locker, getting her books for the next class. I took a deep breath and decisively walked up to the locker, stopping in front of her without a word. She looked up expectantly, but my rehearsed speech fled from my mind. A horrifying sense of déjà vu rushed over me as I saw a flashback of a white sheet of paper fluttering into a black orchestra pit. I stared down and she stared back, both of us as silent and still as statues. As usual, my hair hung before my eyes like a shield, but this time it failed to protect me from the incapacitating assault of her gaze. In a convulsive rush I opened the notebook and dogwood petals showered over her. One flower remained intact. I picked it up and held it out. "For you," I croaked.

She smiled in surprise, a May queen crowned with dogwood petals. Before I could speak, she uttered the words that slayed the hope budding fretfully in my heart. "You know, Mark, that's what I like about you the most. You're such a good friend, and you do such nice things. I wish I had a brother like you."

Friend! Brother! I gasped; I swooned. Plague! Destruction! Woe! Death! The dreaded word—*friend*—gripped my soul and froze the proclamation of love in my throat. I tried to twist my grimace of dismay into a smile but only succeeded in producing a ghastly leer. Incapable of speech, I staggered off in a stupor of confusion.

Friend! How could she say such terrible things to me? The f-word no guy ever wanted to hear from a pretty girl. Was her heart made of stone? Had she no feelings at all? My only consolation was that no one had been around to hear it. In that moment I vowed to take this secret with me to the grave. Oops.

CHAPTER NINETEEN
On the heels of the Tuttle disaster, I buried my devastation in the grand tradition of disenchanted lovers throughout history. I risked my life in foolish adventure. Lacking a Foreign Legion, I made the best of what was available: I took a ride with Darnell.

Fred was a veritable breeding ground for daredevil drivers, but after a few years in high school, Darnell had become the dominant daredevil, the preeminent road hog, the Grand Pooh-bah of reckless driving. His formal title was Darnell Ray: the Terror of the Back Roads, but most folks called him "Darn ElRay," especially if they encountered him driving down a dirt road. He cruised them as if he were headed to Houston on I-10, trailing clouds of glory and dust.

Darnell was much like the Israelites in that his journeys were accompanied by a pillar of cloud by day and a pillar of fire by night. At least, illuminated by the taillights, it looked like a pillar of fire. He could raise a dust cloud on a four-lane highway from the residue that settled in the bed of his truck.

If you were driving down a dirt road, the first clue that Darnell was on the same road would be a vague fuzziness on the horizon. You would pull off your glasses (assuming, of course, that you were wearing glasses) and check them for smudges. When you put the glasses back on, you would notice a dark spot in the smudge. About the time the spot began to assume a definite shape, you would realize that a vehicle was bearing down on you with deceptive speed—a vehicle at the front edge of a dense cloud of dust, as if it were one of Bradbury's Martian ships surfing the leading edge of a raging sandstorm. Before you could get a grip on the window handle, you would hear a cacophony of rattles and your car would be engulfed in a choking maelstrom of grit. You would at least mutter "Darn ElRay," if not lose your religion altogether.

Even Dad, as pristinely correct in his speech as any rational animal, was moved to strong language when baptized in dust by Darnell. "That dadgummed reckless whelp of the earth!" he would exclaim, fumbling with the window. This was serious terminology from a man who normally possessed the equanimity of a tortoise.

The instrument of terror Darnell wielded was a '52 Ford pickup of indeterminate color, christened the Hound of Hell by Dad when he was feeling particularly charitable. The years had added large patches of rust, and Darnell's driving had added salvage parts of various hues, from fire engine red to primer gray. To attempt to describe the color scheme of the Hound would be like trying to describe Texas weather. "Which day?" would have to be the first response.

Darnell's dad, known as Good-Buddy Ray since he called everybody "good buddy," grew up on a farm in Arkansas, its primary cash crop being a liquid derivative of corn. Before you start thinking that he was a foreigner, I should tell you that G. B.'s mama, Darcy, was from Fred and got romanced away for a few years by a sweet-talking Arkansas boy visiting kinfolk in Caney Head. They eventually moved back to Fred after Darcy convinced him that Arkansas lacked the culture and grace to which she had been accustomed in Fred.

G. B. built his first vehicle from parts he found rusting in the Ozark hills and drove it most of the way back to Fred, although it had to be towed the last two hundred or so miles when the fan came loose in Domino and chewed halfway through the hood. He had a priestlike devotion to the service of vehicles, performing repairs with the ritualistic solemnity of a liturgy. If great artists painted frescoes of mechanics on the ceilings of auto-parts stores, G. B. would doubtlessly have been pictured on the ceiling of Harmon Johnson's service station, lying on his back beneath his Kenworth, anointed with oil, his head surrounded by a nimbus of salvage parts.

So, as you can see, Darnell didn't stand a chance. The grease had permeated G. B. so completely that it was genetically passed on with a vengeance that would have even surprised Lamarck. Like a crack baby being born hooked, Darnell was born with it in his blood. It flowed SAE 10W30 in his veins. He drove go-carts all over Fred until adolescence stretched his bones out long enough to clear the dash and the pedals. By the time he was thirteen, he was driving the first incarnation of the dreaded Hound of Hell with which he terrorized the citizens.

Darnell normally drove dirt roads, not out of fear of the law but because they offered more excitement. They were narrower, twistier, and more conducive to fishtails and donuts. Plus, only on a dirt road could he leave a wake of dust as a tangible, if transitory, testimony to his speed.

So the afternoon after I had been so inhumanely abused by Becky, C. J. Hecker came over to give me a guitar lesson. We were in the garage enjoying the Indian summer and annoying the neighbors (the closest of which was a quarter-mile away) with endless attempts at "Born to Be Wild," when a clamor of rattles drowned out our amplifiers. A cloud drifted into the garage. When the dust cleared, I saw Darnell grinning from his truck in his characteristic pose. He invariably skidded up to any destination in a cloud of dust, and when the fog thinned, he always looked the same, as if he expected the paparazzi to jump out at any second for a photo op. The pose consisted of the right hand gripping the knob at the top of the steering wheel, the left arm (usually sunburned) jutting out of the window, a cap jammed on his head at an angle, and a grin straight out of *MAD* magazine.

"Say, doll, let's go swimmin'."

C. J. and I looked at each other and nodded. In a matter of seconds we were hurtling down a back road to the swimming hole that everyone called Toodlum Creek, despite the fact that the county map labeled it as Theuvenins Creek. I was stuck in the middle. C. J. was new to the area and had evidently never been a passenger in the Hound of Hell. He was an aggressive driver in his own right, but now he was in the presence of a master. I detected a substratum of tension under his air of nonchalance. He even gripped the window to the point of white knuckles on a few curves. I was accustomed to it, having spent a few years building up immunity. I calmly followed my normal program when riding with Darnell: I silently prayed like a drowning man.

Despite C. J.'s expectations, we arrived at Toodlum intact. The water was typical East Texas muddy creek water and was home to its share of fish, turtles, and snakes, but the critters usually left us alone, especially if we made lots of noise. It was a popular spot. Sometimes even girls would come down and swim.

We spent the rest of the day drowning our sorrows in the creek, seeing who could swing the highest or the farthest, or who could jump from the tallest tree, or who could stay under the longest. When it started getting dark, we piled into Darnell's truck. As we pulled onto the dirt road, Darnell said, "Hey, let me show you this neat road I found. I call it the Roller Coaster."

I shrugged my shoulders. With Darnell, I was at the mercy of the "Key Rule": The one with the key makes the rules. C. J., on the other hand, was already dreading the ride back, and the revelation that it was about to be lengthened did nothing to lighten his mood.

"Hey, look, I have to get back to Warren, and it's getting dark."

Darnell frowned at him through his greasy glasses and pointed to the sky with one hand. The other hand gripped the ball on the steering wheel and spun it around as he took a corner of at least 120 degrees at forty miles an hour. "Hey, it's still light. You got plenty of time."

C. J. clung to the bar between the window and the vent like it was a spike on the north face of Mount Everest. With white knuckles and a white face, he glared at the sky as if it had betrayed him, the silver fleck in his eye seeming to darken with anger. Under the canopy of green that shielded the swimming hole, we had experienced a false twilight, but now that we were out in the open, it looked like we had a couple of hours of daylight left.

After we rounded the curve and C. J.'s jaw muscles had relaxed to the point that he was able to pry his teeth apart, he made another attempt.

"Uh, my sister needs the car to go to Beaumont."

I was pretty sure that was a lie because I knew his sister was eight years old, but I didn't interfere. Every man must work out his own destiny. I felt certain that C. J.'s destiny included a trip down the Roller Coaster but I wasn't a prophet. Maybe he would be the one to break the heretofore-unbreakable fortitude of Darnell Ray.

If Darnell had any good qualities, and I must admit it was a disputed question, they would be his constancy and his passionate determination to make every moment of life entertaining. He was an unassailable rock of resolution. Once he had embarked, no quantity of supplication could stay his course. C. J. may not have known it before the Roller Coaster, but I was confident he would know it before the end of the ride.

"Hey, look . . . ," he began again, but a vicious S-curve buried in enough sand to start a private beach loomed ahead, and his jaw snapped shut reflexively as he gripped the window and braced himself.

Driving through deep sand at high speeds is almost like driving on ice. Once you start sliding you have little traction, especially if you are skidding because you slammed on your brakes. Darnell knew better. He started into the curve by shifting back down into second gear and punching the gas. The Hound of Hell spun around in a flume of sand as we rounded the first curve going sideways. It's a strange sensation to look straight out the windshield and see fence posts zipping past like cars at the Indy 500.

Halfway between the two curves, Darnell pulled his foot off the accelerator, spun the wheel back the other direction like a cowboy doing rope tricks, and punched his foot back down. We spun 180 degrees and slid around the second curve, watching the pine trees on the other side of the road racing past in pursuit of the fence posts.

When C. J. finally found his voice, he lost his temper. "You idiot! What if there was a car coming the other way?" he screeched in tones capable of shattering a windshield.

Darnell just grinned and continued to stare down the road. "But there weren't."

"But what if there was?" C. J. demanded, bringing his voice down three octaves, which was still several octaves above his normal level.

"But there weren't, so it don't matter," Darnell said deliberately, as if he were explaining something obvious to a retarded child.

C. J. found this answer so infuriating that he couldn't even articulate a reply. Strange guttural noises emanated from his throat, and he lunged across the seat at Darnell. I tried to push him back, but it was Darnell jerking the wheel to the left that slammed C. J. back against the door. A slight correction to the right kept us from plunging into the ditch.

C. J. grabbed his elbow, which had made sudden contact with the window handle, and rehearsed a few phrases in Cajun his brother-in-law had taught him. I had a Cajun uncle, but he never gave me any lessons on these particular phrases, so I can't give you the exact translation. I got the impression it had to do with details of Darnell's family tree. The gist of it was that, according to C. J., if Darnell had one of those big family Bibles on the coffee table with the genealogy in the front, there would be crucial gaps in the record on the paternal side for several generations. This exercise in oral history took some time and distracted C. J. enough for Darnell to make several astounding maneuvers without eliciting further comment.

We traveled on down a dirt road I had never seen before, buried deep in the woods. The sun advanced more quickly than expected, and before long it disappeared behind the tree line. This didn't necessarily mean that night was imminent, since the true horizon was well below the tree line, but it did mean that the light was beginning to fade. And the further we went, the more the pines became mixed with hardwoods that overhung the road.

Before long we found ourselves on a narrow, red clay road that twisted and turned through the hills. Like most East Texas roads it had a ditch on each side, outside of which the ground rose back up level with the road or above it. Fence lines had disappeared, and the trees crowded closer and closer to the edge of the road. As the light waned, soon all we could see was a narrow corridor covered by an archway of trees.

The road was only wide enough for one car, but Darnell sped down it at forty or fifty miles per hour. The further we went, the more pronounced the curves and hills became and the deeper the road cut into the terrain. I watched the walls rise on either side. By the time Darnell was forced to turn on the headlights, we were speeding along a tunnel with six-foot clay walls on either side. I didn't know roads like this even existed in Fred. The curves were so sharp it was impossible to tell what lay around them, and the hills had crowns so abrupt that the headlights shot up into the canopy of leaves and pine needles. Sometimes it seemed possible that there was no road in the darkness on the other side of the hill.

But more terrifying than the uncertainty of the road was the very real possibility of a car approaching from the opposite direction. It took no time for me to become alarmed to the point of panic.

I decided to make a helpful suggestion. "Turn on your bright lights."

"Why?"

I thought the answer was obvious, but I wasn't leaving anything to interpretation. "Because I can't see where we're going."

"You don't have ta see. Yer not drivin'." I realized that he wasn't willing to diminish the thrill of the ride by being able to see the road.

"Yeah," C. J. insisted. "Turn on your brights. We can't see."

Darnell's response was to turn off the lights completely. Cries of dismay echoed through the piney woods. He turned on the lights and we tabled our complaints.

Then, as if to heighten Darnell's delight and my dismay, it began to rain. The canopy of trees prevented most of it from reaching us, but some drops made it through. Darnell turned the wipers on and continued to hurl through the darkness. The wipers slid across the windshield once and quit.

"What's with the wipers?" C. J. complained. "I can't see the road."

"You don't have ta see. Yer not drivin'."

"Why aren't the wipers going?" C. J.'s voice had an edge of hysteria that must have amused Darnell. I can't think of any other reason he would have volunteered the next bit of information.

"If you want the wipers ta work, you have ta hit the dash." Darnell pounded the top of the dash once with a fist and the wipers slid across the windshield once again. C. J. tried it and they cycled again. He began pounding on the dash in regular intervals as we careened down the road.

Since it was evident that pleading would have no impact on Darnell, I settled into my own private sanctuary of terror. I lived each curve and summit in mortal dread of an oncoming car.

After what seemed like hours, but was probably only about twenty minutes, the road flowed into a straight gravel lane with shallow ditches on either side. I breathed a protracted sigh of relief and a prayer of gratitude to see it was wide enough for two or three cars. It was premature, however, because Darnell skidded to a stop, turned the truck around, and headed back into hell.

At that point I was forced to a philosophical crisis. I felt sure I must either resolve my anxiety or go mad. I reasoned with myself and my Creator in this fashion: *I am not in control of this truck. Reasoning with the driver is out of the question, as he is beyond reason. Therefore I will either survive or die. Either way I will meet my fate in a manner entirely out of my control. So be it.* I closed my eyes with the intention of keeping them closed until the truck stopped swaying and dipping, twenty minutes later.

C. J., on the other hand, dealt with his fear differently. After his non-stop remonstration on the outward journey, at which Darnell had only grinned, he had reached his own philosophical crisis when Darnell turned the truck around.

"No, sir! I am not going back through that again. Stop this machine-from-hell; I'm getting out."

Darnell pushed in the clutch, gunned the engine, and turned his face to the passenger side. The green glow of the dash lights reflected off his glasses, momentarily turning them into opaque green circles. Even his lips seemed to turn green as he grinned and responded, "Look, I'll just slow down ta twenty and you can jump out." He slowed the truck down.

"I mean it. Stop this truck."

Darnell repeated his offer with the same ghastly green grin. The illumination from below cast strange shadows on his face, his high cheekbones leaving his eyes in darkness. He looked like a goblin from some B movie desecrated by Ted Turner.

"That does it. I'm getting out of this truck no matter what." C. J. opened the door and attempted to jump. I grabbed him by his belt loops and pulled him back in. While he was off-balance, I reached across him, slammed the door, and locked it. After a few more attempts on C. J.'s part, we were already into the breech, and he had to abandon his escape attempt as Darnell punched the truck up to thrill speed once again.

When Darn ElRay finally deposited us back at home, I was a quivering mass of nerves. We tumbled out of the door onto the driveway, and Darnell sped off in a cloud of dust. I turned to see C. J. staggering after him, hurling handfuls of sand at the truck.

In the Fortress of Solitude, I tuned in a medley of "The 1812 Overture" and "The Battle of New Orleans." I scribbled in my journal with trembling hands and wondered if God would hold me to a promise I made in mortal fear for my life. If so, how could I explain to Dad, the Baptist preacher, that I was going to be a priest?

CHAPTER TWENTY
Some months later I was lying on my bed, in the winter of my discontent, listening to the radio vacillate between Handel's "Water Music" and "Blue Eyes Crying in the Rain" and staring at the poster on the door, which proclaimed "Abandon hope all ye who enter here." This warning was usually directed toward Mom, who said it had been so long since she had seen the floor in my room she had forgotten the color of the carpet. I didn't have the heart to remind her the floor was done in tile.

However, the poster more accurately described my own despair. Despite my *Grit* route, I had no money, a serious crisis for a sixteen-year-old. Without money I couldn't afford a car. Without a car I couldn't get a job. Without a job I couldn't get any money. Without money I couldn't afford a car. Without a car . . . wait a minute, I think I already did that part. Anyway, you get the picture. I was deep in the throes of a recession that showed signs of deepening into a depression with both financial and emotional implications.

I was startled from my melancholy by a blond head poking into the room. "Whatcha doin?" Hannah plopped down on the edge of the bed.

"Nothing. Go away."

"Robert White, Bruce Gunn, and Luther Gorman all asked me out for the Valentine banquet. Who do you think I should go with?"

I snorted. "Don't be ridiculous. You know you're not allowed to date until you're sixteen."

"So what's your excuse?"

I kicked at her but she was already out the door. She hurled some comment about a pigsty over her shoulder as she disappeared down the hall.

Hannah enjoyed tormenting me by pointing out the disparity between her social life and mine. And, with her usual unswerving accuracy, she hit the bull's-eye that marked my current tender spot. My need for cash was not the result of greed. I was hoping an infusion of capital in my personal economy would stimulate interest from romantic investors. My emotions were surfing on the crest of a rising tsunami of hormones, and I was desperate for the tender caress and passionate embrace of some dark-eyed, dark-haired, dark-skinned island beauty with no tan lines. Actually, after the disaster of Becky Tuttle, I was willing to settle for a bucktoothed, dishwater-blond cowgirl with freckles and a brother named Joe Bob.

Unfortunately, neither the island beauty nor the cowgirl knew of my existence. (More accurately, the cowgirl had seen me once at school when I tripped on a carpet stain and disappeared into an open locker. I waited until the bell rang and the crowd disbursed before I clambered out and slinked to class. Or is it slunk? Slank? Oh, never mind! The island beauty, on the other hand, disappeared every time I opened my eyes. Not a trait that encourages a stable relationship.)

On my last birthday I had realized, to my horror, that I was actually sweet sixteen and had never been kissed. (Except by Aunt Edna, an experience I had tried ardently, but without success, to avoid and, once it had happened, to forget.) Other Fredonians of my age seemed to have little trouble establishing amorous alliances. Even Ralph had managed to snag a girlfriend. And he had never been particularly noted for his looks or charm. Well, for that matter neither had I, but that wasn't the point. The point was . . . well, forget the point! The fact was that he had a girlfriend and I didn't.

And as if things weren't bleak enough, Hannah reappeared at my door. "Come on," she said impatiently.

"What?" I asked without moving.

"Dad said to come 'rouse you out of your slough of despondency.' So, come on."

"He said what?"

"Oh, you know how he talks." She made a face. "Just come on. We're meeting in the kitchen." Her summons delivered, she left me to follow. When I arrived at the kitchen table, everyone else was already there.

Heidi was gathering up the college catalogues and application forms she had scattered all over the table. "Now just wait a minute while I get this stuff put up."

I sat down and shoved a pile out of my way.

Heidi glared at me. "Cut that out! I just got that stuff all organized." I ignored her.

Heidi was anxiously plotting the course of her maiden flight from the nest to college, and she jealously guarded all the forms as if they were rare navigational charts. While she was capable of vexing me on occasion, I was grateful to her for at least one reason. She, too, had experienced difficulty adjusting to the social climate of high school, having done so only after months of anxiety and travail, like a woman in childbirth. Hannah, on the other hand, seemed to have entered junior high a complete social icon, as if she were Venus stepping fully formed from the surf of the Mediterranean.

Dad took charge of the situation. "Heidi, don't worry about all that. We'll only be a minute." He pushed his glasses up on his nose and cleared his throat to be sure he had everyone's attention. "Your mother and I have been doing some planning for the past few months. This is the last summer we will spend together as a family before Heidi goes off to college. We think it would be nice to borrow the pop-up camper from your Aunt Edna and Uncle Lucas and drive out to California to see your Aunt Wilma and Uncle Mort." He glanced at Mom for confirmation of the announcement. She didn't notice. "And take in such sights as befall us along the way."

I smiled imperceptibly. Dad was always throwing in odd phrases when he talked. I think he knew it caught the girls off guard, and I enjoyed anything that irritated them, if only slightly.

The announcement sounded innocent worded like that. However, I translated it: *We will take three teenagers halfway across the North American continent (including a mountain range and a desert) in a nine-year-old Ford Galaxy, pulling a trailer that would herniate Babe (Paul Bunyan's blue ox), inflicting Southwestern culture on them (the teenagers) whenever possible, and then return.*

Kind of changes things, doesn't it? Perhaps Dad became a preacher because he was an idealist at heart. And only an idealist could have seen the trip in Dad's terms.

And Dad really saw it in the terms he had used, even when we were enduring it. That was part of the mystery of Dad: the gritty underside of life didn't seem to bother him. Not that he didn't realize it was there. Whatever he was, he wasn't naive. It just seemed to have no effect on him. The gum on the shoe, the pencil lead that breaks in the middle of a difficult problem, the elevator that stops at every floor when you're late for an appointment on the thirty-seventh—all the things that I was doomed to notice and chafe against, Dad seemed to take as part of the equation.

Despite the hazards I saw lurking in the announcement, at the word *California,* I drifted into a trance. Ever since I had seen hippies in Cincinnati, I had been captivated with the concept of the counterculture. When we moved to Fred, I was plucked from an urban environment where flower children flourished, only to be planted in a dense thicket where the light from the Age of Aquarius rarely penetrated. I was like a cultural-exchange student, except I had no interest in exchanging cultures.

Though I was emotionally attuned to the counterculture, I had little knowledge of it and even less exposure to it. Therefore, the vacation announcement moved me profoundly. After a few years of managing on a trickle of information, I was going to actually travel to California, the fountainhead! To be given the opportunity to make the pilgrimage to the

Mecca of Cool at the culturally significant age of sixteen was an omen that my destiny awaited me there. I shivered with anticipation, certain that some serendipitous coincidence would initiate me into the inner sanctum of Hipness. I began to dream of lithe girls in hip-hugger, bell-bottomed, patch-covered jeans wearing headbands to hold back straight hair that hung long enough to sit on. I visualized chance encounters, bumping into each other in a head shop or a record store.

"Oops," I would say. "I'm sorry. I'll get it." I would pick up the eight-track I had accidentally knocked from her hand. "Far out! Iron Butterfly. I have this one. It's one of my favorites."

"Groovy," she would answer. As I gave her the tape, our hands would touch. She would look suddenly into my eyes, as if startled, and the electricity would ignite a pure but passionate desire. The tape forgotten, we would be lost in each other as . . .

Well, the details got a little fuzzy after that, but I had every confidence that if I could only get to California, I would wing it from there. After all, she wouldn't know I was a PK, and I certainly wasn't going to tell her!

"Mark . . . Earth calling Mark." Hannah's voice cut through the haze. My eyes focused on the group surrounding the kitchen table. "Where were you?"

"Oh . . . uh." I fumbled for words. "Sorry. I was thinking about something."

"Then think about food for a second," Dad said. "What kind of snacks would you like to have for our picnic lunches?"

I made some appropriate reply and muddled through the rest of the meeting. As soon as it was over, I rushed back to my room to figure out what I was going to wear while in California. I wanted to find the perfect combination that would perhaps be the catalyst of fate when I crossed paths with that anonymous beauty I was destined to meet.

I dug through my wardrobe of Montgomery Ward mail-order shirts and J. C. Penney clearance-sale jeans. Those jeans must have been made of fiberglass. They didn't fade and fray the way real jeans were supposed to. They stayed distressingly dark and disgustingly whole, regardless of the number of washings or abuse they received. I was certain NASA had designed the material as a heat shield for protecting capsules during reentry. And the shirts! I couldn't decide if they looked more like something modeled by the Beaver or by Timmy from the *Lassie* show. I had acquired this stuff to facilitate my assimilation into Fredonian culture, but now I could see that it would not do at all. My wardrobe had atrophied into a weak and useless appendage.

I was discouraged until I suddenly remembered the white bell-bottoms Mom had picked from some bargain rack. In honor of the election year, they had a donkey and an elephant stitched on the back pockets in red and blue. I thought those should be OK. After all, the counterculture was very politically conscious.

I jumped up, dug them from a pile in the closet, and put them on. Next I located a royal blue, long-sleeved shirt. A pair of flag-design socks and some maroon-and-white patent leather shoes completed the ensemble. I donned a pewter cross on a heavy chain and took stock of myself in the mirror.

It was a measure of the sartorial nadir to which I had descended that I found the combination hip, fashionable, and guaranteed to attract attention. I was right on at least one count. Fortunately for my emotional health, my assessment didn't extend to my physical appearance. The mirror reflected a figure that was dismally pale and remarkably, if not painfully, skinny. (It was no great feat to count my ribs, even if I had a shirt on.) My hair strayed into my eyes, slightly longer than the school dress code allowed. Only through great euphemism and amazing grace could my complexion be described as "not the best." And I had a Texas accent that would mark me for a sucker anywhere north of El Paso. Happily, as oblivious to reality as only a teenager can be, none of those details prevented me from feeling like I was ready to descend on L.A. in splendor.

CHAPTER TWENTY-ONE Planning for the vacation required attention to the bad head gasket on the car. Our budget dictated the shade-tree-mechanic approach to auto repairs, which were frequent. Dad never owned a new car. Consequently, I assisted in many midnight sessions, holding the light like an acolyte before the altar.

These long hours were exercises in patience and restraint. There is only one thing more frustrating and unnerving than spending fifteen minutes trying to thread a slightly cross-threaded nut onto a bolt that is located in a remote cavity deep in the bowels of the engine and accessible only to octopi or species equipped with prehensile tails. That is *watching* someone spend fifteen minutes trying to thread a slightly stripped nut onto a bolt that is . . . you know the rest.

Our current car of choice was a maroon 1963 Ford Galaxy. It was only nine years old, practically new! I was intimately acquainted with it, having assisted in several oil changes, a brake job, rebuilding the carburetor twice, countless tune-ups, and replacing the water pump, the thermostat, the fuel filter, the coil, two mufflers, a manifold gasket, and now a head gasket.

It was late at night, as always, and Dad was putting the head back on the block. I, of course, was holding the light. I was looking forward to a late snack of Dr Pepper and pickled okra over a Ray Bradbury novel when Dad, who didn't own a torque wrench, applied a little too much torque and twisted the top off a bolt.

"Dadgummit!" he exclaimed. This was pretty strong language for Dad. The strongest exclamation I ever heard him make was "Hell's Bells," which astounded me.

"What?"

"I seem to have sundered the bolt, separating head from shaft, effectively decapitating said bolt. Now we'll have to get the shaft out of the block somehow."

"Great. How do you do that?"

"I don't know." He considered options as calmly as if he were deciding whether to have mayonnaise or mustard on his burger. "If I had a reverse-thread bolt, we could drill a hole in this one, thread it with my die-cutting set, and then screw the reverse-thread bolt in the hole. When it got snug, we could turn them both and get that little sucker out of there." His voice dropped off. "But, I don't have a reverse-thread bolt."

I kept my mouth shut. I figured the more I talked, the more it distracted him from finding a solution. We stood in silence for several minutes, both staring at the end of the bolt. There was a ridge where the head had broken unevenly. Dad grabbed a hammer and a screwdriver and tried to tap the bolt in a counterclockwise direction. He succeeded in barking his knuckles a few times and shaving off the ridge.

Then he tried making a new ridge with a cold chisel. Then he tried drilling a hole in the bolt and wedging something in it to turn it. He tried several other things, approaching each as calmly as if it were the first thing he was trying. Each attempt was equally unsuccessful.

I despaired of ever leaving the garage again. I envisioned myself still in the garage a year later. Ralph would stop by to see if I wanted to go swimming. "Sure, I'll be out, just as soon as we get this bolt out of here. Try next month."

Dad broke in on my thoughts. "I know what we can do to get that bolt out of there."

"What?" I asked anxiously, not daring to hope after so many failed attempts.

"We can pray."

The worklight in my hand reflected off Dad's glistening forehead, echoed in duplicate in his glasses. I nodded impassively. As a PK I was immersed in religious concepts and practices, most of which I accepted with little thought or question. I had said the words, prayed the prayers, gotten saved, been baptized–the whole package–but since *The Mysterious Stranger,* nagging doubts plagued me.

Sometimes, while sequestered in my tree house Fortress of Solitude, I would argue with myself. "What if there is no God? I accept it like . . ." I would pace the quaking boards, grasping for an analogy. "Like . . . like I accept the fact that when I ride an elevator, I face toward the door. What if I had been raised in Iran? Wouldn't I accept Muhammad in the same way?" I would look through the trees to the pale blue sky, which looked as empty as a pocket with a hole in it. The whole thing seemed fantastic. Too irrational and unlikely.

However, I never voiced these doubts or challenges to Dad. He wasn't tyrannical, but I somehow felt that to suggest such things would be heresy. Besides, he knew a lot more about these things than I did anyway. That was his job, wasn't it?

So while I believed, I did so with unspoken reservations. I worried that I might one day discover that none of it was true. Placing it all on the line in such an irreversible way for the sake of removing a bolt seemed risky. What if there were no answer?

Taking my silence for consent, Dad placed his hand on the car, closed his eyes, and started praying. I hastily closed my eyes.

"God, You tell us that You see every sparrow and You know the number of hairs on our heads." I thought this was a good start. Nothing to argue with here; it's right there in the Bible.

"If You are interested in what seems to us such trivial information, then You are surely interested in the problems we face in our lives." This seemed like a reasonable conclusion.

"Right now it's late, I'm tired, and there's a bolt stuck in this car." I was deeply moved to shout "Amen," but I refrained.

"You say that if any man lacks wisdom, he should ask and You will give it generously, so I'm asking." Uh-oh. Sure, it says that in the Bible, but I wasn't certain it was a good idea to test it out on something so practical. That's fine as long as it works, but what if nothing happened? The good news is, we could get the bolt removed; the bad news is, we might end up proving God doesn't exist. If Twain's Mysterious Stranger was right, I wasn't sure I wanted to know about it.

"Give me the wisdom to get that bolt out of there. Amen." We opened our eyes and looked at the engine. I glanced at Dad, then looked away quickly, afraid that my doubt was plainly written in my eyes. We waited in silence for a minute or two.

I started wondering what would happen if God did answer the prayer. Would the shaft start turning and drop out on the floor? Would an angel appear and hand Dad a reverse-thread bolt? Would a mechanic appear at the garage door with a toolbox and a nimbus? I looked intently at the bolt, straining to see or hear anything supernatural.

I almost dropped the light when Dad said, "Hey! That just might work." He turned to the workbench and started digging in the trunk underneath.

I regained control of my pounding heart. "What might work?"

178

"I just had an idea." He turned and grinned at me. "What a coincidence, eh?" He rummaged around and pulled out an old brace-and-bit contraption, one of those big hand-powered drills with the crank handle, like the safecrackers in old black-and-white movies used. This one looked like Pa Kettle had tossed it off the truck when he was a kid. "We can turn this forward and backward." He attached a bizarre-looking bit, and in five minutes the bolt was out.

Twenty minutes later I was having a long-delayed midnight snack. Instead of reading Ray Bradbury, however, I was reflecting on the miracle I had just witnessed. I always thought they were accompanied by smoke and lightning and an angel telling everyone not to be afraid. But still the doubt lingered. What if Dad had just sat there ten more minutes instead of praying? Would the idea have come anyway? I felt guilty for harboring this haunting skepticism. I did have to admit that the idea came after he prayed. But I also knew that Dad had a great ability to improvise, financial necessity doubtlessly the mother of sometimes bizarre invention.

It was while planning the vacation that Dad had one of his strangest inspirations. On past trips we had washed our clothes in the homes of people we stayed with along the way. On this trip, however, we were taking our cue from the turtle and bringing accommodations with us. Dad had acquired a pop-up camper, which I christened the Beast. An eight-by-twelve-by-four turquoise slug that mushroomed into bed and breakfast for four.

Dad just couldn't see pumping all those quarters into a laundromat. After several weeks of fiddling around with various twenty-gallon drums, sometime in March he found a resealable, plastic drum to suit his purpose. He called an impromptu meeting in the backyard and announced his plan to a less-than-enthusiastic public.

"OK. Here's what we do. Each morning we take the clothes we wore the day before and put them in this drum." He held up the lid and pointed into the drum, which was half full of water. "Then we add water, a half-cup of detergent, and seal it." He put on the lid, secured the latch, and turned it upside down. "Notice how it is watertight," he added, smiling at this revelation. We all murmured our approval for his benefit. He stepped over to the car. "Then we strap it onto the luggage rack and drive five hundred miles. The normal movements of the car will provide the necessary agitation. At the end of the day, we will remove the clothes, rinse them out, and hang them overnight to dry." He spread out his arms with a flourish as he ended the presentation.

I exchanged glances with Heidi and Hannah while Mom asked, "You're not serious, are you?"

"Of course," Dad answered, his smile slowly fading.

"It's only going to take us three days to get to California. We can wait until then to do the wash. And if not, we would only have to do one or two loads on the trip. That couldn't cost more than $1.50 in a laundromat."

"But this won't cost anything at all," Dad countered. "And we won't have to lose road time sitting around in a hot, dirty laundromat reading back issues of *True Detective*."

"I'm willing to sacrifice the $1.50 to avoid using that thing." She pointed with obvious disgust at the watertight drum. "And I'll bring along a *Reader's Digest*."

"Look, let's give it a chance. If it doesn't work out, we can dispose of the drum along the way. OK?"

Mom reluctantly agreed, probably because Dad seemed so taken with the idea that she didn't want to discourage him.

CHAPTER TWENTY-TWO
As spring turned to summer, Dad held practice drills in erecting and dismantling the Beast. He inspected every crevice and opening, noting where he could pack items that didn't fit in the trunk.

I tried to supplement my wardrobe in anticipation of my cross-cultural experience. I found a denim workshirt in Beaumont, which I wore and washed as much as possible, picking up patches when I could—American flags, ecology symbols, whatever I could find on sale. I had considered adding a peace sign until Dad got some literature in the mail about it being a satanic symbol. (A broken, inverted cross. Everybody knows that!) I gave up that idea without even bothering to ask. It would hardly do for the PK to be walking around Fred advertising for the competition.

I also checked out the love beads and incense burners in head shops and import stores. On the romantic front, I had managed to get the attention of the bucktoothed cowgirl with freckles and a brother named Joe Bob. By April, she acknowledged my existence and had actually allowed me to sit next to her during lunch once. However, the day I came to school sporting a set of love beads I detected a distinct cooling of her interest. Joe Bob went so far as to suggest that I was experiencing problems with my sexual identity. Not exactly in those words.

This setback forced me to reconsider my position. Evidently I was going to have to choose. If I prepared myself for California, I would jeopardize, if not decimate, my chances for social success in Fred. However, cultivating Fredonian culture would impair my transition to the counterculture. This dilemma was the focus of several sessions in the Fortress. By the end of the school year I had made my choice. I was already an anomaly in Fred and evidently would always be one, regardless of my decision. I could not spurn the golden and perhaps only opportunity fate had set before me.

Only one month remained before I was to embark on my odyssey of actualization. I felt as if all the events of my life had pointed toward this journey, this pilgrimage, beginning with the dawning of the age of WLS. Only a few trials lay before me.

First, I had twenty-eight days of preparation. I spent them completing my self-imposed regimen of cultural indoctrination. I memorized the names of every type of incense I could find. I studied album covers and liner notes, finding out who played in which bands. I stood in bookstores reading *Rolling Stone* until the clerks kicked me out. I even contemplated stealing Abbie Hoffman's book (titled *Steal This Book!*) but I figured I'd get caught and maybe blow my chances of going to California at all.

My second obstacle was the week of revival meetings Dad had planned, culminating in the Sunday night baptism service before our departure on Monday morning. Dad decided to lead the music and invited Brother Bates, a former heroin addict turned traveling evangelist, to preach.

On the first night, the auditorium was half full, not bad for a Monday night. I saw Old MacDonald off to the side near the organ, where he normally parked his wheelchair to be out of the way of traffic. The Harmons were a few rows back. I was surprised to see Sonia with

them. Although she had been living with them, she had not been coming to church.

Brother Bates nodded gravely from the podium when Dad introduced him. He was skinny, almost emaciated, with a thick shock of
chestnut hair brushed back from his bony face. He wore a cornflower
blue suit, white shirt, and white shoes. A gigantic black Bible rested in
his lap. After the special music, Dad sat next to Brother Bates. I settled
in for what I expected to be a protracted ordeal. Brother Bates stood,
seeming to unfold and stretch into an impossibly tall skeleton. He
walked to the pulpit, his knees rising up unnaturally high so that his
thighs were almost parallel to the floor. To my surprise, he walked past
the pulpit, down the steps, to the space in front of the table where they
put the stuff for Communion.

He stood there, silent, scanning the room, his large, thin nose jutting
between piercing eyes that matched the color of his suit. The small settling
noises always present in a room full of people died out until we could hear
the breath whistling in and out of his nostrils. Then he spoke, and the
sound rattled my bones. I found myself wishing someone would turn
down the microphone, but he used no microphone. The sound poured
forth from him like the sound of many waters, like a waterfall pouring into
an abyss. And from the abyss he brought forth visions of the torture of the
damned, the agonies of those who die without hope, without love, without
God.

Fortunately, since it was a Baptist church, nobody was sitting on the
first row. Or even the second. The unfortunate souls on the third row, in
addition to having their eardrums pounded by this cataract of sound,
also had their psyches singed by the flames of hell. I'm sure it was small
consolation that the fires were partially extinguished by the saliva and
sweat pouring forth from Brother Bates as he labored to literally scare
the devil out of us. By the time he had preached himself into a frenzy of

apoplexy and back down to a hoarse, rasping plea for our souls, I was so exhausted I couldn't have come forward during the invitation without a wheelchair, and the only guy with one wasn't offering shuttle service to salvation.

There were others in the crowd who didn't share my disability. The altar was crowded with penitents. Even Ralph made his way down, tears streaming down his cheeks, and dropped to his knees. I didn't know what to make of it. I had sat next to him every Sunday for years, and he had never displayed the slightest interest in anything Old MacDonald or Dad had to say. Then I saw Sonia. She was walking slowly to the front, mascara running like a bad Alice Cooper impersonation. Brother Bates welcomed her, seemed to ask her some questions, and they talked for a long time, more than ten verses of "Just As I Am."

When she returned to her place next to the Harmons, I almost didn't recognize her. It was as if someone or something had whisked away what had been Sonia from beneath that perpetual coating of makeup and had substituted another person without even disturbing the dark purple eye shadow or clotted eyelashes. Another person with the same bleached hair with brown roots, same brown eyes, same clothes and body, but another person nonetheless. I studied her like those puzzles where you are supposed to identify the six things that are different between the two pictures, but I couldn't identify any single characteristic that was visibly different. Except her eyes. Looking into them used to be like looking into a well of insecurity and confusion. Now it was like looking into a serene pool of confidence and contentment.

For a week the cycle continued: preparation for enlightenment by day, trial by fire at night. One by one everyone around me walked the plank as I looked on, people I had never suspected of having a single spiritual bone in their bodies. However, Brother Bates' labors were lost on me. He hadn't produced any information I didn't already know or exposit on any principle I didn't already accept, but by the sheer force of the masses of humanity streaming down the aisles, I felt as if I must be missing something, that I was somehow mocking him in my refusal to admit an abject depravity that I didn't believe I shared.

Attendance had been building all week, which meant that on Sunday morning the usual crowd combined with the growing throng packed the building. Brother Bates delivered the goods with his dramatic testimony of drug addiction and salvation. People streamed to the front like there was a blue-light special on salvation. Church members came down out of the choir to the altar before we finished the second verse of "Amazing Grace." After the last tear was shed and the last nose was blown, we bid a reluctant (well, most were reluctant) farewell to Brother Bates, and he left with a sizable love-offering.

The final night was before me, the preamble to my rendezvous with destiny: the baptism service, an early bedtime, and then I would turn my back to the dawn and set out for the Promised Land. I was ready for a return to the more sedate routine of Dad's services. The Sunday night baptism service would be just us home folks, plus the new additions queued up for a stroll through the baptistry.

We started with a few songs, a short reflection on the meaning of baptism delivered by Dad, and then he disappeared to suit up in his hip waders. We sang a few more songs before we saw, behind the empty choir loft, the troubling of the waters that presaged Dad's appearance in the baptistry. There were more than twenty people—segregated and sequestered by gender, of course—in the two rooms on either side of the tank. Dad diligently, and joyfully, worked his way through them like a scythe in a hayfield, alternating between sides. I watched as Ralph dutifully submitted to being dunked by Dad (something that would have earned me a licking if I had tried it at Toodlum Creek) and exited stage right, solemn and dripping.

Sonia descended the steps on the opposite side and was baptized. As she was rising up, water streaming from her bleached hair, the back door of the church slammed open against the wall. Every head jerked around in one accord to see Parker come striding down the center aisle, his good eye bloodshot and burning with intensity. His face was flushed, the scar dead white in contrast. He clutched a small paper sack in his left hand. He stopped two-thirds of the way to the front, swaying slightly, and held out an accusing finger as he scanned the crowd, starting on the back left.

"Meddlin' do-gooders," he hollered. His good eye darted back and forth, and he slowly spun on the heel of his boot. It alighted on me for a second and moved on. I flinched as if the dirty fingernail had scratched my face in its arc through the crowd. "Wife-stealin' hypocrites," he thundered like Brother Bates's evil twin, spewing saliva. He completed his scan on the back right and swung back again, finally locating the objects of his fury—the Harmons.

"Christians," he hissed, as if uttering the most obscene word he knew. "We was married, not in this church, but in the sight a Gawd all the same. 'Til death us do part." He paused for a hit from the bottle in the paper sack.

"Parker Walker, it's about time you got here." Dad's voice reminded everyone that something else had been happening only a few seconds before. Dad was standing on the edge of the podium in his white shirt, black tie, and hip waders, a trail of water leading through the choir loft to the baptistry where he had evidently climbed over the wall.

The sight of Dad in this unlikely ensemble caught Parker speechless. His forehead creased, the scar cutting through the ridges. His one eye squinted as if trying to make sense of what he saw.

Dad didn't wait for comprehension to sink in. "There's been a world of folks praying you would come in here, and now, there you stand. I don't think it's a coincidence."

"You," Parker growled. "Yer the one what put her up to it. Tellin' a wife to leave her own man that she married in the sight a Gawd. Poisonin' her mind agin me. Poisonin' the whole town agin me. What right you got to tell these folks to pray for me? If I'm hankerin' for some prayin', which ain't so likely, I'll tell 'em myself."

"Parker, you're the one who is poisoned," Dad said, slipping the straps of the hip waders off his shoulders. "You've poisoned yourself with lies and with the bottle you think is hidden in that sack." He slipped the waders off, holding them in one hand, standing there in his black trousers and stocking feet. "You've loaded yourself down with a weight that you don't have to carry, and it's driving you mad. But you can take it off, just like I've taken off these waders, and be free of it forever." Dad threw the waders across the podium, and they landed with a wet thud on the floor by the piano.

"Don't you start preachin' at me, you citified Bible-thumper. I ain't no weak-minded woman what can be twisted one way and t'nother. You ain't never dealt with the likes of me, and you don't want to start now, I guarantee it." He spun unsteadily on his heel back to the Harmons. "Where are yer hidin' her? Yer ain't got no right to keep a lawful husband from his wife, not in the sight of the law or God."

Parker was interrupted by a racket that caused everyone to look to the front of the church. There was no apparent cause of the noise, but I noticed the water in the baptistry was rippling against the glass in front. Then Sonia stood up in the back row of the choir, where she had evidently fallen while climbing over the wall.

"Parker," she said, looking at him steadily while climbing over the pews in the choir loft, "didn't nobody steal me. Didn't nobody trick me. Didn't nobody make me leave. Exceptin' you." She finally cleared the rail at the front of the choir loft. "You." She stopped at the edge of the podium next to Dad. "You drove me away. I had ta leave before you killed me. You 'n' that bottle. Didn't have no choice."

"Lies! Filthy lies! Forget this bottle, it ain't nothin' to you." He jerked it from the sack, drained it in one gulp, dashed it to pieces on the floor in front of the podium, and started toward Sonia.

Dad put his stocky frame between them, pushing Sonia back away from the edge of the platform. "Parker . . ."

Mac suddenly appeared between them, whipping the wheelchair around in the broken glass. "Hold on, Parker," he shouted. "You've already killed one good woman. Isn't that enough?"

Parker jerked back as if he'd been slapped. "Mac." He shook as if he'd seen the ghost of Peggy and Kristen accusing him. And for all I knew, maybe he did. Given what he'd been drinking, he could be seeing anything.

"It's enough already. It's time, Parker." Mac's eyes burned with a ferocity that paled the fire in Parker's eyes like the sun overshadows the moon. "God, how I have hated you."

Parker blinked rapidly, looking confusedly around him, slowly backing away from Mac as if from a rattlesnake.

Mac closed his eyes. "I laid there in that hospital, half alive, knowin' you were just down the hall, and I prayed for you to live, and I prayed for strength." His fingers were white as he gripped the arms of his wheelchair. "Just life enough for you and just strength enough for me. To crawl to your room and kill you myself with whatever I could find." He opened his eyes. "And you lived." He leaned forward. "And I finally have the strength." His right hand jerked up as it pulled the armrest from the wheelchair.

Mac looked at his hand as if surprised at what it had done, as if it belonged to someone else. Parker fell to his knees and bowed his head like a prisoner awaiting execution. Sonia let out a cry and started forward, but Dad held her back, shaking his head.

Mac rolled the wheelchair forward, crunching through the glass, until his knees were almost touching Parker's nose. "But there's been enough death. It's time for some life."

Parker's head jerked up, face to face with Mac. He squinted at Mac with his good eye and shook his head, confused. "But . . ."

"Hate is death, Parker. I've killed you a thousand times in my mind, and it's made me a murderer. You and me, Parker, we're the same." Mac threw the armrest to one side. "No, that's not right. You killed by accident, by carelessness at worst. I killed with knowledge and will, and gloried in it. Rejoiced in it. Desired it."

Parker shook his head violently. "No, no . . . ," he blurted out, clambering to his feet and stumbling backward. "No!" he shouted. "I killed 'em. I done it!" His hands flew to his face. "I got the mark to prove it," he declared, tearing the patch from his face. The white scar slashed his flushed face from his hairline to his jawbone across a pale, sunken eyelid. "I don't get no mercy. I been marked for hell, and the devil's done took me." A single eye glared down with fierce despair at the small man in the wheelchair. "You can't change that, Mac. Can't nobody change it."

Mac looked back up at him, tears overflowing his eyes. "You're right, Parker," he whispered. "I can't change it. Won't never be able to change it." He rolled closer. "But Jesus can. Jesus did." Parker watched him anxiously, but stood his ground. "Can't neither one of us bring back Peggy or Kristen. Whether we hate or love, can't change that. But two lives wasted is enough. There ain't no reason for me to waste another life in hatin' you, or you to waste a life in provin' to yourself that you ain't no good."

Parker shook his head. "It's too late. I done crossed the line. I can't come back. Look at me." He held his arms out in a plea, desperation on his face as plain as the scar.

Mac looked at him for a long time. "I see ya," he said quietly. "And I see it ain't too late. You look at her and tell me it ain't so." He spun his chair around and pointed at Sonia.

Parker looked at Sonia. I looked at Sonia. Everybody looked at Sonia. Dad stepped aside and turned back to look at her. I looked, and hard. She looked like Sonia to me. A Sonia without makeup, which was pretty rare. A Sonia with wet hair plastered to her head and clothes dripping a big puddle on the podium, which was somewhat out of the norm, but still just Sonia.

Well, almost just Sonia. It wasn't the same Sonia I had sold a paper to, shut up in a cave of a house. It wasn't the same Sonia I had seen hysterically dropping keys and boots on the garage floor. This Sonia seemed a little more solid, even while looking around self-consciously before looking back at Parker.

That was all I saw, but I was at the end of a week during which everyone around me had seemed to see much more than I did. Now, during what I had hoped would be a reassuringly boring service, I was once again playing the role of the puzzled observer. I turned back to Parker.

Parker looked at Sonia with a wild distraction that made it hard to think he could see her at all. But he did. His eye focused on her, and pain seemed to pour out of him like water through a breached dam. He clutched his head and reeled like a man caught off balance, falling to his knees. Mac turned back to him and held out a hand. Parker buried his head in Mac's lap, his shoulders heaving.

Dad stepped down from the podium and picked his way through the shards of glass to where Mac and Parker held everyone captive. He put one hand on Mac's shoulder, the other on Parker's shoulder, and waited for a long time—his head bowed so that I could see clearly where the crew cut ended and the bare scalp began. When the sobs that wracked Parker's large frame finally subsided, Dad spoke.

"Parker, do you know that all these people here love you and have been praying for you?"

Parker raised himself to a kneeling position and nodded his head, which was still bowed.

"Do you know that Jesus loves you more than all the people here?"

Parker nodded.

"Nobody can undo what has happened, but Jesus can change what happens next. But only if you let Him. Are you ready to do that?"

Parker nodded.

We got home very late that night.

CHAPTER TWENTY-THREE Given the circum-

stances, early to bed, early to rise seemed to be a policy unlikely to be enforced. I did my final packing while Dad and Parker sat late into the night talking in his study. In my suitcase I included the AM radio, Pauline's Bible, which took less space than mine, and for reasons unknown even to myself, Twain's *Mysterious Stranger.* I set aside a stack of books to bring with me in the backseat, mainly science fiction. Then I turned off the light and lay in bed, trying to force myself to go to sleep. The events of the last few hours, the low murmur of voices echoing from the study through the air-conditioning ducts, and the anticipation of the trip conspired against my plans. I pulled the Twain book out of the suitcase and skimmed through it. Sometime after midnight I heard an F-150 start up and pull out of the driveway, followed by the click of light switches and footsteps as Dad traversed the length of the rambling house from the garage, past my bedroom, to his.

Not for the first time I wondered how Dad did it. It was as though he could see through this world into another—through what was, into what could be. Or would be. When Sonia had burst into the garage, all I saw was a frantic, desperate, abused woman. I would have lost a considerable sum if I had been asked at that moment to bet on what her state of mind would be ten minutes later. But then Dad prayed, and I watched her change, literally before my eyes. How could that happen?

The bolt-removal experience I could, and did, write off to Dad's talent for improvisation, even if I didn't mention it to anyone. But you don't change people at the very core with improvisation. From what I could tell, you don't change people at all, no matter how much you want to. Something else did it. The Parker who stormed into the church was no more like the Parker who walked out than I was like Jolene Culpepper. It was almost like in the movies, where something from outer space takes over a person, only backward. This invasion had left Parker more human, less alienated. Once again I watched a person change so completely that even his body seemed different. What could do that? Twain's stranger didn't seem to be acquainted with this side of God. Was a dream that powerful? Could a vagrant, formless thought alone in the universe transform other vagrant, formless thoughts? I woke up with the book in my hand, the sun in my eyes, and the questions still pestering my brain.

I leapt from the bed, suddenly very awake in the anticipation of the day for which I had been preparing for months. But my impatience would have no effect on the measured pace of our methodical departure for a Cloud vacation, events which were steeped in traditions, unspoken, undocumented, but as reassuringly predictable as any religious ritual.

As those traditions dictated, Mom sat in the front reading the jokes from *Reader's Digest* to Dad. We kids in the back listened to see if she would translate the occasional d-word into "darn," or, as she occasionally did, render it in the original French. If we went for the original, we would glance at each other in the backseat and raise an eyebrow. That was living on the edge!

We hit Houston about rush hour and the air-conditioning promptly failed, a harbinger, had we but known it. We resorted to the old reliable, 4-60 air-conditioning. (Roll down the four windows and drive sixty miles an hour.) Of course 4-60 air-conditioning is not effective against June in Texas, particularly during rush hour in Houston. When we got out of town and back up to seventy miles per hour on I-83, we cooled down. Mom gave up reading the jokes from the fresh *Reader's Digest* because shouting over the wind made her hoarse.

We arrived in Austin at the house of Aunt Maureen and Uncle Ernest late that evening, somewhat wilted. My sisters and I sat gingerly in the den sipping iced tea and enduring the baseball game Uncle Ernest was sleeping through. Dad and my cousin, Ernest Jr., tore into the air conditioner and had it fixed by midnight.

Dad came in and tried to get us to load the laundry drum with our clothes, but Mom refused. We all changed to our pajamas, and Mom started a load in Aunt Maureen's washing machine. Then Mom, Dad, Aunt Maureen, and Ernest Jr. talked over coffee around the kitchen table until we kids were dozing along with Uncle Ernest to the lullaby of a test pattern.

Tuesday morning we were back on the road. But not for long. Before noon the car made a few choking gasps, and Dad maneuvered it to the side of the road before it sputtered to a stop.

"Now what?" Heidi demanded of no one in particular. No one in particular answered.

Dad got out and opened the hood. After a minute or so he poked his head in the car. "Everything seems to be OK, but I smell gasoline real strong." He went back and looked at the engine.

"What does that mean?" Heidi asked. Nobody answered. It meant nothing to me, and I knew more about engines than anyone else in the car.

Dad poked his head in again. "Dear, why don't you try to start it while I take a look." Mom slid over and gave it a try, but it wouldn't fire.

"OK. Hold it for a second. I'm going to take off the air filter to dry out the carburetor. I think it's flooded."

We waited awhile for the gas to evaporate. The heat began to build up inside the car. We continued to sit in silence, swaying slightly when eighteen-wheelers whooshed by and shook the car.

"OK. Try it again." Mom turned the key, and gasoline spurted out of the carburetor like a geyser. "Whoa! Hold it! Stop it!" Dad hollered. "I've never seen a car do that before!" He looked at me through the window. "Gas pours forth like a freshet in spring." Then he leaned on the grille, staring at the engine.

"So, what are we going to do?" Heidi asked, undaunted by her previous failures to elicit any response. When nobody answered this time, either, she evidently gave up trying to find out anything and changed to declarations. "It's sure getting hot in here."

Heidi seemed to have a need to fill any lull with sound. I never understood why. I have a reputation for talking, but I only talk when I have something to say. That didn't seem to be a prerequisite for Heidi. She would spout phrases at regular intervals, like a snooze alarm. In between comments I tried to fathom the motivations that drove her to spasmodically engage her mouth without necessarily including her brain in the process. I speculated that when things got too quiet, she felt waves of silence swallowing her. Then she would panic and blurt out something, anything, like a drowning man clutching at driftwood.

Well, that's one theory anyway. Maybe it was chemical; I don't know. I do know that if I was already irritated, it drove me crazy. Especially when she would spontaneously point out the painfully obvious. During the first hour of the trip, when we were driving in the Big Thicket, she said, "There sure are a lot of trees out there." When we got stuck behind a log truck on a back road, she said, "He sure is driving slow." I figured that one day she would finally drive me crazy, and I would hit her in the head with a bat. I was restrained by the thought that if I did she would probably say, "That bat sure is hard."

After several minutes, Dad opened the trunk, moved some hanging clothes, and pulled out the toolbox. Years of experience had taught him not to bury the tools under luggage.

When I saw the tools, I figured he had a plan. I pulled on my shoes and joined him in front of the car, screening my eyes from the relentless Texas sun behind the fresh crop of hair I had been growing for this trip.

"So, what's the deal?"

"Well, I think it's the needle valve in the carburetor. I think it's stuck open and flooding the engine." He wielded a wrench that he used to tap on the side of the carburetor. "I'm hoping that I can jar it enough so that the needle will drop back down into the hole and it will start working properly." He wrinkled his nose to keep his glasses from slipping down. Sweat ran into his eyes, and he blinked and squinted.

I leaned on the fender long enough to realize I had made a mistake. Maroon paint and the Texas sun had rendered the fender hot enough to fry the proverbial egg. I jumped back and rubbed my arms gingerly, checking to see how much hair had been singed off. "How long will that take?"

"I don't know."

I relayed the information to the womenfolk, two-thirds of whom received it without comment. Every five or ten minutes Dad would have Mom try to start the car again, with strict instructions to stop immediately if she saw a geyser of gas. After about an hour of tapping and cranking, the car finally started, and we were on our way once again, however briefly.

Within another hour we were back on the side of the road, stewing. Dad got out and tried his tapping trick again. After a few more roadside sessions, ranging in length from fifteen minutes to two hours, Dad concluded that the air conditioner was causing the car to heat up, which was causing the needle valve to stick, which was causing the car to flood, which was causing all of us considerable frustration. We once again resorted to 4-60 AC, which seemed to reduce the frequency of, but not eliminate entirely, the roadside sessions. Both temperature and tempers inside the car were rising.

About the time we hit West Texas and were sitting, once again, sweltering, on the roadside, Mom reached her limit. "I'm ready to turn around and head back," she announced. "If this is the way it's going to be for the rest of the trip, I don't want to go."

I couldn't imagine a mundane thing like being stranded on the side of the road for thirty minutes every other hour being a problem of sufficient magnitude to stop a Cloud vacation. After all, two years earlier we had taken a rambling trek through Michigan to Canada, Niagara Falls, New York City, and Washington, D.C. En route we had the exhaust manifold replaced in Ohio by a former deacon; the generator rebuilt in London, Canada, by an electrical engineer who had emigrated from Hungary; and the clutch replaced in Alabama by the governor's third cousin on his mother's side. What was a carburetor to that? Car problems were a way of life for the Clouds. The publishers of Chilton repair manuals sent us Christmas cards. Car part dealers had put kids through college because of us.

But Mom was insistent. Evidently the Eastern Seaboard experience had left its mark on her. Then occurred the event that could only happen to the wife of a preacher. (Consider it well, single female readers, and ponder carefully your choice of future mate.)

Taking a break from tapping, Dad was sitting in the car with his feet hanging out of the door, his shirt hanging limply on his back. "You know," he said, "I've been studying James 1 for the past few weeks. Verses 2 through 4 say:

> My brethren, count it all joy when ye fall into divers[e]
> temptations; knowing this, that the trying of your faith wor-
> keth patience. But let patience have her perfect work, that ye
> may be perfect and entire, wanting nothing.

"I guess this is just the Lord teaching us patience in a practical way," he concluded. He wiped the sweat from his face with a sleeve that had the cuffs unbuttoned and hanging loosely from his forearms.

I recognized this stuff right away. It came just before the part about asking for wisdom. He was at it again.

That ripped it as far as Mom was concerned. "I don't want to learn patience on the side of the road in West Texas. Let's go back to Fred, and I'll learn it in the air-conditioning."

I weighed the options. In one sense I was with Mom. If I had to sit on the side of a West Texas road in hundred-degree heat to learn patience, I could do without it. My interest in refining my soul had a limit, and that was definitely beyond it. On the other hand, I was fervently anticipating our arrival in California, the land of Ultimate Cool. I was willing to endure considerably more than occasional turns tapping on the carburetor in order to get there. My vote was to get to the nearest town of consequence and have the carburetor fixed. However, I was not consulted and kept my own counsel, not being one to volunteer advice where none was sought.

Heidi, however, had no such reservations. "Why don't we stop at the next town and get the thing fixed?"

Dad sighed. "A new carburetor would cost several hundred dollars. If we did that, we would have to turn around anyway because we wouldn't have enough money to finish the trip."

"Oh." *That's what you get,* I thought. A bit presumptuous, too, I figured, since she hadn't taken a single turn tapping on the carburetor.

Once again we were down to Dad insisting on getting practical with the Bible. It had worked with the broken bolt, but this was different. That time getting practical had brought a quick resolution to our impasse. But in this case, it seemed like getting practical meant prolonging the difficulty, enduring the problem rather than solving it. Would that really bring patience? While I tapped on the carburetor, which was now beginning to look like a part bought from a demolition-derby scrapyard, I listed a few other things it might produce, like frustration, rage, ulcers, heatstroke, or apostasy. It didn't seem to be having the desired effect on Mom, at any rate. Just how long was it between the trying of the faith and the producing of patience? I was afraid to ask.

Regardless, we forged fitfully ahead at an erratic, if not leisurely, pace. By late afternoon we had only traveled two hundred miles and were approaching Abilene. Based on our progress during the day, we could see there was no point in trying to make it to the planned Tuesday night destination. We consulted the map and opted for Abilene State Park, a few miles outside of Abilene near a watering hole called Buffalo Gap.

The road to the park turned out to be a long, twisting drive through scrubby mesquite trees, leading quite a ways from the main highway. At about the moment the sun was kissing the horizon, Dad uttered an exclamation and began wrestling with the steering wheel as if some invisible force were fighting him for control of the car.

"Power steering just went out," he explained through gritted teeth as he tried to navigate a road that rivaled San Francisco's Lombard Street for sinuosity. Inspection revealed a broken power-steering hose. Five minutes later I was riding with Dad as he grappled his way back down the winding road in the gathering dark, leaving the women behind to make camp and fix supper. We took the car into the town of Buffalo Gap to pick up some ice and see what could be done about the hose. In the days before auto-part franchises, there wasn't much chance of finding something open after sundown, so I wasn't sure what Dad's intentions were. But I adopted my usual policy of wait and see.

CHAPTER TWENTY-FOUR Before we proceed to plumb the depths of the resourcefulness of fathers, I need to have a little talk with you, the gentle reader. The experience that I am about to relate catches Dad at a disadvantage. We glimpse his humanity and are given occasion to have amusement at his expense. I don't know what your experience with parents was like. (Or is like, if you're just a kid. Shoot, I don't even know what you are like, for that matter. Remind me to ask you about it later. I'm a little busy right now.)

Anyway, based on my experience at the time, I saw parents as creatures of conservative reliability, sober and reserved.

Here's something that will give you an idea of how I saw Dad. I remember at age six sitting in the garage helping him work on some little project, when he made a comment about being wrong about something. I was astounded. "But you can't be wrong," I protested. "You're a daddy!" He assured me that even daddies could, on rare occasion, be wrong. It revolutionized my entire worldview. In light of these attitudes, you can see how, as I grew older, I found it remarkably refreshing to witness an event wherein a parent was placed in a humorously awkward position. I was amused primarily because these events were very rare in my experience.

For example, once, back in Ohio, the family sat down to a meal. The normal beverage for our meals was iced tea. It just so happened that there was only enough tea for one glass and we all wanted it. Mom, as moms are wont to do, gave it to Dad, the rest of us having to suffer with KoolAid. Dad said the blessing, and when we opened our eyes, we all looked up to the head of the table at that glass of tea. Dad put his napkin in his lap and reached for the glass of tea. All eyes followed his every movement. Conscious of the attention focused on the glass, he slowly and regally raised it to his lips. But just as the glass crossed his plate, the bottom fell out and tea flooded his plate and the table.

If my parents had been buffoons, then perhaps these events would not give me such pleasure. Well, now that we have settled that little detail, let's get back to the silent teenager and his father, who is wrestling a reluctant maroon road ship toward a one-horse town in the darkening twilight. (But, don't forget. We'll get to your dad in a minute.)

As was his habit when in need in a strange town, Dad sought out a member of his fraternity, the clergy. Very few towns in Texas, regardless of size, lack a Baptist church. As we crept through the streets, squinting in the failing light for some sign of a church, we came across two barefoot boys toting cane fishing poles. Dad slowed and called out the window, "Say, can you boys tell me who is the pastor of the Baptist church in this town?"

They stopped and looked at us closely, then at each other. The taller one spoke. "Oh, you mean Elder Nelson."

"I guess that's who I mean. Is he a Baptist preacher?"

"Yup, sure is. That's the church, right down there." He pointed to a building about three hundred yards away. "His house is right next to the church, on that side."

"Thank you." Dad drove on.

"Elder Nelson? How could he be a Baptist preacher if he's called elder?"

"There are many different variations of Baptists. Southern Baptist, American Baptist, Independent Baptist, and so on. There is one variety called Primitive Baptist, sometimes called Hardshell Baptist. Some Baptist denominations," he continued, "call their pastors elders." We pulled up in front of the house, a frame structure that had at one time long ago been white. "Heck, I'm just as much an elder as he is."

We emerged from the car and walked to the gate. The yard was largely dirt; a few sparse tufts of grass straggled by the walk. On the porch two barefoot kids of five or six were playing in the gloaming.

"Is your father at home?" Dad asked. The kids skittered into the house, leaving the screen door waving open. We walked up the sidewalk, which jutted from the dirt like a causeway, and stood at the foot of the porch steps.

Presently a woman in a plain cotton dress appeared at the door. The kids followed, grabbing her legs and peeking out from behind her skirt. The woman was slender and sturdy, with the cares of raising children on too little income plainly written on her face. An older boy, about ten or eleven, stood behind her, half-obscured by shadow.

She eyed us cautiously. Dad hadn't shaved since we left Fred, much to Mom's dismay, and his two-day growth gave him more hair on his chin than he had on the top of his head, which didn't exactly lend him an air of respectability.

"Is this the home of Elder Nelson?"

"Yes, it is."

"Well, I'm Elder Cloud." I looked at Dad, taken by surprise, but my reaction was nothing compared to theirs. The woman looked startled, and the older boy yelped out a barking laugh of one syllable. The younger ones continued to stare brazenly as though we were performing animals.

"I pastor a Baptist church in East Texas. We're on vacation, and we've had a little problem with our car. We were wondering if he could direct us to a garage that would give us a fair shake." He took off his glasses and smiled. I stood by, woodenly, as was appropriate for a teenager.

"Sure. He's not here right now, but he should be back soon. Why don't you come in and wait?" She opened the door and we filed in, taking a seat on a lumpy couch that was probably past its prime before I was born. On the other hand, with these kids, it might have been new last week.

"Would you like some iced tea?" We assented and she disappeared into the recesses of the house. The older boy stared at us for awhile and shuffled out the front door. The younger kids continued to stare from around corners and doorways.

Always curious about how other people lived, I looked about the room. Here were others who shared my fate, being a preacher's kid. *Perhaps they haven't felt it yet,* I speculated. *Perhaps they never will.* My own sense of PK isolation developed after the symptoms of that dreaded malady, adolescence, had manifested.

I wondered how different their life was from mine. The room was sparsely furnished. Other than the couch, there was an armchair, a rocking chair, and a coffee table—all past their prime except the rocking chair, which looked like it was built to outlast several generations of indigent pastors. A threadbare braided rug attempted vainly to disguise the fact that the wood floors had lost their finish long ago. On the far wall was the inevitable, albeit small, bookcase filled with reference books and magazines.

The living standard seemed below what I was used to, but upon reflection I realized that I was used to a nicer house only because the church in Fred had built a rambling, brick parsonage with volunteer labor just a few years before we arrived. If we had been forced to buy or rent a house on Dad's income, it wouldn't have been as nice as the one I was critiquing.

The woman eventually returned with our drinks. I sipped at mine. It had a strong mineral taste, making the tea almost undrinkable. I resigned myself to holding the glass and making token sipping movements every few minutes. The woman went back to whatever she had been doing, and Dad and I waited in silence. The house seemed to discourage conversation. Dusk deepened toward genuine darkness and still we sat, holding sweating tea glasses and meditating on the metallic taste in our mouths. In the twilight I could feel the relentless stare of those kids, like the never-sleeping eye of God, inspecting my every movement and nuance.

After an eternity, steps sounded on the front porch and a tall, genial-looking man walked in. Dad rose awkwardly from the couch, and I followed suit as Mrs. Nelson entered the room.

"This is Elder Cloud," she said, smiling.

The man registered surprise. "Really?" He grinned at Dad.

"Yes. I pastor a Baptist church in a small town in East Texas." He proceeded to explain our dilemma to Elder Nelson, who directed us to the Ford dealership in Abilene. Of course, both being pastors, they were incapable of concluding their business immediately. I slumped in the requisite adolescent stupor while the two elders talked shop. I knew I was in for the duration, much like my experience with Darnell on the Roller Coaster, only with less panic. Eventually they both talked themselves down to a fine powder, and we made the preliminary overtures to parting.

The parting ritual took almost as long as the conversation. I endured it with obvious stoicism. Finally the rites led us out of the house, lingering on the porch, tediously inching down the steps, through the yard to the gate. We moved deeper into the humid night and the warm cocoon of cricket song and fireflies. As we stood near the car, the denouement fell like a flourish of timpani.

In the darkness, the periphery of the porch light silhouetting our features, Elder Nelson said, "This has really been an experience. I've never met anyone else with the first name of Elder before."

It seemed to me that the crickets fell silent and the universe quivered, slightly. I staggered as nonchalantly as I could to the car, rolled up the windows, and fell into spasms of laughter on the vinyl seat. I don't know what Dad said to get himself out of that one.

I was still laughing when he got into the car several minutes later, a quiet and humble man if I've ever seen one.

We awoke Wednesday morning at sunrise, the birds being our alarm clock. After breakfast and cleaning up, Dad opened up the laundry drum.

"All right, everyone drop your dirty clothes in here," he said.

Mom made a last attempt. "You aren't really serious, are you? We only have a few days until we get to Wilma's. We can wait until then."

"I didn't strap that luggage rack on the car and figure out a way to secure this drum for nothing. We're going to use it."

We all deposited our clothes from the day before. Dad handed me a box of detergent. "Fill the drum to the line with water and add a scoop of this," he instructed. "I'll put on the lid to make sure it's sealed."

I did the laundry while everyone else broke camp. Then we wrestled our way into Abilene, repaired the hose, and struck out across West Texas. I will not weary you with an account of each time the carburetor flooded out. Suffice it to say that we found ourselves sitting on the side of the road twenty-two times due to the needle valve, in all manner of terrain, from desert to mountains. By the time we reached California we had completed a graduate-level course in the trying of our faith, producing patience, and counting it all joy. However, not everyone graduated with honors.

I interspersed my reading with staring out the window, obsessed with visions of the land of Ultimate Cool. In Fred I was strange in a stranger land. I fit in about as well as a fish in a rodeo. But I figured it was just the

Ugly Duckling Syndrome. I told myself that all I needed was the proper environment for my awkward layer of gawky adolescence to molt, revealing a brilliant new coat of sophistication and charm. I pondered without enlightenment on my primary dilemma: how to determine the locus of fate and, more importantly, how to get there.

I alone was aware that this vacation was in reality a pilgrimage to the Mystical Mecca of Hipness. I had not breathed a word of my aspirations to anyone. Heidi would consider it childish, Hannah would mock it, and Mom and Dad couldn't possibly understand it. I was forced to scheme silently and unaccompanied. The itinerary of the average family vacation is not conducive to providing opportunities for meeting and converging with the counterculture. I needed a ruse that would provide transportation to some cultural marketplace while at the same time gaining independence. I couldn't make contact with the counterculture in the company of my hopelessly uncool family.

In spite of the difficulties, we covered 350 miles by nightfall and pulled into a campsite near Tijeras Canyon, New Mexico. Everyone piled out of the car. I headed to unhitch the Beast and set it up, but Dad collared me. "Come here."

I dutifully followed, having been saddled with the very job I was trying to avoid. He unstrapped the laundry drum and handed it down. "Rinse this out very thoroughly. When you're through, hang the clothes on the rope that I'll stretch on the back side of the camper."

The drum was too heavy to carry, so I rolled it to the faucet, wondering if this was some kind of sadistic payback for laughing too heartily as I recounted the Elder Nelson story to Mom and the girls. I poured out the soapy water and ran fresh water. After three rinse cycles my musings turned from self-pity and resentment to amazement mixed with exasperation. I had never realized how much work a washing machine does. The camp was set up, and supper was cooked before I was through. I vowed, and not for the first time, that I would not be a preacher. Or if I did become a preacher, I'd be a TV evangelist and make enough money to have my laundry done while I was on vacation.

CHAPTER TWENTY-FIVE Thursday morning we

drove into Albuquerque to fill up with gas. Hannah went to the bathroom. We were sitting in the car waiting when she finally returned. She bounced in and asked Dad, "Is that supposed to be doing that up there?"

"Is what supposed to be doing what up where?"

"Is there supposed to be something dripping under the front of the car?"

Dad turned off the ignition and climbed out of the car. As I followed, I heard Heidi groaning, "Now what?"

Sure enough, something was dripping from the engine: gasoline. Dad diagnosed the problem as a leaking fuel pump, which prompted a discussion on an administrative level. It ranged from counting it all joy to counting it all lost. Eventually it settled on the immediate problem, and Dad ransacked his memory. I had no doubt that he would dredge from the bottomless well of his memory some antediluvian acquaintance who was now living in Albuquerque.

"Hey, didn't old So-and-So move to Albuquerque after he left Buna?" Dad asked.

"No, he went to Lynchburg," Mom replied.

"No, he didn't. He graduated a year early by going summers and got that little church in Red Lick. From there he went to Buna, was moderator of the Association one year, I remember. I think they moved to Albuquerque in '70 to work in that mission."

"No, that was Whats-His-Name. So-and-So went to Lynchburg."

"Are you sure?"

"Yes, I'm sure."

"Who did he marry, Such-and-Such?"

"No, it was Whats-Her-Face, the one who sang soprano in the choir."

And on it went until they had nailed down who had moved to Albuquerque, his complete job history, a partial family tree, and his voting record at the annual convention.

We called Whosit. Before long we were at his house. It was morning, so there was no need for me to hold the light. I got to swim with Heidi and Hannah while Dad and Whosit replaced the fuel pump. By the afternoon we were on the road again.

For about twenty minutes. Then the carburetor threw a fit, jealous over the attention lavished on the fuel pump. Like indulgent parents with a strong-willed child, we obligingly catered to its whims, tapping it lovingly with a crescent wrench and pleading impotently like a follower of Dr. Benjamin Spock. Due to the delay caused by the fuel pump combined with regular ministrations of the carburetor ritual, we only covered 150 miles on Thursday and camped outside Gallup, New Mexico.

As I irritably rinsed out the clothes in the laundry drum, I reflected on Fate. Fate. Destiny. I spat with disgust into the swirling suds flowing into the dusk. I had expected Fate to orchestrate my assimilation into the counter-culture in a romantic tryst. Instead, the fickle muse had stuck me on the edge of New Mexico, doing a chore with which I was as painfully familiar as the carburetor tap, and which I hated more, if possible. I was in the frame of mind to write a sequel to Ecclesiastes.

We got up plenty early Friday morning and crossed into Arizona. We had no mishaps other than the now familiar carburetor and a flat on the

Beast. Our first tourist stop was the Petrified Forest in the Painted Desert. Coming from East Texas, I thought of a forest as a cool, shady place. I knew the trees had been petrified, but I was disappointed to discover that they were all lying around on the ground. There was no shade for miles.

We also took a detour to see the Meteor Crater. This was more impressive. Trying to imagine the impact that would blast a hole in the ground a mile wide occupied my mind for hours. *Heck,* I thought, *I could fit the entire town of Fred, Texas, inside this crater. Let's see, if this platform is the south city limit sign, Fred Grocery would be about there, and there would be the church. The parsonage would be right by that boulder, and the post office would be there by that little shack. Over there would be the other city limit sign, with a tenth of a mile to spare before I hit the other side of the crater.* My primary disappointment was that I was not allowed to hike to the bottom.

Because of the sightseeing, we had another 150-mile day. However, we had more to show for it than a new fuel pump and a dented carburetor. Friday night we camped near Flagstaff, where once again I did the laundry. I began to hate the sight of the drum. I decided that I would volunteer to spend my own souvenir money if necessary to avoid two hours of rinsing.

Saturday morning we broke camp and detoured up to the Grand Canyon. Nothing I had seen, not even the Meteor Crater, prepared me for the Grand Canyon.

I had seen pictures and movies of the Grand Canyon, had read about it, but the sheer enormity is impossible to capture in any medium I have ever seen. Nothing but actually standing on the edge can deliver the impact of a hole more than ten miles across, almost three hundred miles long, and more than a mile deep. It was a moving, almost spiritual, experience that left me speechless for quite awhile. Before we left I bought a book from the gift shop. I watched the roadside to catch glimpses of the canyon, but I began reading the book as soon as the canyon was definitely out of sight.

In one section, the book discussed the geological history of the canyon, describing the various layers that are clearly visible in the canyon walls. Practically every geological age is visible—all the way back to the Precambrian Era, two billion years ago according to modern geology.

"Wow!" I said, getting everyone's attention. "Listen to this. According to one of the theories on how the Grand Canyon was formed, it took only two to three million years to cut." I laughed and tossed back my hair. "Only three million years! I think I've been grounded longer than that before." I thought my little joke was clever, but nobody laughed. Hannah just rolled her eyes and returned to her Nancy Drew book. Heidi forced a strained smile and looked out the windows.

"Based on dates from the Bible," Dad said, "Bishop James Ussher calculated that the earth is only six thousand years old. If the Bible is true, then the Grand Canyon couldn't have taken three million years to form." Of course, I knew the "if" was rhetorical. In our family there was no question about whether the Bible was true. I might as well ask if gravity really worked. "When you look at the Grand Canyon, what does it remind you of?"

It didn't remind me of anything I'd ever seen before. It was too massive to be familiar. I tried reducing the scale in my mind. "Well, it sort of looks like the gullies washed out of a river bank after a storm," I guessed.

"Exactly. But it would take one heck of a storm, probably one heck of a flood, to wash out something like the Grand Canyon, don't you think?"

I picked up on his inference immediately. I wasn't a PK for nothing. "Like a storm that lasted forty days and forty nights? With a flood that lasted over a year?" (That's Noah and the ark stuff, for you who haven't guessed it yet.)

"Exactly! A flood of those proportions could have devastating effects on the landscape."

I considered the idea. "But, why would these scientists think the earth was . . . ," I consulted the book, ". . . more than two billion years old? I mean, they're not stupid. You have to be pretty smart to be a scientist."

Dad caught my eye in the rearview mirror. "It's possible to be too smart for your own good."

"How could you be too smart for your own good?" I thought intelligence was an asset. I rated it pretty high, at any rate, because it was one of the few assets I possessed. I didn't see how I could ever be too smart.

"When you are so smart you think you don't need God." His eyes flashed back and forth from the road to the mirror. "'What shall it profit a man if he shall gain the whole world and lose his own soul?'"

"Yeah. I guess you could be too smart for your own good." I drifted back to the book, my mind grappling with the ideas Dad had brought up.

Of course the Bible was true. It was the Word of God. If there was a God. I looked out the window at the landscape flitting by at seventy miles an hour. It seemed stunted and barren. Brittle spikes of grass and yucca under the shadow of angular outcrops of granite. Scrubby, deformed pinion and juniper, blasted by the elements, broke the monotony of the mesa. The world felt empty, devoid of beauty, perhaps even devoid of meaning, no more than the bizarre and grotesque dream of Twain's Mysterious Stranger. While standing on the edge of the majesty of the canyon, overwhelmed by its magnitude, the grandeur of God seemed obvious. But now we were surrounded by miles of wasteland not even worth fencing in. It had futility written all over it. I had to struggle to conjure up the conviction of divine purpose and meaning.

I had lain on my back on a midnight hill in the wilderness of Fred, deeply aware that the heavens declare the handiwork of God. The magnificence and complexity of nature suggested an even more magnificent and complex mind behind it all. But I had also seen that nature was cold and relentless. The nourishing rain may fall on the just and the unjust alike, but devastating floods also destroyed the just and the unjust alike. The mind behind nature sometimes seemed as unconscious and aloof as a machine blindly churning out results, matter indifferently following the principles of particle physics. How could I get a sense of majesty and futility from the same source?

I eventually abandoned that riddle and returned to my book about the Grand Canyon. A chart in the back showed the different levels at which fossils could be found, some separated by hundreds of feet. It didn't have to take millions of years to accomplish that. If they were all drowned in a giant flood, they still might settle at different layers. Then I saw that fossilized footprints had been found on four layers, each separated by five hundred feet of rock.

My pulse quickened. If it was all laid down during the Flood, how did tracks have time to form and harden before five hundred feet of debris was piled on that layer? Four times? I looked up, irrationally fearful that Dad knew what I was thinking. He drove on, oblivious to the revolution brewing behind him. I considered challenging his Flood theory, but decided against it. For all I knew, I might be too smart for my own good!

As if to juxtapose the absurd with the sublime, we made a stop at the set where the TV series *F-Troop* was filmed. It had the characteristic tourist-trap ambience, replete with a gift shop full of dreck. Inevitably, Dad took pictures: the kids looking down from the tower that collapsed in every episode; the kids surrounding a cannon with a surface temperature of 150 degrees; the kids staring at a mangy buffalo. You know the pictures. You probably have a few yourself. Vacation shots.

I still can't erase the image from my mind of a picture Dad took in the Painted Desert. There, preserved for eternity, I stand next to the Beast wearing lime-green, knee-length cutoffs and a homemade "Charlie Brown" shirt, red with the black zigzag stripe. The image is replete with nerdism— the dirty blond hair hanging in my eyes, the deathly pale skin. And a thoroughly revolting grin that says, "Mystical land of Ultimate Cool, here I come." I think of it now and shudder. I hope it has been burned.

CHAPTER TWENTY-SIX The last of the major tourist traps behind us, we pressed toward Prescott, Arizona, and the mountains. We reached the foothills in the afternoon and began the ascent. Afternoon crept along, and soon the sun disappeared over the peak. As we topped the mountain, we saw the sun again, still a good distance from the horizon.

Then began the descent. Approaching the mountains from the east had been easy enough, but the west slope of the mountains looked like something from a Snuffy Smith cartoon. Being a flatlander, I got chills riding along with an immense density of rock on one side and an eternity of air on the other.

With the weight of the Beast breathing down the neck of the Galaxy, the usual measures of gearing down for the descent were inadequate to keep the car at a reasonable speed. Dad was forced to use the brakes with increasing frequency. Before long we began to detect an acrid odor.

"Yuck," Heidi complained. "What's that smell?" She tried to lean across me and roll up my window, but I whacked her hand with my book. "Ow!" She jerked her hand back and silently dug an elbow eighteen inches into my ribs.

"That smell is the brakes," Dad replied tersely, concentrating on getting us down the mountain.

"Why do they stink like that?"

"They are getting too hot from trying to slow down all this weight."

"Great," I answered. "Let's throw Heidi out. That'll lighten things up."

Hannah laughed and Heidi made a jab with her elbow again, but I had anticipated the move and she hit a copy of Asimov's *I, Robot* instead. "Ow!"

"Could y'all keep it down back there?" Dad was uncharacteristically abrupt. "You aren't making this any easier."

"Making what any easier?"

"If the brakes get too hot, they'll quit working."

"Oh." The implications were so obvious that not even Heidi needed to inquire or comment any further.

Dad used the brakes as sparingly as possible, rolling down the mountainside at a rate too fast for my comfort. I envisioned a fiery, plummeting death as the smell grew stronger and our speed increased. No one talked as we all gripped armrests. Heidi, who was in the middle and had no armrests to grip, mangled Hannah's and my legs as surrogates, leaving what I assumed would be permanent furrows. We were both too petrified to protest.

Dad grimly gripped the wheel, squinting into the setting sun. His week-old beard bristled on a chin set with determination, making him look like a cornered desperado steeling himself for the final showdown. After several lifetimes, we arrived at the base of the mountains physically, if not emotionally, intact. I watched the sun set across the flattest land I had seen since West Texas. We stopped at a gas station and choked down some tuna fish sandwiches.

The temperatures had been fairly cool in the mountains, but on the plain it was in the nineties. The sand radiated the heat it had been absorbing all day, and the air seemed to trap it and hold it close to the ground like a blanket wrapped around a delirious patient. No breezes relieved the stifling intensity of the heat.

Lacking air-conditioning, the administrative decision was to cross the desert at night. I knew from my vast, self-administered reading program that regardless of how hot it seemed now, the desert was supposed to be cool at night, perhaps even cold. We might have to turn on the heater, but we had nothing in that car if not plenty of heat. I wondered how long it would take for the temperature to start dropping.

Darkness closed in quickly. By the time we had the ice chest loaded, it was genuine night. We had already traveled more than two hundred miles, and Los Angeles lay four hundred miles away, a good day's drive by anyone's definition. Being without air conditioning, we had no choice but to forge on ahead.

Forge on, we did. I had told everyone about how deserts get cold at night, and now Heidi and Hannah began looking at me like it was my fault the temperature was still in the nineties. The windows were down, and we were continuing our regimen of sweating every available molecule of moisture. *Surely,* I thought, *anytime now the last of the absorbed heat will dissipate and prove me right.* I kept waiting for a change.

About midnight we got a change; the wind began to build. *At last,* I thought, *it's going to cool down.* I tried to get comfortable enough to sleep in the oppressive heat when I was rudely awakened by stinging pinpricks peppering my face. "Ow!" I put my hand up and felt a layer of grit.

"Oh!" Heidi echoed. It was Hannah's turn in the middle, and Heidi had been sleeping with her head against the door. "Yuck, what is this stuff?"

"Roll up the windows," Dad ordered.

"But it's ninety-five degrees."

"Just be quiet and roll up the windows quick."

I looked up and saw a cloud racing toward us on the ground. I recognized it from my research on deserts. It was a haboob, a wall of sand on the leading edge of a windstorm that could reach as high as five thousand feet.

I grabbed the handle and started rolling. In seconds we were enveloped. Cries of pain, astonishment, and indignation rang out. Dad had to fight gusts of wind to keep the car on the road, and visibility was on the level of a dense fog. We slowed down and crept through the sandstorm, for that is what now assaulted us. The sauna heat in the car was unabated as we were forced to proceed with our windows up. I closed my eyes to avoid the sullen stares of the girls and finally drifted off to sleep in a delirium.

Sometime in the night we made it through the desert. Dad just kept driving, possibly under the delusion that he was the Vacationing Dutchman, cursed to forever roam the highways with a camper, a camera, and Bermuda shorts.

Just after dawn, Sunday morning, the trance broke and he took an exit near San Bernardino for a pit stop. The rest of us were awakened by his exclamations and the swerving of the car as he attempted to pull to the side of the road. I looked up to see what had happened. The windshield was a blaze of glaring pinpoints, sparkling in the sunrise. I looked behind. The back window was obscured by some brown, opaque film.

Dad rolled down his window, stuck his head out, and drove around the cloverleaf to a truck stop. When the car turned away from the morning sun, we were able to see again. He pulled into the truck stop, and we got out to inspect the phenomenon. We discovered that the sandstorm had pitted the windshield with millions of miniature pinpricks, which caught the sunlight and transformed what was once transparent glass into a sparkling wall of light. But only when we were heading into the sun.

The back window was another story. During the sandstorm, soapy water from the laundry drum had leaked down the back of the car. The heat caused the water to evaporate quickly, leaving a sticky film of soap that was covered with sand and then baked rock-solid, like pottery in a kiln. Once again, all eyes focused on me, the keeper of the laundry drum.

"Mark, it looks like you didn't put the lid back on right," Dad pointed out.

"Yes, I did." If I had possessed greater presence of mind, I would have accepted the blame and sorrowfully admitted that the task was beyond my abilities. However, I hated to take the blame for anything, even things I had done. And I knew I had put the lid on tightly Saturday morning.

"I think the evidence shows otherwise."

I unlashed the drum from the luggage rack and inspected the lid. It was sealed perfectly. Then I noticed a trail of soap and sand that led to a hole in the drum, evidently eaten through by the sandstorm. "Aha! There's the leak," I announced triumphantly.

Dad took a closer look and cleared me of all charges of incompetence. Feeling like the Hebrew children delivered from slavery after four hundred years, I tossed the drum into the dumpster since it could no longer hold water. However, being acquitted of the charge of incompetence didn't relieve me of the chore of chipping away the spontaneous cement from the window. Nothing could be done about the windshield except to avoid driving into the sun. Fortunately it was dawn and we were headed west, only a few hours from our destination, barring carburetor delays. We hit the road again.

So it was with a defaced windshield, an erratic carburetor, a new fuel pump, and an inexpressible sense of relief that we coasted into Los Angeles and to the home of Aunt Wilma and Uncle Mort seven days after we had left Fred. I had arrived in the Mecca of Mystical Hipness at last. We parked that car and didn't touch it again until it was time to return to Texas.

CHAPTER TWENTY-SEVEN Although we had arrived in plenty of time to get ready for church, we did something unimaginable in our family—we didn't go. We had all slept in the car except for Dad, who had been awake for twenty-four hours. Instead, we all took showers and crashed into real beds for several hours of ecstatic sleep.

Sunday night we went to Uncle Mort's church, the Church of Christ. My whole family on both sides had always been Baptist, with a capital *Southern*. I found out later that when my Aunt Wilma decided to marry Uncle Mort, it sent a few shock waves through the family. Not only did his church believe all that stuff about not having instruments in church, but they actually believed that nobody else but Church of Christ members would go to heaven. Of course, we knew the Baptists would be at the front of the line, and anyone else who really believed the right things but just happened to be a member of the wrong church would come next in line. After all, we lived in America, where we have a right to be wrong if we absolutely insist on it.

Being a PK, I rarely had the opportunity to visit other churches, especially ones that weren't Baptist. As soon as we walked in I noticed something was missing—the piano. While Uncle Mort was introducing Dad to the minister, I looked around for an organ or something, but nothing was there. I turned back to the men standing next to me.

"Matt, here, is also from Texas," Uncle Mort was saying. He was smiling, although I was at a loss as to why. I didn't try to figure it out. Uncle Mort was always joking about something. He would walk up to complete strangers who had nametags, like workers in a fast-food joint, and greet them by name as if he had known them for years.

"Is that right?" the minister asked. He seemed to be in his late sixties, brown hair mostly gone gray. He had a weather-beaten look to him, as if he spent a lot of time outside. "Where in Texas?"

"A small town in East Texas," Dad replied. I wondered, not for the first time, why he always said that instead of just coming right out and saying "Fred, Texas." Perhaps he wanted to avoid the inevitable conversational detour that would require him to explain where Fred was and that he had no idea where the name came from.

"Brother Paul, here, is from Texas," Uncle Mort said, still smiling. "It's one of the reasons we picked this church. Nice to have a touch of home every week."

"Yep," Brother Paul said. "I grew up in Mansfield, south of Fort Worth."

"Matt, here, pastors a Baptist church back home," Uncle Mort said, and the penny dropped. Three men, three expressions: Uncle Mort smiling quietly, Dad subduing a brief look of irritation that flitted across his features, the minister raising eyebrows in interest.

"Is that right?" the minister said again. He inspected Dad as if looking for visible evidences of heresy.

"Yes." Dad's voice was even and emotionless. "A small church in Fred, Texas."

It was a nice gambit, but Brother Paul didn't pick up the bait. Instead he just said, "Well, I hope you enjoy the service," and left with a nod. I could tell that Dad would have rather attended the service incognito, but he didn't say anything to Uncle Mort, who seemed content to enjoy his little amusement without further comment.

When the song leader got up, he started off the first song by blowing a note on a pitch pipe, which I suppose didn't qualify as an instrument. Reflections on the difficulty of using a pitch pipe as an instrument in an ensemble occupied most of my attention through the lackluster music. Then we all sat down, and the minister took over.

As the sermon progressed, it appeared to be aimed at a certain part of the room. In fact, it seemed to be an impromptu catalog of those points on which the Church of Christ differs from Baptist doctrine, with a full exposition of how they were right and we were wrong. At each point Dad bristled, certain the preacher was unsportsmanly shooting at fish in a barrel.

I treated it all as a purely academic exercise and eventually got bored and looked for some reading material. I picked up the bulletin. The front had a line drawing of the building and some words:

Grove Avenue Church of Christ
Minister: Paul Jordan

My head jerked backward as if I had been slapped. Indeed, I felt as if I had been slapped. Paul Jordan? A preacher from Mansfield, Texas? Not possible. I picked up the Bible I had brought with me and looked at the faded gilt letters on the front: Pauline Jordan. I flipped through the pages to the envelope that was still unopened and inspected the front, trying to decipher the smeared address. Was that a CA on the front? I searched for more clues, but the only legible items on the envelope were the Chicago postmark and the "Return to Sender" stamp, and the inscription "You made your choice" on the back.

I looked up at Brother Jordan, searching his face for a glimpse of Pauline's features. It had been too long—five years—and I had only seen her a few times. His eyes were brown. Were hers? I couldn't remember. I looked around the room and saw a slight woman sitting on the front row on the right. There was no doubt that this woman was Pauline's mother. The resemblance was unmistakable. *"I have the Mark,"* echoed in my mind.

I was still staring at Mrs. Jordan when the sermon ended with a prayer and we were dismissed. Dad stood up and said, "Let's go," evidently hoping to avoid a confrontation with Brother Jordan, who was walking down the aisle like the proverbial canary-gorged cat. His wife followed. I stood rooted to the spot, unable to move. Dad grabbed my shoulder as he tried to exit the other direction. I pulled away and stepped into the aisle directly in front of Brother Jordan. He looked at Dad. I held out Pauline's Bible toward him like I was holding a crucifix in front of a vampire.

"So, did you enjoy . . . ," he started, but his eye caught the Bible and his voice trailed off. The satisfied look on his face faded into a blank stare. Mrs. Jordan stepped around to greet us, her gaze following his. Her gasp was so loud it even got Dad's attention, and he reversed his retreat and came to stand next to me.

The silence was unnerving. I looked at Mrs. Jordan, whose hand fluttered at the collarbone protruding from the parchment skin stretched over her slight frame. Her eyes were wide and her breathing rapid with some emotion I couldn't identify, almost like fear. Brother Jordan's eyes were dull and his face had gone slack, as if the breath had been kicked out of him.

"It isn't . . . it can't be," he whispered. Then he seemed to regain a sense of where he was. "Where did you get this?" He jerked the Bible from my hand. "How did you get this?" Around us people stood in small groups, visiting. Those closer looked up at the tone that carried across the sanctuary.

Dad put his hand on my shoulder and started to object, but I shook it off and blurted out. "In Ohio."

"Ohio?" Brother Jordan looked confused.

"Yes, sir. I met your daughter in Ohio." Mrs. Jordan took the Bible from his grip and opened it to the front. She let out a ragged breath and ran her fingers across the inscription. I looked back to Brother Jordan. "Pauline is your daughter, isn't she?"

"I don't have a . . . ," he began, but then he saw the envelope Mrs. Jordan was pulling from the pages that had fallen open to Psalm 51. She turned it over and read "You made your choice," scrawled on the back. It was more an accusation than a look that her green eyes flashed at her husband. She shoved the Bible into his hands and tore the envelope away from the letter. She read the letter aloud in a quiet voice.

> Dear Papa,
> I thought you ought to know you got a grandson.

Mrs. Jordan closed her eyes and swayed slightly for a second.

> His name is Enoch, right out of the Bible, the one who pleased God. He's 3 months old and ain't got a hair on his head or a tooth in his mouth and looks like a little old wrinkled Enoch, sure enough.
>
> Vic is gone and I'm not sorry, but he did seem like he was getting back to the old Vic for awhile. Oh, I guess you don't know about that. It's been rough on him and he got backslid there for awhile, but it seemed like things was getting better, but then he left. It's probably all for the best, and God's will be done.
>
> Anyway, I wanted you to know. I didn't try to write before because I didn't think you wanted to hear from us after the things you and Vic said that nite a long time ago. It was hard on me at first, but now when I look at Enoch sleeping while I write this letter, I know you meant well. It ain't always easy being the papa, or the mama I'm finding out, but you always want the best for your baby and sometimes it

seems like your heart will break with carrying so much love in it.

So, now I know that you didn't mean no spite. For a long time I didn't think I could forgive you, but now I see that there weren't nothing to forgive, there was only me not understanding how you loved me so much you just wanted the best for me. But now I know and there goes my heart again, too small to hold all the love God give me.

If you have a mind to see your new grandson, I will come bring him to you. Just me and him. I don't know where Vic is, and that is probably just as well.

Tell Mama I love her and write me back if I can come home. I got some money set aside for the bus.

Love,

Pauline

Mrs. Jordan looked through her tears to her husband and clenched the letter in her fist. She held the inscription on the envelope up to him. "You made your choice?" she asked, challenging him to explain what she must have recognized as his writing.

A small group had gathered, some coming to visit, others attracted by the scene that seemed to be developing.

"I didn't realize . . . How could I know . . ." Brother Jordan turned from his wife and glared at me. "How did you get this?" he demanded again, thrusting the Bible in my direction. The newspaper clipping fluttered to the floor.

Mrs. Jordan threw the letter at him. "Oh, you made your choice all right, but I never got to make mine."

Brother Jordan flinched from the letter and bent over to pick up the clipping.

Mrs. Jordan composed herself with a visible effort and turned to me. "How did you meet Pauline in Ohio?"

"She was sick, and I brought her some soup." I looked at her with a feeling of helplessness. How could I possibly explain all that had happened to this woman's daughter? "She got better. She told me about you." I said.

She struggled unsuccessfully to keep her composure. Suddenly the silence was broken by the sound of the Bible hitting the floor. The newspaper clipping fluttered back to the floor. Brother Jordan stared blankly ahead. Dad picked up the clipping and began reading it.

"What?" Mrs. Jordan rushed to him. "What is it?" Several people stepped from the crowd, reaching toward them.

"Gone," he whispered to the air. "She's gone. Dead."

"My baby?" Mrs. Jordan dropped into a pew and began weeping.

Brother Jordan was startled to an awareness of his surroundings. He saw his wife crying and sat next to her. "She said there was nothing to forgive." He took her in his arms ineffectually, unable to shelter her or himself from this storm. "She said she knew we loved her and there was nothing to forgive."

The guy who had led the music stepped through the crowd. "What's going on?"

Dad handed him the newspaper clipping, and he stared at it dumbly. "They have just received the news of their daughter's death."

The man looked up in confusion. "Their daughter?"

Dad nodded, and we left the Jordans to the care of those that knew them best. Or thought they had known them.

CHAPTER TWENTY-EIGHT The touristing we

did en route to California was a mere hors d'oeuvre for the gluttonous
feast we devoured once we arrived. Disneyland on the Fourth of July,
Knott's Berry Farm, Hollywood and Vine, Grauman's Chinese Theater,
the Sidewalk of the Stars, China Town, the Sequoia National Forest—you
name it, we went there. Every day Mom and Dad and Aunt Wilma and
Uncle Mort would plan out an itinerary of the classic tourist spots, and we
would trudge through them. Not that Disneyland was boring. Actually,
most of it was fun, but I was obsessed with finding some way of making
contact, a close encounter of the third kind with a new and alien culture.

During every extravehicular activity, I scoured the landscape for hippies, Flower Children, the Beautiful People. To my dismay, it seemed that
the counterculture didn't frequent tourist traps. At least not openly. They
may have been there incognito.

Convinced that the orthodox agenda was not going to produce the
opportunity I needed, I attempted to effect a minor excursion of my own.
After all it was Friday and I was running out of time. I selected Mom as
the best target and shadowed her until she was alone. Then I sauntered
casually into the room.

"Hey, Mom. Do you think somebody could drop me off at a record
store or something?" If I had asked Dad this question, he would have said,

"Well, which is it? Do you want to go to a record store or something?" Mom spared me the harassment.

"Why do you want to go to a record store? You can do that anytime."

"Yeah, but they probably have a better selection out here."

"Oh, you don't want to spend all your souvenir money on records. You should use it on something that will remind you of the trip." She was putting up more resistance than I had expected. Maybe I should have asked Dad.

"Yeah, but I think a record I bought out here would remind me of the trip. Besides, who really needs a set of Mickey Mouse ears or a mug shaped like a redwood tree? A record would be something I would use a lot."

Mom must have been in an uncharacteristically contrary mood because she began to sound like Dad, the master of enumerating difficulties to get out of doing something. "But what if the record has a skip on it? You won't be able to take it back from Fred."

"I could listen to it on Uncle Mort's stereo, and we could take it back if it was bad."

"Honey, we're on a vacation. We're going to be really busy getting in all the sights. We don't have time to make a lot of trips to record stores."

I tried a last ditch effort, the plaintive cry of "Mom."

She softened slightly. "We'll see."

I turned to leave in defeat. A verdict of "we'll see" was the next thing to "no."

"Maybe when we go to the beach this afternoon there will be one on the way," she added as a consolation.

The beach! I left the room with my mind racing. Why hadn't I thought of that? The beach was the perfect place to find the counter-culture. Fate had come through at last.

The day turned out overcast, and the temperatures stayed low. Since it was Friday and we were scheduled to leave Saturday, we had little choice. If we were going to see the Pacific Ocean, Friday was the day. I was used to swimming in creeks that stayed cold, even in August, so I didn't expect the weather to be a problem. Which showed just how limited my experience was.

We arrived at the beach, and I scurried into a bathhouse to hastily change into a pair of cutoffs, the swimwear of choice for Fredonians. Leaving everyone else behind, I ran to the water and plunged into the surf. And instantly turned a light shade of pale blue. Every nerve in my body sent panic signals to my brain, inquiring who was the fool who had just immersed my body in water on the verge of turning to ice.

I bounded back to the beach, running along the top of the water like a creature in a cartoon, bewildered and shivering. Salt water and waves were supposed to be warm. Anybody who had ever been in the Gulf of Mexico knew that.

But I purposed to tough it out. I was going to swim in the Pacific if I had to do so with an ice pick in each hand. Nothing was going to prevent me from being present when Destiny took a walk down the beach. I pressed resolutely back into the water, commanding my protesting body to ignore the distress signals from my nervous system. Swells of liquid ice poured over me. Still, I staggered stubbornly into the surf.

Heidi and Hannah ran out, touched the water with their toes, and ran back squealing. They wrapped themselves in towels and watched from a safe distance. Mom and Dad sat in lawn chairs, admiring the beauty of the ocean. I swam bravely, firm in my faith that if I persevered, Fate would reward me. Besides, motion was the only thing that prevented me from freezing into a block of ice and floating away.

After several minutes of agony, I squinted up and down the beach. It was practically deserted. Some old man wearing a sweater was flying a kite. A middle-aged man in hip-waders was surf fishing. Scattered here and there were a few courageous individuals submerging their ankles as they strolled down the shore. It looked as if Fate had taken a rain check. I was indignant.

Then my body unleashed a primal scream of protest. In a violent paroxysm of outrage, it demanded unequivocally that I get the heck out of Dodge. Relenting, I retired to the showers to change.

As I neared the bathhouse, a bright yellow VW microbus turned off the road and onto the beach. I froze in my tracks, mesmerized by the psychedelic designs painted in neon colors on the side. It couldn't be! The van veered from the drive in my direction. I was incredulous. It was really happening! All those months of waiting, hoping, planning, yearning weren't in vain. To my amazement, a girl with long dark hair under a woven headband leaned out of the window and hollered at me. The flowing sleeves of her paisley blouse rippled in the wind. Several sets of beads swung from her neck. She was the perfect incarnation of my fantasies, as if my dream creature had sat for a portrait and then walked from the frame into a minibus for a ride.

My pulse raced and my mind groped for the proper action. This was it! The rendezvous with the counterculture that would transform my mundane life to a romantic journey into Otherness. The specifics of this Otherness were hazy in my mind, but that didn't concern me. Any Otherness at all was preferable to the cultural desert I had sojourned in longer than the children of Israel. I knew I would soon be drawn into a world where intelligence was not scorned, where awareness was understood and appreciated, where I didn't have to shoot woodland animals, drink beer, play football, and spit tobacco juice in order to achieve acceptance. Where people wouldn't say "Never heard of her" when I mentioned Alice Cooper.

As the van approached, I heard "Good Vibrations" on the stereo and saw a windowful of grinning faces staring in my direction. I was awakened from my reverie by the stark realization of what the girl was hollering. "Ooohhhh, look at those white legs!" she cackled.

I smiled and waved weakly as the van lurched past me, laughter spilling out like salty surf spray to the accompaniment of Brian Wilson singing, "I don't know where but she sends me there." I walked into the cinder-block showers, washed the sand of that western shore from my body, and emerged the same pale, skinny kid that had left Texas. We left California the next day.

CHAPTER TWENTY-NINE Saturday morning found us once again peering through a sand-pitted windshield, rolling east with the Beast in tow. I mentally braced myself for the return trip, hopeful that we had passed the lesson on counting it all joy and were starting the unit on counting your blessings.

We were nearing Barstow, and I was getting bored. I skimmed over my resources: a Ray Bradbury book I had already read three times, a brochure on turquoise jewelry, and the book on the Grand Canyon. I chose the latter.

We were past Barstow when I was startled by a grinding screech with sickening implications. Dad pulled to the shoulder, got out, and walked to the passenger side. Slender tendrils of smoke snaked from the rear hubcap, right by my door.

"Yup," he said. "This really is unbearable."

I was amazed that after dozens of breakdowns on the westward trip, he was finally going to have a breakdown of his own. "What's unbearable?"

He grinned faintly, closing in for the kill. "We lost a bearing." His eyes sparkled. "Wheel bearing, to be precise."

"Great," Heidi sighed. "What does that mean?"

"It means," Dad said as he slid back behind the wheel, "that we're pretty lucky. It could have frozen up instead of making that grinding noise.

If the wheel had locked while we were going seventy miles an hour pulling a trailer, who knows what would have happened."

"So what do we do now?" Heidi asked as I visualized a maroon car and a turquoise camper tumbling across the highway like some art-deco demolition derby. She always wanted to know the next step, while I was still wondering over the last one.

"We drive back to Barstow and see if we can get it replaced." Dad checked the rearview mirror and made a U-turn back to the west.

I considered the implications. "But, what if it freezes up now? Won't that cause a wreck?"

"Not if we're driving slow enough that it will have little effect."

Slow enough turned out to be ten miles per hour. By the time we arrived in Barstow and located a place to fix the car, it was well after noon. The decision was made to find a place to set up camp and start out fresh the next day. Before long we were in a trailer park, seated in metal patio furniture and eating sandwiches at a metal table shaded with an orange-and-yellow umbrella. Mom and the girls walked to a nearby shopping center and left Dad and me to take in the scenic beauty of Highway 57 and the laundromat across the street.

The Grand Canyon problem weighed on my mind. I looked over the chart again. I was sure that my analysis was fairly conclusive, and I wanted to see what Dad thought about it. However, what if he pronounced me as being too smart for my own good? He had seemed so sure about the six thousand years and the Flood. Was questioning it like doubting, or even sacrilege? Maybe it was more like a civil crime, like treason, dissent in the camp. I struggled over whether to mention it and risk court-martial or to sit safely in silence with my own private doubt.

Dad solved the problem for me. He pulled the book to him and peered over his glasses at the chart. "So, these fellows think the Grand Canyon is three million years old, eh? I guess you can believe just about anything if you want to escape God."

I gulped. "But why would a scientist make this stuff up? Isn't his job to find out facts and figure out how the universe works? It seems to me that if he just made stuff up, it would be like a fireman going to a fire and throwing gasoline on it."

"Exactly. A fact is neutral, but the explanation of the fact is not. It is based on the prejudices of the explainer, and that is such a powerful motivator that it can make people do the opposite of what they should. Say a guy, let's call him Larry, is at the office, and he decides to go to an Italian restaurant for lunch. He walks in and sees his wife, let's call her Bertha, holding hands across the table with a guy he's never seen before. There are the facts. What is the explanation?"

This seemed like a very long detour from our topic of conversation, but I knew from many long years of conversations with Dad that we would eventually get back to the Grand Canyon, even if we did have to go through Giovanni's to get there. "Well, I guess Bertha is having an affair."

"Which is probably what Larry thinks, also, if he doesn't trust Bertha. But what if Larry completely trusts Bertha? He might be willing to hear an explanation before he jumps to a conclusion. He might find out that this is her cousin she hasn't seen in years, and she has just been bragging about how generous Larry is by showing him her wedding ring."

His speculation set my imagination into gear. "Or maybe he's a palm reader and he's telling her future, like she's about to get a divorce because Larry isn't going to buy her story about the long-lost cousin."

Dad gave me an indulgent but unamused look over the top of his glasses. "Possibly."

"Or maybe it's a Treasury Department agent trying to talk her into testifying against Larry for tax evasion. He just told her that Larry is a crook, which naturally upset her, and now he's trying to calm her down."

Dad's look became less indulgent. "Perhaps."

"Or maybe he's a medium trying to help her contact the spirit of her dearly departed mother to find out why she named her Bertha." I figured, as long as we're in Giovanni's we might as well enjoy it.

Dad gave me a steely stare, but I was enjoying myself. "Or maybe Bertha really is having an affair, and the guy just told her he's not going to leave his wife, as he has promised for the past three months, and he is holding her hands to keep her from slapping him!" My mind raced as I tried to think of another, more exciting, scenario.

Dad, on the other hand, was ready to leave Giovanni's and get back to the Grand Canyon. "Yes, I see you get the picture. Well, as I was saying, many times the explanation offered is colored by the prejudices of the person doing the explaining. It used to be that scientists accepted the view that God made the world. And because an intelligent mind designed it, they expected it to fit together and make sense, and so they set out to discover the principles that govern how the world works. Since the 'enlightenment' of the Renaissance, however, science has gradually become dominated by men who view religion as superstition and find any reference to or dependence on God distasteful."

I nodded, feeling like the kid who asked for a bedtime story and got the first three volumes of the *Encyclopedia Britannica* instead. I was still thinking about Bertha and Larry.

"In the modern view, the universe didn't have a beginning because to admit to a beginning is to admit to a beginner. So, when something like the Grand Canyon comes along, scientists will naturally prefer an explanation that accommodates their prejudices, which is that it took billions of years to make the Grand Canyon."

The mention of the Grand Canyon brought me back to the subject. Perhaps we were finally getting to the crux of the matter. "Well, actually, they say it took millions of years, two or three million."

"Million, billion, what's a few millennia among friends? Either way, it's a lot longer than six thousand."

"Yeah, well, I was sort of looking at this chart and thinking about what you said about the Flood and everything . . ."

"Sure, just look at it." He flipped to a page with a wide-angle picture from the South Rim. "One explanation is that it took a long time for the normal rates of erosion to create. But it's just as possible that a catastrophic event accelerated the pace of erosion and dug this thing in much less time. It makes sense if you just look at it and think."

"But . . . uh . . . I was noticing the fossils they found at all these different levels." I turned back to the chart. "See, they're hundreds of feet apart and—"

Dad broke in. "You know, if all these animals were drowned in a monstrous flood, you would expect them to be at different levels as they were washed down the river."

"Yeah, but it says here that they found fossilized footprints on four different layers. See this?" I pointed out the layers. "Trilobite tracks in the Cambrian layer; and then animal tracks on the Pennsylvanian layer, 1,100 feet up; and then tracks in the Permian layer, 300 feet up; and then reptile tracks in the Triassic layer, 500 feet up."

"OK," Dad said, waiting for my conclusion with evident interest.

"Well, for tracks to form and harden into rock, it has to dry out, which takes some time. If all these skeletons got dumped down at one time and buried, how could each of the layers dry out and harden before the next layer got dumped on it?" There, it was out. I looked at Dad from behind a barricade of hair. He looked at the chart in silence. "I mean . . . it just seems . . . well, it just makes you wonder, you know . . ." I faded off into silence myself. I was breathing fast and shallow, anxious about Dad's reaction. I forced myself to take slow, deep breaths.

Finally Dad spoke. "That's a good question." He took off his glasses and looked closer at the chart.

I realized I had stopped breathing completely. I tossed my hair back, took another deep breath, and tried not to look so amazed.

Dad looked up at me. "Now, let me ask you a question. Remember when we were driving through the Painted Desert and it looked like there was water on the highway up ahead?" I nodded. "Did we ever reach it?" I shook my head. "Sometimes things look like one thing when they are another. It's like a magic trick. It looks like the lady really is floating in the air, but once we hear the explanation, it seems very simple."

I grew a little impatient. "I know, the explanation can be affected by our prejudices."

"Yes, but I mean something even more than that. Sometimes we have to decide if we are going to believe our eyes and our logic, or if we are going to believe God. For example, if you saw a man walk out of a bar and stumble, what would you think?"

"I'd think he was drunk."

"Right. Now what if that man was me?" He raised an eyebrow. "What would you think then?"

I knew Dad hated alcohol, almost as much as I hated country music. Then I remembered a time, back when we lived in Ohio, when he had gone into a bar to hand out tracts and to witness. "I would think you had been handing out tracts and that you tripped on something on the way out."

"Why?"

"Because nothing else would fit."

"Or, maybe, because you know me and you have faith that what I say is true?"

"Yeah, that's the same thing."

"Then if I know God and have faith that what He says is true, I won't let a piece of circumstantial evidence make me think God's Word isn't true." He leaned back in his chair as if resting his case.

I wasn't satisfied to leave it at that. It annoyed me that the whole issue had been reduced to a loaded question of who was right, God or man. In our house, there was only one way you could answer. I countered with a question of my own. "But why can't they both be right? Does the Bible say the Earth is only six thousand years old, or is it only Bishop Whats-His-Face who says it? Maybe the bishop was wrong. I mean, the Bible doesn't say how long it was from when the world was created until Adam. Maybe it was millions of years."

Dad replied with the air of someone pointing out the obvious. "Genesis says God created the Earth in six days, not millions of years. And," he added, "his name was Bishop James Ussher."

"OK, Bishop Ussher. But what about the verse that says a day to the Lord is like one thousand years? Couldn't those six days be longer than just a day? Like a whole era or something?"

"Some people think that, but the Hebrew people were very practical people. They didn't usually think in ethereal or abstract terms. And their language was, accordingly, very practical." He put his glasses back on. "The word translated 'day' is *yom* and is defined in terms of evening and morning, a very practical and observable phenomenon. Every other place in the Bible where this word is used with a number in front, like 'the first day,' refers to a literal twenty-four-hour day. Therefore, it is highly unlikely that the author of Genesis had in mind a vast, vague, and undetermined period of time when he wrote, 'And it was evening and morning, day one.'"

I had to admit I was out of my depth there. Dad was the expert on dead languages, not me. "So, you're saying that based on how the words are used in the rest of the Bible, it makes more sense to think it means a twenty-four-hour day in Genesis."

"Yep. Obviously, not everybody thinks that. But this is America. They have the right to be wrong if they want to," he said, smiling.

"Even Bishop Ussher?"

"He wasn't American." Dad's smile grew.

"Even people who study ancient languages?"

The smile didn't fade, but the twinkle in Dad's eye did. "Meaning?"

I knew I was pushing it. Best to retreat and minimize the damage. The voice from one shoulder said, "Now you've got him! Just get it all out on the table and see what he does." The voice from the other shoulder said, "It's not too late to back off and smooth things out. Just say you were kidding. No harm, no foul." The problem was, I didn't know which voice had the halo and which had the pitchfork. They were just two voices, two choices—although I did seriously question a voice that would say, "No harm, no foul." What kind of a voice was that?

Dad was still looking at me. The glasses were off, the smile was gone, but the twinkle was back. I decided to ignore the second voice. Any voice that said, "No harm, no foul." was asking for it, in my opinion.

"Meaning . . . ah, well . . . yes, uh . . . maybe the scientists aren't the only ones who look for answers that match their prejudices. Like hearing 'Elder' and assuming it's a title and not a first name."

The twinkle in Dad's eye froze and shattered like an icicle dropping silently into the snow. His eyes narrowed slightly and his look grew harder for a second, but then grew vacant, as if he were thinking of something else.

The silence seemed suddenly ominous. "A rather unusual first name," I added, lamely.

My addendum roused Dad from the reflection he seemed to have fallen into. "So, you dare to suggest that the emperor is underdressed?"

"Huh? I mean, what?"

"It seems you have given this a lot of thought. The Grand Canyon, I mean. And other things, apparently, but for now, we'll stick with the Grand Canyon."

"OK." That was fine with me. I feared I had gone too far with the Elder comment.

"So, what exactly are you saying?"

I slapped my hand down on the Grand Canyon book like Pastor Bates closing in for the kill amidst a crowd of heathens. "OK. So, we have these scientists who are all pretty smart, even if they might be too smart for their own good, and their job is to figure out how things work. Right? So, they have thought about this thing for a long time, and they figure it took millions of years to make the Grand Canyon. OK, so maybe they see it this way because they want to, or maybe they see it that way because that's what really happened. Don't people who believe this Bishop Ussher guy also have prejudices? Can't they also decide that the Grand Canyon didn't take long to make because that's the way that fits their prejudices?" It was all coming out in a rush, and I didn't want to stop for fear of what I might hear, so I kept babbling on.

"Even this *yom* thing might be seeing the things the way we want to. I mean, people who study ancient Hebrew think that when people back then used this *yom* word, they meant only twenty-four hours. They're really only guessing, right? What if the scientists are right and the people who study ancient Hebrew are wrong? Maybe Moses, or whoever it was that wrote Genesis, didn't necessarily mean a twenty-four-hour day. Maybe he just used that word because they didn't have a word for 'geological age.'"

I came to an abrupt end and dropped the book on the table. There it was, all out in the open. And then there was the other thing. The one I didn't want to mention.

Dad had listened to my diatribe quietly, but with interest. "But they did."

"Huh?"

"They did have a word that meant 'an era' or 'a long time.' It's *olam*. So if Moses had meant an era, don't you think he would have used *olam* and not *yom?*"

That's the danger of going to the play-offs where the other team has the home-court advantage. Sometimes I just can't get a break to save my life. I had one round left in the chamber, but I was afraid to use it. I felt like I was using a musket against a grizzly bear. Against some targets you should shoot to kill or don't shoot at all. But I had spent two years wrestling with Twain's Stranger, and I was gorged with questions like a seedpod about to burst open. The time had come. I pulled the trigger.

"So, what if Moses was wrong? What if the earth is really billions of years old but that idea didn't fit Moses' prejudices, being from a very practical people, and so he wrote it in the only way he could understand it, even though it didn't really happen that way?"

Dad looked at me thoughtfully. "So, what you're really asking is, 'What if the Bible is wrong?'"

"Yeah. I mean, yes, sir."

A silence grew, stretching out like a tendril from a vine crawling across a wall. Dad looked at the Grand Canyon book, then at me. "That's an even better question."

"It is?" Of course, I thought it was, but I was surprised that he thought so too.

"Yes. It shows you're thinking, not just following along. That can be dangerous, but it can also be good."

"OK, but what if the Bible is wrong?" Now that I had the question out, I wanted an answer. Two years is a long time to a teenager.

"Then we among men are most miserable." I looked at him, uncomprehending, but didn't say anything. I figured he would eventually explain himself.

"Deciding if the Bible is true or not is not really an intellectual question; it is a spiritual question. When we get home, I can drop a stack of books on you that will list all the factual and historical reasons why you should take the accuracy of the Bible seriously. It's entertaining if you like that sort of thing, which I do. But it's really nothing more than a different kind of crossword puzzle."

I continued to look at him blankly. I figured I would prefer Bradbury and Asimov to whatever books he had in his library. And I wasn't getting it.

"The real issue is not what scientists say, or what layer in which you find a fossil, or what word Moses used in Genesis. If you want to find out if the Bible is true, you should ask Parker Walker. Or Sonia." He sat silent for a moment. "Or maybe," he added, quietly, "the daughter of Pastor Jordan, if you could."

I wasn't following him, but I figured I had asked enough questions for one session. I picked up the Grand Canyon book and resumed my reading.

CHAPTER THIRTY That night I lay in the belly of the Beast, canvas angling above my head and netting on three sides, daring sleep to overtake me to the lullaby of eighteen-wheelers growling down Highway 57. I reflected on the vacation. The breakdowns and counting it all joy, the fiasco of Fate and the counterculture, the majesty of the Canyon, however it was dug.

All year long this trip had haunted me with the assurance that my destiny awaited me in California. I thought of earlier times, of nights lying in the dark in Ohio, where the AM radio whispered nebulous promises of another world in my ear and visions of sugar cubes danced in my head. I thought of my first steps toward Camelot, picking out the right color of paisley shirts with M. And the untimely death of that dream.

I thought of the netherworld of culture where I had spent the last half-decade in free fall, adrift in the doldrums and finally tacking against the prevailing winds as I caught a glimpse of that long forgotten vision of Avalon. Of the vacation that had rekindled the hope deferred.

I had expected Fate to usher me into a new existence, to finally be accepted for who I was and not what I was expected to be. I had been vigilant, examining every moment for the possibility of enlightenment. Boldly I rode, and well, to the dunes of the beach, plunged in the freezing spray, mine not to question why, although someone had indeed blundered.

The haunting laugh of a girl in a yellow microbus had slapped me back to my senses. In the bathhouse, despair had poured over me like the water that washed away the salt of the sea and of my own tears. I knew the chance would never come again, and even if it did, it didn't matter. I would never be more than a pale, skinny preacher's kid, standing on the outside looking in.

I was startled back to consciousness by a realization. I had actually challenged one of Dad's ideas. And instead of accusing me of blasphemy or rebellion, he had taken what I had to say seriously. He hadn't demanded that I snap to attention and march in lockstep with him. He listened and offered his perspective, but he also allowed me to come to my own conclusions. Stunned, I realized that Dad's approval was more important to me than the acceptance of all the Flower Children in Eden. The meeting that Fate had for me wasn't on a beach with a willing and nubile nymph in hip huggers and a headband. It was under an orange-and-yellow umbrella with my own dad. He had been the one to accept me for who I was and not what I was expected to be.

Not that he agreed with me, but he wasn't making me walk back to Texas. At least he didn't say anything about it before we went to bed. He could be saving it as a surprise.

Awake again, I wondered what he meant, that I should ask Pauline Jordan if the Bible was true. I thought about the scene at Pastor Jordan's church. I had finally learned the contents of the letter. I thought about it in the light of my discovery. It looked as if she had been seeking the same thing: her dad's approval. But she had discovered something more. Even though her dad had banished her along with Vic, she said there was nothing to forgive.

For years I had wondered about her death. When she rushed out of the alley with a knife, I was certain she intended to kill the man who had stolen her son. But instead, she died saving his life. The tortuous paths of

her ramblings were hard to follow, but I thought I might have finally discovered the secret to her confusing end. Could she have forgiven Vic? Or
maybe come to the startling revelation that there was nothing to forgive?
Could her forgiveness have been the act that had saved his life and ended
hers?

For the first time, I wondered how Vic had dealt with her sudden
appearance. He probably had not realized she was stalking him, probably
had not even given her a thought for years. Then, on an innocuous spring
night, he was plunged into a nightmare of violence, only to see the woman
whom he had so egregiously wronged appear from the shadows and give
her own life to save his. Had it changed his life?

An image of Parker kneeling amidst broken glass, head buried in
Mac's lap, flashed into my mind, followed by a picture of Sonia's bruised
face wet with tears, overwhelmed with the discovery that the Harmons
still loved her like a daughter. Dad's advice had been to ask Parker,
Sonia, and Pauline if the Bible was true. I didn't follow him then, but
now I saw the scarlet thread that joined them all. It seemed I had been
surrounded by stories of redemption and had been too dense, or self-
absorbed, to realize it.

I reached up to wipe tears from my face and only then realized I was
crying. In my mind I saw the Mysterious Stranger, perfect and aloof, with
his message of despair and abandonment. I sensed I was at a crossroad. I
could accept his rational but bitter interpretation of the seemingly mind-
less machine of nature, or I could embrace the image of God, tortured and
bleeding, hanging on a cross in a desperate attempt to communicate an
incomprehensible message of love and forgiveness.

I quietly groped in my suitcase, extracted *The Mysterious Stranger,* and
slipped out of the Beast. The box of matches was next to the grill where
we had cooked our supper. I watched the flames, feeding in pages until the
last one crumbled into black ash. I then returned to bed, turned the AM

radio to a low volume, and put it under the pillow like I used to do so many years ago in Ohio. I fell asleep to the Staple Singers promising me they would take me there.

The next morning we retrieved the car, hooked it to the Beast, and shook the dust of California from our feet. The return trip was anticlimactic. Spurning all those sights we had wondered over when driving west, our one goal, contrary to the instincts of most of the population, was to arrive in Fred as quickly as possible. We sped as swiftly as the stall-outs would allow us, like nomads fleeing a distant evil.

With a literal cheer we crossed the Texas state line; traversed the vast expanses of West Texas, as well as the rolling hills and black dirt of Central Texas; and had reached East Texas when our final adventure befell us. Somewhere around Madisonville, the Galaxy blew out a tire. The right rear tire. If that tire sounds familiar, it should. It was the one that had been replaced only days before in a shop that used air tools. Dad and I emerged from the car and began to change it. The lug nuts were incredibly difficult to remove. We had to jump on the tire tool to turn them. After Herculean effort, we removed all but one.

Dad, always inventive in the face of insurmountable odds, used a Craftsman socket and a break-over handle to no avail. He added an extra length of pipe for more leverage and got a split socket for his pains. An extended survey of our options left us with one choice. Dad fished the cold chisel and a hammer from the toolbox and began chipping away at the nut, cursing (in an entirely wholesome and family-appropriate fashion) the inventor of impact wrenches.

For those unfamiliar with the wholesome, family-appropriate form of cursing, it went something along these lines: "A pox on the miserable cur who in a drunken frenzy of iniquitous pride ever blasphemed the Name of all that's holy by inflicting the innocent and unsuspecting saints with such a diabolical device as the impact wrench." This was sometimes followed by a string of inarticulate, guttural sounds, reminiscent of a bobcat chewing on a porcupine while caught in a wolf trap, which I took to be groanings too deep to be uttered.

We took turns cursing and chiseling, and succeeded in peeling the nut from the lug after only an hour in the baking roadside heat of a Texas July. We took pictures to commemorate the event and proceeded on our way. Three weeks after our departure, we rolled into the greater Fred metropolitan area. We had survived yet another Cloud vacation, one like no other. I was confused by my emotions, never dreaming that I would be happy to return to Fred.

Our last stop was the gas station, for a fill-up and a lug nut. Mr. Johnson recognized the car and came out to welcome us home. "Well, now, Preacher, I see yer finally decided to come back." He faltered, his gaze arrested by the three-weeks' growth of facial hair on the pastor of the big church.

"Well, knock me down and chop me up for cord wood," he muttered. "Preacher's done gone off to Californie and turned into a dang hippie."

Yup, we were back in Fred, all right.